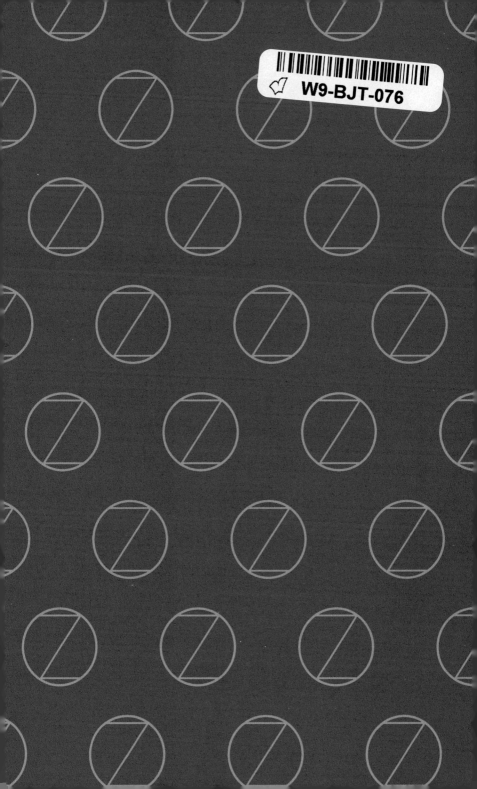

MEET THE AUTHOR

TEASERS,
TRAILERS & MORE...

Wine People

"In her hands, wine is many things at once: a sometimes-destroyer of relationships, yes, but also an ancient art that bottles time and place. Smart and very funny, satirical but deeply felt, *Wine People* is an ode to the complexity of working friendships—as well as a shrewd, clear-eyed love letter to wine and the people who make, import, and drink it."

—CHLOE BENJAMIN, author of *The Immortalists*

Praise for

Bread and Butter

"Three words for you: Food Nerds Unite."

—*The New York Times*

"As she did in *You're Not You*, her compulsively readable literary debut, Wildgen couples vivid description with crisp prose, putting the reader right in the scene—and right at the table."

—*Miami Herald*

"Wildly entertaining . . . a novel that's as much about the complex dance of family dynamics as it is about the mysterious world behind the kitchen door—and a divinely delicious read, to boot."

—*O, the Oprah Magazine*

". . . filled with tasty insider details."

—*Vogue*

Wine People

· A NOVEL ·

MICHELLE WILDGEN

ZIBBY BOOKS

NEW YORK

Library of Congress Control Number: 2023934627
Paperback ISBN: 978-1-958506-02-8
Hardcover ISBN: 979-8-9852828-3-2
eBook ISBN: 979-8-9862418-5-2

Book design by Neuwirth & Associates
Cover design by Mumtaz Mustafa and Graça Tito
www.zibbybooks.com

Printed in the United States of America
10 9 8 7 6 5 4 3 2 1

FOR EMILY

There's a secret we "wine people" know,
and it is that everyone else hates us.

—TERRY THEISE

PART 1

golden girl

· CHAPTER 1 ·

In her five years in the wine business, Wren observed many roads into the industry—an affinity for chemistry, history, or travel; an auspicious mix of boredom and family money; unchecked hedonism—but surprisingly few ways out.

Wren herself had arrived here after working front of the house at a James Beard Award–winning restaurant in Madison, Wisconsin, where she'd spent several years pouring Lionel Garrett's wines before joining his wine importing company. People arrived in the wine industry from restaurants and bars and sales jobs and Ph.D. programs and culinary schools, but once ensconced in the business they all sorted themselves into three types of colleagues. Some realized early that the highs of tastings, dinners, and parties weren't worth the endless bureaucracy and physical toll; those people departed for saner industries by the age of thirty-five. Others stayed in the wine business when they shouldn't, desperate and resolute, their teeth growing ever more stained and their enviable international anecdotes ever longer, until they were gently escorted from the wine business by their spouses, doctors, or AA literature.

And then there were the lifers.

Wren was a lifer, and she knew the rules. To stay in wine, you had to be both romantic and pragmatic, never losing the love of this ancient substance even as they figured out how to balance its excesses with ruthless physical economies. She nursed the same dream they all did: fifty years in the business and dying upright at the table, a glass of her ideal wine in hand. (The perfect final wine was ever-changing and an ongoing topic among wine people, who didn't find the conversation morbid.)

Until today she'd thought that the owner of Lionel Garrett Imports shared that dream. But then, at a meeting in preparation for everyone's spring buying trips, Lionel had done something he never had before. He started talking about endings.

"Who knows?" he'd said, in response to someone's offhand joke about the future. "By then I'll have stepped down and one of you could be running the place."

For someone else, this might not have been notable, except that Wren had never heard Lionel envision a world in which he was doing anything but ruling it. He was not physically imposing—rumor had it he'd been an indefatigable boxer in an earlier life, and he still had a compact pugilist's build—but his opinions carried more force than others'. It was something about the absolutism in his brilliant black eyes, the vulture's cast of his nose, the way his balding head gleamed in the office lights like something powerful and ancient.

Maybe he had a slight hangover that morning, an accepted occupational hazard. Lionel was known for his impromptu weeknight bacchanals with other wine titans. Every now and then he deigned to invite one of his employees.

Then someone said, "I guess by then Jonathan will have taken it over."

Jonathan was a minority partner, and a decade or so younger than Lionel. But Jonathan waved this notion away with a chuckle, his messy white hair flopping. "God, no," he said. "When I became a partner, I made Lionel promise me he'd never stick me with the whole thing."

Lionel looked to be deep in thought, which was odd for him. He was leaning back in his chair at the head of the long oval conference table, gazing around the room, when he shrugged and said, "Obviously Jonathan will always be here, but he's right. You don't take one of the best palates in the business and make him focus on paperwork instead. I'm just saying you all should start considering what your futures look like at this company. Maybe someone else needs to think about stepping up."

A silence fell over the twenty or so people gathered around the table. This was unheard of, especially from someone like Lionel Garrett, who hoarded his empire around him. They'd never seen him give up anything. He didn't even share appetizers.

"But . . . when?" Thessaly said. Wren shot a look across the table. Thessaly was one of the company's top salespeople, and Wren thought she ought to have more emotional intelligence than to ask. Thessaly must have thought the same thing. She flushed the moment the question fell out of her mouth, and her word *when* broke the spell.

Lionel seemed to shake off his brief flash of melancholy. He planted his feet on the floor and popped upright in his chair, as if his true self had reasserted itself. "When?" he said. "Good lord, I was just musing out loud. Let's get down to business. Buying trips next week. France. Germany. I want to hear how each one of you is going to ensure we sell every last drop of our imports and then some. And none of this 'meeting last year's numbers' bullshit. We're aiming higher this year, higher every year. We have an office to pay for."

He gestured around the room. The company had moved into this building only a few months earlier. It was the culmination of Lionel's lifelong dream to get out of Long Island and into Manhattan—specifically, the eighth floor of the Hartnett-Klein Building on the West Side Highway, a layer cake of a structure that looked stunning from the outside and had seen better days on the inside. The building had a sharp chemical smell, as if the drywall were still curing. Lionel said the building was an Art Deco gem, but the rent was expensive and so was the staffing.

Working for Lionel meant jogging alongside a fast pacesetter. His dark eyes were never still, his feet forever in motion. Every time Wren thought she might relax even for a moment, he turned around and asked for more. But this was what led to success.

All the more reason, Wren decided, to take any retirement musings with a grain of salt. Lionel liked to keep everyone on their toes. It would not be unlike him to perform some light psychological experiments just to see what motivated everyone most.

"Gavin," Lionel was saying, "start us off."

Now, *that* felt more familiar. Gavin, the national sales manager, leaned forward and began a rundown of who was going where to taste what. Gavin had a penchant for lengthy, penetrating silences, suits cut close to his lanky frame, and attending to the perfection of his meticulously groomed dark beard.

Wren listened to him with one part of her brain, but secretly she was also hurtling down another track. If Lionel were going to groom a successor in the next few years, could she be in consideration? This was unlikely—she was only an import liaison now—but what if she moved up in a few years with the kind of momentum that made her an undeniable candidate? Even if Lionel did what he was likely to do and chose one of his existing golden children, like Gavin or Thessaly, Wren could at least make a case for herself, and that might lead somewhere too.

Suddenly her upcoming buying trip to Europe—which was at once the core of the business, the best part of the job, and an exhausting frog-march fortified with immoral quantities of food—looked ten times more exciting than it had a few minutes earlier.

Except for the addition of Thessaly, who would be joining her and Jonathan in France and Germany. Wren considered her across the table, the colleague she'd kept at a friendly, professional, watchful distance for years and could no longer avoid. It wasn't that Wren disliked her, exactly. It was more that Thessaly was the wine-importing version of a supermodel—it didn't behoove Wren to stand right next to her.

Thessaly was a golden girl by birth and by training. The daughter of a prestigious Sonoma grower who supplied grapes to some of Lionel Garrett's top domestic producers, she'd been reared to expertly work the global dining room that was the wine industry. Wren had seen her haze the bros on the sales team, be respectful but self-possessed with the higher-ups, talk shop with the growers and winemakers, and perform some alchemy of all of it with her restaurant and retail clients. Even after a couple of years of working with her, Wren still had a tinge of fear and envy for the ease with which Thessaly wore lug-soled boots in a field or heels in a dining room, both of which they were called upon to do. Thessaly was one of those people of irrepressible confidence, unbothered by a strong nose Wren would have tortured herself over: not long or hooked or upturned, but a firmly placed triangle slightly thick across the bridge, as if it had once been broken in a horseback riding accident or by a Mayan sculpture falling from a shelf. It was the perfect nose for Thessaly's high cheekbones, bright dark eyes, and chocolate Patti Smith bangs.

Wren liked Thessaly as much as you could like someone born into the pot of gold at the end of the rainbow, which was to say, with caution and some resentment she tried not to admit even to herself. And she didn't fully trust her. Not because she thought Thessaly was untrustworthy, but rather she feared her own skills looked wan in comparison. Wren didn't have as much opportunity to shine in her less-glamorous operational role, and it was hard to break out of your mold once you were labeled.

All the stock wine types worked at Lionel Garrett Imports. There were the Inquisitors like Gavin, who loved nothing more than firing questions at new people to be sure they had a clear grasp of their ignorance, but shouldn't be confused with Educators like Amit, who handled Midtown West: nerdy, erudite, excitable, thrilled to share their joy in picking out nuances like kumquat skin or mushroom stem. There were the Pocket-Square Guys like Oliver, who worked on the Upper East Side, seemed British but weren't, focused heavily on Burgundy and Bordeaux, and ate a lot of game birds. The Chemists sank deep into the processes that created the wines, identifying the story in Brix levels and yeast strains and pH. The guy who'd had what was now Thessaly's territory—he'd been fired for low sales, not spared even by being one of Gavin's best friends—had been a Chemist.

Their top-selling salesperson, Bob Harvill, was a Wine Dad. Wine Dads were the suburban reps who wore polo shirts and khakis, knew untold volumes but were reluctant to burden you with them, and made bank without bragging about it because they did so selling such unsexy wines. Bob lived upstate and covered four hundred miles of territory without ever enjoying the lifestyle that had drawn the rest of them into the business in the first place.

And then there were the Poets. They were often into biodynamics and natural wines, more literary than mystical. A not-insignificant portion played bass in bands with names like "Residual Sugar." In describing a wine, their references ranged from seventies cinema, to Ovid, to baseball, to descriptions of musky scents and flavors that sounded intoxicating and a touch unsavory and took a while to register as being thinly veiled references to oral sex. Jonathan was a Poet.

Only recently had Wren started to notice what the taxonomy did not include: she'd encountered few Asian, Black, or Brown wine professionals, and maybe one or two Black winemakers, in her whole life. Lionel Garrett Imports was almost entirely white. At nearly every American vineyard Wren had visited, the hardest work was done by Brown people, yet they were underrepresented in the better-paying parts of the industry like sales and distribution. She was devoted to the industry, but no one would say it was a humanitarian oasis.

Most of the time, Wren loved her job. She could now talk to winemakers without stammering, assess a room and a wine list for opportunity, sleep soundly on international flights. She could not imagine life without her work, not after she'd built her whole existence in the shape of it. But sometimes—just sometimes, every now and then—she did wonder if she'd somehow made a mistake leaving fine dining for wine importing. Restaurant jobs were demanding but finite; when she'd walked away each night, Wren hadn't thought of it again until she returned to work. Now she often struggled not to obsess over her past and future decisions; she sweated through her blouse every day. Would she ever work and not obsess? Sometimes she feared her ambition would always keep her slightly miserable.

•

After any meeting with Lionel, it was de rigueur for the sales team to go out for drinks and dinner. Actually, they did this most nights, after *any* meeting, usually at a place of Gavin's choosing. They sought out cheap, oily noodles, endless tapas, Trinidadian curried goat, Italian trattorias. But these dinners weren't just about sharing good food—there was subtle one-upmanship at play: Who could bring the best bottle of wine to pair with the cuisine? Who could best withstand the prickly, taxing nature of team building as Lionel defined it and Gavin enforced it? Your attendance ensured you were in the game and that people remembered you when it was time to move to a better territory or ask for a favor.

Thessaly was pretty sure this was the reason, several years earlier, she'd been able to move out of customer service and into sales when a spot opened up in Westchester. And again when she left Westchester to sell to the Lower East Side. As always, Thessaly was drinking away across the table from Gavin, effectively keeping herself top of mind.

This was why Thessaly never missed a dinner, and why every few months, almost as a challenge for herself, she tried to get Wren to come out too. Thessaly was often the only woman at these things—the other female sales rep, Sabrina, had handled the Upper West Side since long before Gavin started with the company. Sabrina managed to do this job and have a family and keep her intimidating Italian eyewear sparkling and her chestnut hair in a smooth pageboy. She had no interest in proving she could drink as much as the cool kids in some far-flung neighborhood, and she seemed to have no desire to be a mentor.

During her first week on the job, hoping for an ally, Thessaly asked Sabrina to lunch. Sabrina reluctantly agreed to coffee, where she ordered an espresso, never put down her phone, and at one point raised a finger to quiet Thessaly so she could place an order for lamb chops at her local butcher. Just as Thessaly was starting to get angry—she knew she was inconsequential; she didn't need Sabrina to drive home the point—Sabrina had taken off her glasses and rubbed the bridge of her nose where the pads dug in. Without the frames, her eyes were large and hazel and slightly protruding and vulnerable. "Don't take it personally," she said. "No one gets more than thirty percent of my focus, that's all. Lionel's never really forgiven me for having kids *and* talking to them."

Sabrina was not deliberately unfriendly, Thessaly realized, just completely booked both personally and professionally, from dawn to dusk. Thessaly had no interest in children herself, and secretly thought there must be easier ways to live than trying to please several dictators at the same time. She also had a hard time imagining Sabrina moving up in the company. Lionel respected her institutional knowledge, but he wasn't going to twiddle his thumbs while she placed an order at Citarella.

Wren and Thessaly had never had lunch together, just the two of them, and that was fine with Thessaly. They didn't cross paths a lot because Wren worked on Jonathan's portfolio of wines from Switzerland, Champagne, and Germany, and Thessaly sold not just his portfolio, but everyone's. Wren was one of those worker-bee types—not a salesperson, more of a numbers drone and transporter of goods across state lines. Every now and then she caught Thessaly's attention by saying something insightful about a wine, but no one would say Wren was the company's prime source of razzle-dazzle. That made it easy for Thessaly to concentrate on more pressing matters, like persuading a surly sommelier that their order needed to be doubled or that her wine should stay on the by-the-glass menu, where much of her money was made.

But at the meeting that morning, amid the excitement and chaos of twenty people imagining themselves king in the wispy fantasy of a post-Lionel future, Thessaly had glanced over and seen the most fascinating look on Wren's face. She'd been sitting there with both hands around her coffee cup as if for warmth, though the conference room temperature had just risen ten degrees in flop sweat, and she was gazing at the table as if it held a meal she'd dreamed of for decades, or a man she used to love. Thessaly now understood that as the competiton played out over weeks, months—who could say?—she would have to factor in Wren.

Wren must have sensed Thessaly's gaze. She looked up and her face went back to its usual inscrutability. But for the first time, Thessaly was interested in who she was dealing with. She and Wren didn't have to be pals; she just needed to know what she was up against.

She stopped by Wren's desk later and said, "We're going to Casa Mono. You in the mood for some chorizo and Rioja?"

For the first time, Wren seemed about to say yes.

Thessaly hadn't really expected that, and immediately wanted to walk it back.

"Who's coming?" Wren asked.

"The usual. Gavin, of course. Legs. Maybe Amit. Greg." Thessaly was careful to keep her tone neutral when she mentioned Greg. Lionel had met Greg at a Bordeaux tasting and promptly hired him, declaring him one to watch. Greg was only a few years out of

Vassar, one of those scary wine obsessives who'd grown up drinking the Burgundy his parents paid for and issuing cutting opinions about a product he'd never be able to make himself. Thessaly might have a degree from a chichi liberal arts college herself, but she also had a farmer's contempt for people who could not produce, only critique, who had plenty of time to study wine when they didn't have responsibilities like rent. (Greg still lived in his parents' brownstone.)

Wren's gray eyes hooded by the tiniest fraction; she had been looking slightly interested until Thessaly mentioned Greg. She smoothed a blond curl unnecessarily against her skull, though it was already brushed back like a prison matron's. Her straight dark brows made her look as if she were permanently anticipating some disaster. "I'm pretty swamped," she said. "Getting ready for France."

Thessaly made sure her relief was not visible. "No problem. We can catch up then."

"Oh," said Wren. "Yes. I knew you were coming. We'll touch base then."

Well, fine. They could be awkward on another continent and tonight Thessaly could go have a few drinks with people who were fun. People who knew how to throw back some Tempranillo and work their recent sales numbers into the conversation.

Several salespeople were already at the restaurant when Thessaly arrived, hunched over their massive glasses of red and a lone plate of jamón ibérico.

"Kitchen's slow," Gavin said, nodding at the ham.

"Thank god," Thessaly said. She poured herself slightly more than a measured glass. It would have been wise to pace herself, as this would be the first of many wines to taste and compare. Then again, this had been a day. "I was afraid you'd all lost your appetites at the mere notion of life without Lionel."

Gavin smiled thinly at this. "More will be revealed," he said, reminding her that as her boss he knew more than she did, "but I wouldn't worry about it yet. I didn't hear anything concrete in Lionel's words, did you?"

"I guess not," Thessaly admitted. But she didn't trust Gavin when he was being reassuring. Comforting people went against the fiber of Gavin's being.

"He's probably just trying to motivate us," said Greg. He took the last slice of ham without asking if anyone else wanted it. "And I'm all for it. It's how we got here, right?" He cast an appraising look around the restaurant, as if to confirm it deserved him. Thessaly thought pettily that if Greg wanted to be a man-about-town, he would have to quit dressing like a toddler at Easter, in neat little shirts buttoned all the way up and with his blond hair flopping across his forehead.

"Hear, hear," said Legs, raising a glass. The server set down a sizzling plate of chorizo, from which Legs made a point of plucking a slice with his fingers to show he had evolved beyond pain. Legs was their resident misfit, a leggy beanpole with a deeply seamed face, black hair pinwheeling out in all directions, and decrepit leather pants, which, he often made an unsettling point of noting, he could always wipe clean. He'd had a storied youth in punk and now sold to the East Village, because people loved buying fine wine from someone who could tell you the precise ways in which the Mudd Club had been unsanitary. Thessaly had done the math and suspected Legs either was stretching the truth or had been sneaking into the clubs at about thirteen, both of which seemed likely. Legs's refusal to answer questions about his

14

current address and the region of his childhood was friendly but absolute, though he was always glad to tell them the most appalling, debauched stories of his youth. "This motherfucker," Gavin had once said, an arm slung around Legs's skinny neck, "is in the background of like seven Nan Goldin photographs." No one had seen them, but everyone believed it.

"I think I've shown plenty of motivation," Thessaly said. "Don't you worry, Greg. You'll claw your way out of Hoboken." But she said it merrily and reached across the table to toast him.

Greg frowned at the spot where her glass had touched his. "Hoboken's up-and-coming," he said.

"That's what I'm saying," Thessaly agreed. She pretended not to perceive Gavin's steady look in her direction. Okay, so she was gaslighting Greg just a bit, but this was a boy who talked over everyone at meetings, who'd been known to take credit for other people's discoveries, who never missed a chance to remind them that international travel at an early age was, in fact, quite taxing.

She made a show of casually pouring herself a fresh glass. She was already getting that easy, loose-limbed feeling that let her stretch out after a day spent running and striving. If it wasn't her job to be a professional drinker, it might seem like a problem.

"Well, since you're all so motivated," Gavin said, "let's use it. How about a little sales team competition?"

Legs suppressed a sigh. Greg leaned forward. Amit, who'd been pacing outside the restaurant on his phone, joined them at the table in time to hear the last few words and said, "Aw, Jesus, I was gone for ten minutes."

Gavin laughed. He was never happier than when he was issuing a challenge. "You're all going to new territories next week.

Whoever comes back and sells the most from the region they visited gets a reward. Maybe a blowout dinner. Maybe a trip. Maybe a little face time with Lionel to secure your futures."

He allowed this to sink in and then summoned the server for one of his lengthy harangues concerning the wine list, in which he would run a finger up and down the columns, commenting at length, until he'd finally engaged in sufficient Socratic dialogue with himself to order another bottle. Before the server arrived—she was moving slowly, probably sensing her immediate future—he added, "Impressing Lionel now counts more than ever."

Those final words had the desired effect: They all sat up a little straighter, more eager, and hungrier. Gavin had skillfully made the big unknown a much clearer, nearer goal, with a fresh dimension of their professional pride at stake. As far as Thessaly could tell, she was the only one who saw the flaw: Yes, it was good to impress Lionel. But did any of them really have a better chance than Gavin at becoming Lionel's successor? Realistically, they would not be advancing themselves as candidates to take over for Lionel one day—they were advancing Gavin.

Gavin smiled at her and Thessaly gave him a knowing grin back, just so he knew *she* knew what he was doing. Sometimes she forgot Gavin had gotten where he was by being a top-notch salesperson himself.

Thessaly had other long-term goals. Selling wine was research for her, a useful way to learn the aspects of the business she hadn't been exposed to growing up on her family's grape farm and tasting the output with her parents. She never told anyone she didn't plan to be shilling wine her whole life, but of course she didn't.

Her family were growers on the Sonoma Coast, a forbidding, foggy, hilly place that yielded some of the best Chardonnay and

Pinot grapes in the country. Her parents had started buying tiny parcels of land decades earlier, working it and adding to it bit by bit, until now their acreage stretched over a significant chunk of the hills and valleys near the Pacific coastline. Her family was land-rich and cash-poor, the land and its operations always demanding a tiny bit less than they gave. Both Thessaly and her older sister, Arielle, had gone into wine as well, but avoided the never-ending task of farming. Ari had majored in business and taken a job with one of the many corporate California producers, skillfully managing the tasting room of a winery in Sonoma and never getting worked up about their extremely commercial, suspiciously consistent wine. And Thessaly had wound up here.

Her goal was to make wine, and not on a massive, life-draining piece of land like her parents did, but something more intimate, more changeable, and weirder. She didn't want to turn out thin withholding wines in bottles with elegant ivory labels and loopy script. Her bottles would be personal, artistic. Was that even possible these days? So much of Sonoma seemed expensive and sleek, which was why she couldn't see herself working in one of the huge commerce-driven wineries with an on-site chemist, a shiny pamphlet, and the same look-alike tasting rooms—with weathered wood tables and benches, white walls, exposed beams.

When Thessaly pictured her future, she saw herself in an as-yet-unnamed small city where she could walk out of her wine-making room and down a street when she needed something. She'd make esoteric little blends and spotlight unknown, oddball varietals that she'd give funky labels and witty names. She'd sell, in other words, unfamiliar wines to people who didn't know they wanted them. And after her time selling wine around Bronxville and Yonkers and Scarsdale and Tuckahoe, and now to a lot of extremely grouchy Lower East Siders, she was pretty sure she could do it.

But she was not *positive*. A few years after college, she worked up the nerve to tell her parents about her dream. She was nervous that what she wanted was not what they'd built, and less practical than what Ari was doing. "I was thinking maybe you could reach out to one of the winemakers who use our fruit," she had said, after briefly describing the broad strokes of making tiny wines for like-minded people. "They might let me apprentice with them," she added tentatively. Her father's hawklike face had remained immobile, and, as Thessaly said the words aloud, her dream had started to sound a little spindly and half-assed to her: handmade labels, magically sourced fruit, imaginary real estate that was both spacious enough for equipment and squarely in town. She stopped talking.

"Maybe eventually," her father said. "For now, your mom and I both think you need to keep learning." That was it. No next steps, no reaching out to contacts or encouragement for her to do so either. He wasn't the type to throw her a parade, but she'd been stung by how much the exchange felt like a tactful avoidance of the truth: her father believed that she was not up to this.

And if he were just some dismissive guy like Greg it wouldn't matter—she could have disregarded him. But Thessaly's father always seemed to *know* things, and he was usually correct. He had spent decades working directly with winemakers. He understood why so many tried to make wine and gave up. He'd long known that Thessaly dreamed of trying herself, even before she'd worked up the nerve to say it.

He hadn't given his blessing. No, he'd told her to "keep learning."

She knew she shouldn't care what he thought. She didn't shy away from debates with him—most of their conversations turned into a throw-down about politics, tariffs, ground cover. She'd spent her childhood eavesdropping on her father and his friends arguing over dinner about Brix levels, about pH, about the joy of arguing. But even after she learned to needle them all in return, she still feared that underneath her loud, well-timed points, her will was soft, wobbly goo. And when her father had implied she wasn't ready, deep down she agreed.

She *wasn't* ready. Her greatest fear was that she never would be. Her father was a pain in the ass, but he had nerve and vitality. So did her mother. Her parents had ditched the suburbs and bootstrapped their way into owning and successfully farming some of the most temperamental crops on the most expensive land in the country. Their work hadn't been any easier back then. (Although, in fairness, it had been cheaper. Land was now far too expensive for anyone like Thessaly to do what her parents had done.)

By pure chance, when she'd happened upon Lionel Garrett and they shared a glass of Sardinian Carignane, she discovered that sales came easily to her. The possibility of success was too tantalizing. It felt too good to have the bragging rights, the lifestyle, the travel. Here, no one ever looked at her as she was building her sales numbers month after month and said, "For now, you need to keep learning." Not one fucking person.

· CHAPTER 2 ·

No matter how many times she walked into a grand French tasting room, Wren could not stop being privately amazed to find herself in this glorious place: her hand touching a three-hundred-year-old tabletop with a finish as silken as fabric, her footsteps echoing over the patterned parquet floors, her breath stirring the air that smelled so deliciously of grape skins and rising bread. The first few years, when she was a brand-new customer service rep and not expected to have an opinion, some part of her had waited to be asked to leave. The other part of her breathed in extra deeply, as if to anchor herself in this world just by drinking up its atmosphere. And perhaps it had worked, because here she was.

"*Bonjour!*" She exchanged the requisite four cheek kisses with Fernand and Mireille, the owners of this massive estate in Champagne. They were both in their fifties, with engraved Gallic faces and ash-blond hair, and were as slim and elegant as a matched pair of whippets. Their exquisitely impersonal French manners reminded Wren every year that the couple displayed their estate to countless people, as their predecessors had done and their children would too. The family had been making

Champagne for centuries, their practiced demeanor implied, and they would do it for centuries more.

"Wren, my dear, *bienvenue*," said Mireille. She had barely finished speaking when Thessaly darted forward from behind Wren and emitted a stream of pretty French. Mireille looked taken aback and pleased at once, and the two headed into the tasting room.

Wren turned and saw Gavin looking at her. He seemed pleased by Thessaly's maneuvering—Gavin saw operations people like herself as competition for his salespeople. Wren's direct boss, Jonathan, was the one making decisions about what to import from this region, but Gavin liked to remind everyone that without his team, the company was nothing but a warehouse full of unsold wine. That was why he was here, after all; he didn't usually come on this trip to France. Wren wondered if this was all because of Lionel having whatever mini-stroke had led him to start speculating about stepping down someday far in the future.

Unless the future was closer than she'd thought?

They settled at the table, the producers at the head, Jonathan to their left, Gavin to their right. Wren and Thessaly wound up beside each other. Wren could see this was going to be trouble. If Jonathan was secretly thinking about moving into Lionel's role, importing might not be his only goal for this trip. Wren worried that despite his demurrals, he was in fact closely evaluating them all, watching how Thessaly talked so easily like the salesperson she was, and how Gavin was nodding gravely as he and Fernand conferred about the weather. Wren was the only one of them who was not in the mix and making herself at home. It had never bothered her before. She'd always felt she was doing well, learning and taking care of business without fuss, but now that was simply not enough.

She leaned over and whispered to Thessaly, "Hey, what do you think about doing the yellows? They're a pain, I know, but talk about a great way to really learn the list."

The yellows were a massive binder of carbon paper that tracked the names of each wine, how much Jonathan was reserving, plus your own tasting notes. It was a tricky job because Jonathan rarely looked at the keeper of the yellows and said, "Sixty cases of the nonvintage." Instead, he ho-hummed and chatted and sometimes a number slipped out, which he assumed someone would catch. To do the yellows well, you had to listen attentively to the conversation and to Jonathan's every murmur. The book was sitting between them on the table, and Wren subtly pushed it a quarter inch closer to Thessaly.

Wren had requested they bring along one of the customer service newbies to perform this exact task, but Lionel and Jonathan said it was an unnecessary expense. What they meant was that Wren would do it, even though she'd been promoted twice out of her original customer service position. Was it anti-feminist that she was trying to pawn it off on her female colleague? Probably. But Wren had to work with the situation she was given, and Gavin and Jonathan would never do it. Asking them would be so ludicrous it would create a scene.

Thessaly's head snapped in her direction. "Isn't that the sort of thing you and Jonathan need to handle?"

"I can do yellows in my sleep," Wren said with a shrug. "It's all about having as many skills as possible. Don't you guys have a little contest going? I heard Greg say something about seeing the Tuscany producers this year. Man, Tuscan wine—people just beg for that stuff. Jonathan's book requires more knowledge and skill. I'll do the yellows."

Thessaly looked Wren dead in the eye, her chocolate eyes narrowed, her full berry mouth, which was almost always turned up mirthfully on one side, pressed thin. "I know exactly what you're doing," Thessaly whispered, "but if you need the schmoozing practice, I'm happy to show Jonathan I'm a team player." She took the yellows book from Wren and opened it, a pen poised over the first page as the tasting began.

The handoff didn't feel quite as triumphant as Wren had hoped, but it didn't matter. She was telling the truth that this would help Thessaly sell. She'd walk away from this trip with the quality and quantity of wines they chose deeply embedded in her brain. It just so happened that it would also help Wren find air to speak while she kept Thessaly busy with admin work. She'd have done the same to anyone.

Jonathan ran these visits in a precise format. The first few minutes were spent on kisses, greetings, and check-ins about the nearby villages, the producers' families, and whatever the current American president was doing to vex the Europeans. Then they'd begin tasting nonvintage blends, specific recent vintages, and finally the finest and oldest Champagnes that had been aging for several years longer, being rotated one-eighth of an inch at a time in the great chalk cellars beneath them. Jonathan would say things about the weather that had affected the harvest, effortlessly distinguishing between the many different harvest years represented at the table. There would be some coded regret over the wines that had not sold so well the year before, and less-coded pushback on the bluntness of the American palate.

Fernand and Mireille were going to be difficult today because a few of their wines had sold poorly last year. Jonathan would have no choice but to fall on his sword if he wanted to keep the relationship, which he did. This was a prestigious house that hadn't deigned to sell to the American market until Jonathan wooed them for several years straight, and it would look terrible to lose it as a partner. Every producer had an off year, which had contributed to the sales problem last year. But no one would ever say *that* to the winemakers.

As Fernand poured the first wines, Wren thought how different these people were from everyone she'd grown up with. She came from a land of comfy, rounded people in soft pale clothing, who could talk for hours about nothing much. She had grown up being the quiet one simply because she had nothing to say about family gossip or church. That habit of listening had served her well, but she knew it was time to start talking now. She just was not exactly sure how.

She took a breath and focused on the glass of wine in front of her. Of course. She didn't need to provide commentary on French politics or the new café in Aÿ. They only wanted her to talk about their wine.

"This is a deeper gold than last year," she said. "Though I loved that pale grassy tint too."

Jonathan was nodding. "Aged a touch longer?" He took a sip and smiled. "This reminds me of a slightly richer version of that nonvintage I loved so much about six years ago, with maybe ten percent more Meunier. And that was one of your best."

The couple looked pleased; Jonathan's prodigious memory was both a necessity and an effective party trick. He committed every detail of producers' work to memory and called upon it effort-lessly, and Wren had yet to see anyone resist the flattery.

Wren had learned so much from Jonathan that she would've followed him on a tasting of the pine saps of Scandinavia. You'd never guess that an unassuming man with prematurely white hair in disarray and wearing his ever-present sport jacket was slowly changing the way Americans drank wine. But he absolutely was. Jonathan was the first to see the potential for German Riesling and small-grower Champagnes—he single-handedly created new markets in the U.S. even if no one wanted one to exist. He'd be part of determining the future if Lionel really did step down.

Jonathan *had* to be looking at all of them through totally different eyes now, the way Wren was, and reporting back to Lionel about who needed to be swept aside to make way for the ones who'd run the company.

The big chilly room went silent but for the sounds of scratching pens, wines sloshing in mouths, and spitting into heavy silver canisters. Wren considered a Blanc de Blancs and reached for the spittoon once she had gotten what she needed. There was an art to spitting, which felt unnatural and frankly nauseating—until you tasted one hundred wines without spitting and lived the true meaning of *nausea*. Although Wren could never quite quash the feeling that she was insulting the makers of the wine, it had to be done. The key was to purse your lips and lift the tongue in one move to create a focused, petite jet into the bucket. No dribbles. No hesitation. Jonathan had a magical ability to spit almost silently, and Gavin always looked slightly peeved, as if he were rejecting the wine. Thessaly's spitting sang against the silver spittoon walls, practically birdsong.

The fervent attention to each wine, as they moved on to two vintage cuvées, circulated the air like an electric current. Wren loved the solemnity and intensity of these moments. Back in the office, it was tempting to be the one with the most cutting quip when a wine revealed itself to be inferior, or to be the one who best understood the finest points of an impressive blend. But here, with the people who had worked for years to tend to these bottles, such quick judgments would have been deeply offensive.

Wren focused on tasting and writing in her notebook, closing her eyes and capturing the images that came into her head: fresh linen, baking bread, the juice trickling down the crisp white flesh of a green apple. People thought Champagne was celebratory, but so much work went into creating it. To Wren, good Champagne felt searching, even soulful, the weight of it asking something of her.

Jonathan was the only one who could break the silence. Once, Gavin began to speak, but Jonathan started talking over him as if he hadn't said a word. Wren tried not to show her shock—it was such a power move from someone who almost never felt the need to make them, and it made her wonder why Gavin was here at all if Jonathan didn't want him here, because he clearly didn't.

Thessaly's eyes darted from Jonathan, to Gavin, to the wine-makers, with an occasional questioning look at Wren, who pretended not to see. She would not ally herself against Jonathan, not even with a glance.

They worked their way through several rounds and several orders, but the feeling at the table was increasingly tense. The numbers Jonathan was offering were too low to make the producers happy, too high to make Gavin happy. Finally, Fernand stood abruptly and went over to a sideboard and returned with three bottles. "A few rosé Champagnes," he said, with an air of defiance. "I know they are underappreciated. But still."

Jonathan perked up and the other three all blinked. Pink Champagne was a subset of a subset, a sliver of the American market, but the rosy, baby-cheek color made Wren happier just watching it tumble into her glass. "*Méthode saignée*," Fernand added. He was too polite to assume any one person might not know the winemaking term, so he added, "Crucial to bleed the juice off the skins and seeds at just the right time."

They took a sip and began paying attention to their own experiences. Gavin—always a little pretentious, which was how he exerted his power over the more lumpen boys on the sales team—stroked his perfect beard, his gaze fixed on the wood of the ancient table. Thessaly looked relieved, her jaw working slightly. And Jonathan was hunched over his glass and nodding to himself as if he'd just remembered something. Finally, he looked over at Fernand and Mireille and broke into a smile. A bubble of laughter and relief rose above the table and burst; renewed, they began to taste the other wines: one older vintage; one young and still slightly disjointed; a faintly strawberry-hued blend. Was that last wine as delicious as Wren thought, or was it just the moment?

Apparently it wasn't just the moment. "I'd love to order twenty cases of the Saignée," Jonathan said, "I can't get over it. It's the nimblest juice bomb I've had in a very long time." Gavin and Thessaly (and probably Wren too) all looked shocked at the vulgarity of the term, but Jonathan delivered it with such delight that Fernand and Mireille laughed.

They were also taken aback by the numbers: twenty cases was a nominal order for the new-release Champagne, but a fat one for rosé. Where would they possibly sell it all? There was only one Valentine's Day. Then again, Jonathan had managed to persuade thousands of people that German wine was worth drinking and that Swiss wine existed. If he thought he could sell it, he probably could.

Mireille cast a significant look at her husband. He got up one more time and brought out a final bottle, coated in a thick feathery rime of mold and cellar dust. He opened it gently and slowly, the cork releasing the characteristic whisper that said all the bubbles were still where they belonged, and poured an inch of something rich and golden into their glasses. It was understood that this was not one to judge or sell. It was simply one to share, a reminder of what old Champagne truly was, for almost none of this made it to America.

Nervously, but in keeping with the singularity of the moment, Wren swallowed and said, "*Je vous remercie, monsieur,*" which she hoped was a formal enough thank-you. Gavin looked at her in consternation, as if his shoe had spoken.

Fernand's thick white eyebrows rose a millimeter before he gave her an expressive Gallic nod of acknowledgment. He directed a phrase her way—and did so in French, which was a compliment in itself—but he spoke too quickly for her to comprehend, and she stuttered as she tried to think how to express herself without inviting further conversation.

Naturally, Thessaly followed up with, "*Merci mille fois, monsieur, vraiment,*" in a much better accent. (Jonathan's French was minimal; he was too successful now for it to count against him.) She was going to have to work on this.

Wren had to shake off self-doubt and focus on the moment. This final wine was the leonine bronze of an old coin, its mousse roaming languidly over their tongues. She forgot everything else but that wine, its age, its delicacy, its hidden rooms opening up.

Mireille flicked her eyes over to Wren. Immediately Wren's cheeks grew warm. Her host was looking at her frankly, openly, curiously. Wren didn't know what this meant. Maybe her good manners and her French phrases hadn't hidden a thing. They could see exactly who she was, a girl of no distinction and little education. She waited for Mireille to shift her attention to the more important people in the room. But instead, the woman reached past Fernand for the dusty, precious bottle and stood to pour another taste into Wren's glass, her arched eyebrows raised questioningly. She seemed to have decided that this visitor might be inconsequential but would be treated respectfully nevertheless. Wren straightened up and thanked her, as gravely as she could, handling the r more adroitly. Mireille acknowledged the effort with a crisp nod.

Thessaly had perked up when Mireille lifted the old bottle, and Wren waited for Thessaly to get a fuller pour than she had, or for Thessaly to say something adorable in reply. Thessaly smiled and nudged her glass forward, but Mireille did not offer her any more of the bottle. She offered it to no one else, in fact, no one but Wren. She simply set it back on the table and sipped from her own glass. And although Wren had no idea what she had done to earn this small boon, she felt it transform her entire day.

Thessaly looked confused, as it must have dawned on her that she had been ignored. How foreign it must be for her to not get the special pour, the extra sliver of foie gras. When, at last, her gaze came to rest on Wren, Wren took another calm, delicious sip.

It was ten o'clock in the morning, and she was in France, and she would never go back to bars that smelled of beer and fish fry. This moment would not last. It would change—the wine itself would change—even before they'd left the room. But right now? She was here, and she had earned her way to the table. That was more than she could say for some people.

•

Wren wasn't one of the protégés Lionel brought into the company. Often, Lionel would appear at the office one day with a mysterious new person at his elbow, nodding seriously as he strode through the office pointing out this and that, and the whole place would hear his booming voice talking about the tasting where they'd met, the fascinating wine the person had ordered at the next table at Le Bernardin, which obviously required a conversation with Lionel about that entrancing choice, and so on.

Wren was usually sanguine about these new hires. Some, like Gavin, thrived, and some flamed out spectacularly. They were always older and always men, until Thessaly. Thessaly had apparently met Lionel at the bar at Cru. Enough time had passed that fewer people looked at her askance, but the rumor had just enough of an unsavory ring that it had lingered longer than most. It was hard to hold it against her when she was out elbowing the boys in the ribs, being friendly and energetic in customer service, and slogging up and down the narrow parkways of Westchester without complaint for her first sales assignment. Other people often took pains to let you know they were used to finer neighborhoods and better wines than their first low-totem-pole positions afforded them. Thessaly never did, though Wren had overheard enough to know Thessaly had grown up traveling the world to visit other producers.

Nothing could be further from Wren's chilly Wisconsin childhood. She had grown up in a tiny bungalow with an overworked mother and an intermittent father. Wren had not gone to college (not yet) and hadn't stepped on a plane until she was twenty-one. Her parents hadn't served her bowls of daube and glasses of watered Bordeaux. Far from it. She suspected her colleagues knew this, aware that she struggled to participate in conversations about college or a meaningful childhood food memory.

There was no wine in her house when she was growing

up—none as long as her father, Barry, boomeranged in and out of AA, before he eventually left the family. Alcohol was verboten during her parents' marriage, but soon after her father left, Wren's mother had brought home a box of wine. (She hadn't gone back to school yet for her RN, or it might have been better wine.)

The memory of her mother pushing aside the food in the fridge to make room for the box, opening a cabinet to unearth never-before-seen wineglasses, was blazed into Wren's mind. Her mother washed and dried two of them and filled one halfway with cold pink liquid. Wren was sitting at the table waiting for dinner as she observed this event, but instead of cooking, her mother said, "Let's have a little time to relax first." She poured Dr Pepper into a second wineglass and the two of them sat at the kitchen table and sipped their drinks. Wren fixated on that glass of wine the entire time, entranced by the arcane knowledge her mother had been harboring without telling her. She examined her mother's dark wavy hair pulled back in a ponytail, her bare ears small and tight against her head, her dark eyes watchful and tired, but slowly coming to life. She wondered why her mother filled the glass only halfway; she admired the frosted sheen of condensation and the way her mother held the glass by its stem instead of gripping the bowl, how doing this shaped her fingers so gracefully.

They had never just sat together before. They had never partaken in a ritual like this, with special glasses and conversation. It felt very civilized and elegant, but mournful too. She knew the only reason her mother had brought wine into the house was because Wren's father was never coming back. But Wren had also felt excited. If her father could not stay here sober, then they had this, at least, this pretty drink, with its sharp smell on her mother's breath, its delicate vessels. It made her feel both monstrous and intrigued.

She'd never mentioned this story to her colleagues. Wren figured that once she was further up the ladder, she might be more open and self-deprecating about her humble beginnings, to show how far she'd come. But not yet.

She would have liked to be able to confide in someone about this. To have someone give her a reassuring but honest appraisal of her work and say, "You're worrying too much about that but you could do more of this." She wished she had someone to meet for coffee and long walks on weekends. Her past boyfriends didn't count; they came and went. Wren needed a friend who stuck around. But she spent all her time at work, where the closest possibility was the person who made her feel so inadequate, and who was left if not Thessaly? Sabrina, who was fifteen years her senior and after their years as colleagues was only now retaining the most basic facts about Wren? Gavin? Come on.

She was turning this over in her head as they departed the estate. To her surprise, Thessaly caught up to her on their walk to the car. "Hey," she said, glancing around to see where Gavin and Jonathan were. "Nice work getting that extra pour. If Lionel were here, he would have given you the Nod."

The Nod was Lionel's favorite public approval tactic: a little eye contact, a slow dip of the chin, all very serious. Wren got it once when she'd tracked down an expensive delivery that disappeared on its way to a restaurant. It was only at the wrong restaurant, but it was a big order that she'd located quickly enough to earn some respect. Maybe other people did not count the Nods they'd earned, but she did. Especially because half the purpose of the Nod was for others to see it.

"Thanks," Wren said. She hesitated, not wanting to seem vulnerable or grateful in any way. So she'd gotten a nice pour, so what? Jonathan hadn't even noticed.

Suddenly the fineness of the day dimmed a little. How was she supposed to make herself noticed to the whole company when her own boss overlooked her? Up ahead of them, Jonathan was getting into the car on the passenger side while Gavin got in to drive. She and Thessaly would be stuck in the backseat like kids, while Dad and Dad decided where to go and how to get there.

Wren gave in to a tiny moment of despair and exhaustion. "You know what," she said, "thanks for doing the yellows, but I'll just take them. You can . . . do whatever."

She expected her colleague to shrug and hand them over. But to her surprise, Thessaly refused. "Don't be an idiot," she said. "I told you: I know what you're doing, but when I say I'll do something, I do it."

"So I guess the yellows really will help you in Gavin's competition."

Thessaly looked surprised. "Okay, you're right. But"—she lowered her voice—"what he doesn't say is that if we show these great numbers, it doesn't really benefit us personally. Our little competition just makes Gavin look good to Lionel. Who else would Lionel promote if not Gavin?"

Wren blinked in surprise. It seemed wildly unlike Thessaly to break the honor code of the sales team. Gavin would be appalled.

"That's what I thought." Wren didn't know why she bothered to murmur; Jonathan and Gavin had no idea the women were not right behind them. "But then I figured, you never know. I know Lionel might just be motivating us, but then again, why bring it up to everyone if he isn't genuinely considering it?"

"Because he likes tantalizing people to see what we'll do,"

WINE PEOPLE

Thessaly said. "Listen, even if we think Gavin's the ringer, it benefits us to make a good showing."

"Definitely," said Wren. "Besides, Gavin doesn't have operations knowledge. Just sales."

Thessaly frowned. "True. But operations are nothing without sales."

Shit. Wren turned away, thinking that Gavin could learn operations but she was still not going to be great with sales. She didn't want Thessaly to perceive her faltering confidence. "Anyway," she said, "nice of you to keep the yellows. Let me know if you need help with Gavin's sales tournament."

Thessaly started walking briskly toward the car. "I'm not nice," she said over her shoulder. "And I don't need your help. I'm showing you I can do this stupid bookkeeping *and* my job at the same time *and* still show Gavin and Jonathan all the brilliant insights I have about these wines, so they go home remembering nothing but me."

"You don't think I can do it?" said Wren, walking more quickly to close the gap between them. "I've been doing this for longer than you."

Thessaly shot her a grin that was white-toothed and feral and beautiful. "And you're just now realizing how to do it so someone notices? Jesus Christ, Sparrow, I'm gonna be your boss even sooner than I thought. Get in the game."

34

· CHAPTER 3 ·

Thessaly was enjoying herself. Ever since the first visit that morning and through the three visits to producers that followed, she'd been feeling like she used to when she played basketball: light on her feet, full of sweaty energy and vital alertness. What a pleasure it was to show up someone by doing her job and yours! What fun to let Wren know Thessaly understood exactly what she, Wren, was trying to do and then turning it back in her face. (Thessaly had fouled out a lot in basketball.)

She wasn't even mad at Wren. Perversely, she found herself liking her for the first time. Thessaly needed a jolt. Sales was no easy task: she worked desperately hard to hold the company's ever-growing catalogue in her head and to charm the suspicious buyers of middle-of-the-road restaurants, and had spent endless, crushingly boring time alone in the car or on the subway. She'd needed some one-on-one competition.

And Wren *was* good competition, something Thessaly was both annoyed and pleased to discover. She'd started using her opportunities more concertedly after they left Fernand and Mireille, performing just enough to one-up Thessaly and not be obnoxious. All damn day, she'd been making astute observations,

35

noting the whisper of Arbane in one blend and divining the weather from three years earlier, even before Jonathan, in another. At one point she startled everyone by calling a passing hound by name.

Jonathan looked bemused, the estate owners delighted that someone had remembered their beloved ancient canine, and Gavin looked straight at Thessaly as if she had egged on Wren. Thessaly scribbled away at the yellows and pretended she didn't see him. Out of the corner of her eye she saw Wren stroke the dog's massive head with a serene smile.

Now they were finally on their way to dinner, and Thessaly was ravenous. Outside the window the manicured hills rolled by, dotted with the occasional Gothic abbey and charming village, rows of wine barrels and tractors puttering along the streets. She was always hungry, but buying trips with Jonathan made it worse because he categorically refused to eat lunch. There were too many people to see and wines to taste, too much palate-busting vinaigrette and no point—no point!—in eating a jambon-beurre on a fragrant baguette and perhaps an oozing satiny little wedge of Camembert. Or the tiniest sliver of one of those fruit tarts with pâte sucrée crust and crème pâtissière.

Thessaly had failed to bring enough snacks.

Which was dumb on her part because she knew of Jonathan's well-deserved reputation for this no-lunch quirk. Lionel had finished their last meeting (after tantalizing them all with the possibilities of wealth and advancement and untold power once the king stepped down someday) with the announcement, "Jonathan, consider this your annual reminder not to starve the employees." Jonathan had laughed the evasive chuckle of someone whose colleagues would have no choice but to consume a box of Tic Tacs behind the car to make it through another twenty-five wines before dinner.

She'd hoped Wren was the type to carry almonds in her purse, probably with a Bible and a sewing kit, but when she'd asked, Wren's gray eyes took on that fervent holy look people sometimes got on an empty stomach and ambient alcohol.

Oh well, they were almost to the restaurant. And no matter how exhausted Thessaly was from jet lag and her hand cramped from scrabbling at the yellows all day, and how god-awful sick she was of Champagne, this had been a much more interesting day than she'd expected.

Jonathan startled her out of her reverie. She'd never heard him raise his voice before, and a glance at Wren's face told her Wren hadn't either.

"You had no right to tell Duvillier we'd even consider a visit," Jonathan exclaimed. He was hunched over, arms crossed, in the front seat of the car. "Obviously I'm aware of their offerings—they'll certainly never run out of the stuff—and if I'd wanted to go, I would have. I've been coming here for thirty years, you realize."

"I *didn't* make any promises," Gavin said. The harder Jonathan stared at him, the more he affected relaxation, tapping out a rhythm on the steering wheel as if to underscore who was driving. "I simply had a conversation with them, on the off chance we had time, and I did it because—"

"We don't have time," Jonathan said shortly. "So that's that."

"Because Lionel asked me to," Gavin finished.

A terrible silence filled the car. Thessaly had been inside dramatic pauses like this herself when her parents were having major disagreements about some direction for the vineyard. It

37

was not the signal of a truce but a gathering of arms. For the first time, she understood something about this company that she never had before: Jonathan and Lionel, though partners and colleagues going back thirty years, did not see eye to eye. And Gavin, who knew it, had just made it clear where he fell: on Lionel's side.

Thessaly had always assumed Lionel was the head and Jonathan the heart. Lionel was the one who roosted at one of the best tables at La Paulée every year, the annual Burgundy tasting that was half harvest party and half battle royale to see who'd brought the finest bottles. Lionel was the one who'd begun his career by selling cases of wine out of a rattling Volvo. (He'd met Jonathan when they worked together at a liquor store on the Upper East Side, traveling to Europe to drink the wines they couldn't quite forget, until finally they realized they'd have to sell some to finance the next trip.) Jonathan's esoteric rare wines were the counterweight to Lionel's big commercial plonk, and Jonathan, come to think of it, would understand Thessaly's hopes for the future: this man understood why you'd want to make a few barrels of something like, say, Cabernet Pfeffer, instead of lakes of middling Chardonnay.

Pfeffer was a great idea, actually. She filed it away for the ramshackle farmhouse-in-town of her future.

"Well," said Jonathan. His voice was very soft. "If Lionel wants it, then why don't you set it up? But if I don't like their wine, then you get to be the one who explains it to them."

Gavin cleared his throat. "I wouldn't dream of putting you in a difficult position," he said, with breathtaking dishonesty.

Thessaly finally dared a look over at Wren, now that the two in front were both focused firmly ahead of them. Gavin's hands were gripping the wheel and Jonathan was glowering at the road as if he had to keep the car on the asphalt with the power of his thoughts.

Wren was watching her. For a moment their eyes met and Thessaly read a furious mixture of emotions moving through Wren's gray eyes, her straight dark brows. One blond curl had escaped her chignon and a pink flush stained her cheeks. She looked affronted and uncertain, as shocked as Thessaly that this disagreement not only existed but was allowed to play out before the employees.

At the restaurant, Thessaly found herself alone with Gavin for a moment, which she seized to ask him what was going on with Duvillier.

"We're in the neighborhood," Gavin said, and Thessaly glared at him. "Okay, fine. Lionel's pushing for it. Retirement may be a little more imminent than he lets on. And what does Lionel always want?"

"More," said Thessaly.

Gavin laughed. "Come on, did I not train you at all? He wants to feel sure his baby is safe and thriving and basically rich before he can step away. That's why he pushed so hard to get Big Sky going last year, to get us that office in Manhattan." Big Sky Red and Big Sky White were Lionel's private-label table wines, two blends with catchy labels and unintimidating profiles. Thessaly had once heard Jonathan describe them as "present." But they sold. A lot.

Jonathan and Wren were headed to the table, Wren looking frighteningly purposeful all of a sudden. What did she know? What had Jonathan said to her about this whole Duvillier thing, and was this going to come back on Thessaly? Flustered, Thessaly focused on unfolding her napkin. "How long have you known about all this?" she hissed at Gavin, figuring it was worth one last try.

But Gavin must have had enough of confidences because he said only, "About what?" and then it was too late to say anything more.

•

Their first day was behind them, the first four-course dinner of poulet de Bresse and langoustine bisque and ethereal pastry, and finally Wren was alone in her hotel room in a nightshirt, her feet throbbing. Wren had rarely been so glad to be by herself, even on trips like this. She'd never had a day exhausting in quite the way this one was: Who had invited Thessaly and Gavin? She and Jonathan would have sailed through this alone! She'd have taken her notes and kept track of the yellows and receded into the background and it would have been *fine*. But Jonathan would hardly have noticed anything she did and she wouldn't have gotten to taste more of that old Champagne. In fact, she would have been little more than a secretary. Maybe the exhaustion was worth it. Today she'd been . . . she'd been pretty great.

Oh, it felt like madness to attribute any of this triumphant day to Thessaly with her big jackal's grin or to Gavin for deciding now was the time to antagonize Jonathan at Lionel's bidding—but hadn't these factors been the difference? Hadn't Wren been the person she'd been today *because* Thessaly had pissed her off enough to make her want to work on her French and greet the producers as if she belonged and point out the things she tasted in their wines, because Gavin had made her think maybe she'd better be less trusting of everyone around her? And the wines themselves had opened to her like a book. She'd tasted like . . . whatever had absolutely flawlessly attuned taste buds and three times as many of them as other creatures. *That* was how incredible her palate was today. She knew it; she'd known it even as it was happening, and she had watched Jonathan take it in with growing pleasure and Gavin getting more and more frustrated that he had another person to contend with, whom he'd previously never bothered to notice.

Maybe whatever was going on in this company was going to be changed for the better. It wasn't just Lionel dangling succession in front of them while pushing around his own business partner in the meantime. Maybe Wren herself was changing.

She washed her face, spackled a layer of prescription toothpaste on her teeth as a prophylactic against the sensitivity that plagued everyone on these trips, thanks to all that harsh young wine they swished all day. Then she lay down on her bed to let it work on her teeth. The hotel was nothing special, but it was still a blessing compared to her apartment, a soulless brick box in Astoria that looked like a dentist's office and contained a decent couch, a cheap dining table, and a seventy-dollar bottle of grower Champagne, which she had bought before realizing she ought to have someone to drink it with. Plenty of people would drink it alone, the whole bottle, but Wren was ruthless about watching her alcohol intake. Besides, there were just some wines you wanted to drink with another person.

She'd been in New York for five years and was still figuring out how to be an adult. College appeared to be where most of her colleagues had learned basic life skills, while Wren was playing catch-up, paying attention to how people in her new world dressed and presented themselves and to the things they

seemed to regard as normal parts of life. They argued over
health insurance bills instead of being relieved to have insurance, period. They understood their tax withholdings. They
never looked nervous or ate too quickly when they shared meals,
because they never feared there would not be enough food or
that they would not have enough money to pay for it. One afternoon, Wren had eavesdropped on a twenty-minute conversation
between two sales reps about dining table shapes and pendant
lamps. She'd been aware such items existed, of course, but it
had truly never occurred to her to research, consider, and
choose. Her mother had never once held up two colors of curtains and asked Wren which one opened up the room. When
Wren looked around her studio with its sloping floors and beige
walls, she hoped for a future in which she could put this information to work.

She'd made it here thanks to her mother, Jeannie. Jeannie
was a tiny, trim NICU nurse who had raised Wren to be watchful, kind when she could be, and to build up what she called,
uncharacteristically, a fuck-you fund. (She never swore otherwise.) "You save it up and then just forget you have it till you
need it," she'd explained once, when Wren was thirteen and
babysitting for movie money. "Maybe it's a bad husband. Maybe
your boss grabs your butt and you need to quit before you have
your next job. Which I don't recommend, but sometimes cir-
cumstances force your hand. People will think you don't have
choices, but you will."

Jeannie delivered this explanation not long after she'd kicked
out Wren's father and gone back to nursing school. For Wren,
Barry had always been mysterious but affectionate, more inclined
than her mother to hug or ruffle her curls. Jeannie didn't show

love with kisses and nicknames; she showed it through work, by meeting every single need she could for her daughter.

Barry was less predictable. He could be very winning when he wasn't drunk: Every now and then he would help build an elaborate snow fort in the yard or reveal a hidden talent for drawing comics. When she was in sixth grade, he was sober for almost a year, his longest stint. He came home when he said he would, grilled burgers, and whistled Beatles songs like any other dad, and relief and cautious optimism seeped into her and her mother like radiation. Wren allowed herself to look forward to that one-year anniversary. Maybe they'd have a cake. She felt guilty for having any doubt, which could ruin the whole thing if her father sensed it. Life seemed to have changed.

Then came the day when she needed food coloring and Alka-Seltzer to make a homemade lava lamp for science class. Her mother was working and Barry was making dinner, but when Wren went to find him, the kitchen was dark, the burners off. She found her father stretched out on the couch, the TV flickering, and asked him to take her to the store.

Barry slid his eyes, only his eyes, in her direction. She knew immediately; the knowledge was a hot-ice sensation unfurling all the way to her toes and fingertips, even her chin somehow. He sat up, moving like a puppet with some strings cut. "Let's go," he said, slapping his knees.

"Never mind. It's not due till Friday," she lied.

"Hey, Wren," Barry said, his voice suddenly penetrating, intent. For a moment she thought he was going to tell her a secret. He bent over slightly, as if to her level, and looked at her, hard, with the same gray eyes as hers. "Go get my keys, since you want them so fucking much."

It wasn't the swearing that made her eyes fill up but the sensation that the other selves her father had shown her had been masks and only this was real, the true self he no longer managed to hide. He had never hit her, but his face and voice were so indifferent that she realized she was no safer with this man than she would have been with any other stranger who'd entered the house.

Later, of course, Wren had understood that even though her mother refused to bad-mouth her father, she would have divorced him long ago if she had had a fuck-you fund of her own. Some part of Wren felt guilty about the savings account she opened with her babysitting money, and later her fast-food-worker money, and still later her waitressing money. But she knew her mom would be proud every time she went to the bank drive-through with another stack of velvety twenties that smelled like frying oil.

Through most of high school she built up her fund by working at a diner in the suburbs of Madison. Back then, downtown was considered dicey, so she and her friends rarely bothered to check it out, when there were bars lax about IDs closer to their neighborhood. But one evening her senior year, she and two girls from school had nothing else to do, so they walked up and down State Street, which was packed with UW students, and circled the capitol. They were on their way back to the car when Wren lingered before a bank of windows lit with warm yellow light, people seated in the frame of each, talking earnestly to waiters standing beside their tables. At least Wren thought they were waiters, but no one was wearing a uniform. They wore dark dresses and lipstick as if they might be dining there too.

She saw brick walls and paintings, tables set with goblets of golden or ruby liquid. No one rushed. People held up their glasses to admire the light through the wine, or to gently touch the bells of crystal across the white tablecloth. This was a different universe from that box of pink wine. The place seemed enchanted, exotic, and even foreign, but, at the same time—right there. It occurred to Wren that she could walk inside the door. Now. She would be too terrified to ask for a table, but she could enter.

The next week she went back to the restaurant in her best clothes, her hair tamed with a rubber band, and got a job as a back waiter, basically a busboy. The restaurant was called Heirloom. Her first day, she sat down for the staff meal before the rush began and listened hungrily to the swirl of knowledge around her. At first it was the food, which was rich and often French and unfamiliar and which, to her astonishment, she was expected to taste. But it became clear that the food was nothing without the wine, not to her anyway. She could taste things in wine—a whole story in a good glass of it—that made the wine director pause and listen to her.

The first time she tasted a real glass of wine was at that place. She wasn't supposed to, she was still underage, but a bartender had sneaked her a tiny pour of some old Bordeaux, because a table had left the last glassful of one of their most expensive wines for the staff. "Be cool about this," the bartender said. She was tall and blond and soignée and she seemed to find Wren either amusing or slightly in the way, like a pet rabbit. "You have to taste it, because I don't know when else you'll get the chance."

The restaurant had emptied of customers, but they were behind the employee-only door that led to the offices upstairs, where no one would see. Wren hoped the bartender would leave, but for some reason she stayed. So Wren sipped from her glass as she'd seen everyone else doing, letting some air enter her mouth with the wine so it could roll over her tongue.

She was so shocked that she looked up at the bartender as if she'd been stung. What was this? It seemed to start off with a wisp of smoke or leather, but then that lowered, somehow, into something rich and mushroomy and close to the earth, and at the same time there was something tart and spicy and fruity in there that she couldn't place—a berry, maybe. She swallowed reluctantly and took the kind of swirling sniff of the glass she'd seen people do, which was almost as stunning as tasting it. How could so many things be in this one liquid? How could it be that she had had one sip, one sniff, and now a second sip, and it had been half a dozen different little stories already—she had never realized wine could do this, that it could change not over years but moments. "What the fuck is this?" she'd finally asked, and the bartender laughed so loudly they both looked over their shoulders at the closed door. "An '85 Haut Brion," she said. "You will not see its like again. Or maybe you will, I don't know. You might get rich." Then she patted Wren on the shoulder and went off to close up, leaving her to finish the last few sips of wine, seated at the bottom of the employee stairs, feet braced against the door so no one could disturb her.

Anyone could cook, she learned, but not everyone could taste. Not everyone retained reams of information about varietals. By the time she was old enough to order wine, she'd absorbed a whole education in it. It hadn't felt like work. Wine felt like pleasure and it felt like magic. It felt like the thing that got her everywhere she wanted to go. It was, in fact, literally the thing that got her where she wanted to go: Heirloom's sommelier was a longtime admirer and buyer of Jonathan's portfolio, and he was the one who'd gotten Wren her first interview with Jonathan.

But there was always a drumbeat underneath, the fear that this wasn't passion but plain old addiction. Maybe her father had felt transported by his own first sip of Coors. How would she know? All she could do was be careful, she'd decided, always keeping track of how much she'd consumed and never wasting her time on a less-than-compelling wine. The only other option was not to drink at all, pursue chocolate-making or waitressing or some other line of work that didn't feel vital and right. She resolved that if she started to slide toward ruin, she'd stop drinking and get a job in something unconsumable. The key was never to start slipping.

Wren's eyes opened, and for a moment she was disoriented: she'd drifted into a semi-sleep and expected to find herself back at Heirloom, looking at its brick walls and white ceilings, but instead she was in a little French chamber of a hotel room, sprawled on the bed with a mouthful of expensive toothpaste. She got up to rinse her teeth and then crawled back into bed.

•

The next morning, Thessaly woke up in her ivory-walled room. She felt superhuman, probably because she had slept for the first time in thirty-six hours.

She brushed her teeth with Sensodyne, but already she was feeling twinges of sensitivity, and it was only the second day. She went downstairs to find breakfast.

Wren was sitting at one of the tables, a cup of coffee and a basket of croissants on the table before her. She was writing something furiously in the notebook she carried everywhere with her.

Thessaly didn't want to join her, but sitting somewhere else would have been too pointed. She stopped in front of Wren and waited for her to look up. Wren kept writing and said, "Have a seat."

For a time they didn't speak, and the silence was unexpectedly comfortable. Wren wrote, Thessaly consumed pastry and began peeling an orange, both of them gulped coffee with cream.

"Do you want more?" Thessaly finally asked, raising the carafe of coffee. "I won't tell Jonathan this is your third cup if you don't tell him it's mine."

Wren hesitated, then nodded. "Deal," she said. "Make sure you get plenty to eat. Though dinner tonight should be pretty amazing. Jonathan's been looking at this place ever since last year."

"Do you ever get any say in the dinners, or is it all him?" Thessaly asked. She took a sip of coffee and tried to hide the jolt of the heat hitting her sensitized teeth.

"Your teeth okay?" asked Wren.

"Totally impervious," Thessaly lied.

Wren shrugged. "If you say so."

"What's the restaurant known for?" Thessaly asked, just for something to say.

"Oh, boudin blanc or something like that. Jonathan's the dinner person, but he usually turns us all loose one night this week. Then we can do whatever we want." She paused, probably realizing it had sounded as if she were inviting Thessaly. "We could find something new. Or you and Gavin can go off on your own, whatever."

"You can come with us," Thessaly said impulsively. She'd regret it, most likely, because Gavin would want to use any alone time to strategize, but after yesterday Thessaly was curious to see what Wren would do.

Wren rolled her eyes. "I find minimal Gavin time sufficient," she said, looking around to be sure no one was nearby.

Thessaly laughed. "Once you figure out how to handle him, he's not so bad. I mean, he certainly keeps the sales team tight."

"Well, sure. All that compulsory socializing."

"You could go, you know," Thessaly said.

"I always thought it seemed exhausting," Wren said.

"It is. But you could hold your own. You did yesterday with all the producers."

Wren looked pleased. "Well, that's different—producers have to be nice. Gavin doesn't."

Thessaly tore a corner off a croissant and spread apricot preserves on it. "Let me tell you the key with a guy like Gavin. Or any of those guys, really. You can't curl up. It just makes them give you a hard time. You need to hand it right back."

Wren raised an eyebrow. "Forgive me for saying this, but what a bunch of dicks. That's how you guys spend your time? Just going after each other?"

"Well, no one goes after Legs, and he doesn't go after anyone. He's kind of his own thing," Thessaly said. "But Gavin does set a certain tone. Hate it if you want, but I'm just saying if you want to be in there, this is how to do it. I don't care if you're there or not. I'm sure you and Jonathan have your own team thing."

Wren said nothing. She opened a carton of Petite Suisse and let the cylinder slide into a bowl, where she sprinkled brown sugar over it and stirred it with a spoon. Thessaly watched her do this, thinking that as little as Wren let slip about her life, she knew a few things, like not to eat Petite Suisse out of the carton like yogurt. After yesterday she should have figured as much, but she was realizing she'd overlooked Wren and had largely done so the whole time they'd worked for the same company. The sole reason she'd noticed her at all was because they were the only two women of about the same age at their entire company.

"So. I mentioned something about Gavin. Do you want to give me any insight into Jonathan, or is this just one-way?"

Wren looked surprised. "Is this an exchange of information?"

"It could be. For example, *I* thought the thing between Gavin and Jonathan yesterday was extremely illuminating. And I want to see what happens at Duvillier." She hesitated, not wanting to share anything Gavin had said the day before. She didn't need Wren getting even better at her job, which she would if she knew Lionel was closer to leaving than he let on. She decided to hold on to that for now. "Perhaps you also think things and occasionally share them."

Wren looked dubious. "Well, I'm not the one snubbing all the commercial wines like Duvillier. I'd prefer to carry some wines that you can appreciate without a dissertation on Grüner Veltliner. That's all Jonathan. If you ask me, life would be a lot easier if we worked closer to what people know. But it's not my decision."

"I'm shocked," Thessaly said. "I always thought you were both into obscure little wines." She looked her colleague over carefully, a face she'd seen each weekday for years, but perhaps had never really taken in: her almost painfully clear gray eyes, the determined set of her jaw. Thessaly understood for the first time that if this were an Austen novel, Wren was not the governess. She was the country mouse who gets taken in hand, educated in the ways of society, and winds up married to a duke. Thessaly said finally, "But it sounds as if, maybe, you have a thought or two about yesterday. Maybe."

Wren gave her a look of annoyance. Then she glanced around the empty room again before saying, "Maybe. Listen, I've never seen that before—Lionel getting his hands in Jonathan's territory.

I've also never seen Jonathan that pissed. I mean, what is Lionel, seventy-two, seventy-three? I wonder if he knows he has to start planning his exit but doesn't want to. He might be sick, even. Maybe he's exerting as much control as he can, because he's losing all control soon and it freaks him out."

Thessaly was momentarily stunned into silence. Wren had nailed it so easily. Thessaly wondered if Wren could see through her just as clearly: Wren was probably looking straight into her brain at her procrastination at winemaking, her fear of failure, her radioactive guilt at being such a candy ass.

And Thessaly had not even considered that Lionel might have other reasons, like health, for stepping down.

Wren went on, "I think Lionel should just leave the business in Jonathan's hands, let Jonathan buy him out. He's at least ten or fifteen years younger."

Thessaly said, unthinkingly, "Nah, Jonathan's a minority partner for a reason. I don't think he wants to be Lionel when Lionel's gone. More likely Lionel could sell the business. Maybe he's getting everything into shape for a buyer."

A shadow crossed Wren's face and Thessaly realized she'd forgotten herself. She wasn't drinking with the sales team; she was talking to the other team, and the other team did not take kindly to her speaking so dismissively of Jonathan.

She began to think that she'd had one chance to make an ally of Wren and she'd just torched it. It wasn't just the failure in strategy either—she had realized she enjoyed shooting the breeze with Wren, even if their conversations were tinged with competition and secrecy. She hadn't had a female acquaintance since she'd moved here—her job and the men who populated it took up too much of her time, her psychic space, to let her look around for someone she could just hang out with. It occurred to her too late that maybe Wren could have been that person.

Thessaly had moved to New York four years earlier, after a brief stint working with her father on their vineyard. At that point, she'd finished college, during which she worked in a bakery, a restaurant, and a few tasting rooms, and she'd thought it might be time to learn how to farm. The job went well at first, until her father revealed his lack of confidence in her becoming a wine-maker. After that, every task on the farm, every morning coffee with her parents, had suddenly felt intolerable. She'd dragged herself around for weeks, until she couldn't stand it anymore and persuaded them to float her the first three months in New York City. There was no plan beyond New York. Wine store? Sommelier school? More restaurant work? All she knew was that New York was the farthest possible distance from California.

She'd found a Carroll Gardens apartment on Craigslist, occupying a futon in a third bedroom that was more of a dining room. The financial reality began to sink in. Wine stores paid minimum wage, and good restaurant work was shockingly competitive. She knew her parents would not give her more money. They weren't that kind of family.

When desperation set in, she made puff pastry. Arcane, exhausting tasks had always brought her comfort. Like bashing a block of butter into a thin rectangle and folding it up in dough like a letter in an envelope, then rolling it out again, folding it again, and doing that over and over for several hours. Her room-mates were appalled by the butter; Thessaly sometimes forgot that people who hadn't worked in bakeries did not see blocks as fat as she did. To her it was a tool that made her dough act the way she wished it to. To her roommates, who subsisted on vodka and yogurt, it was arsenic.

If only to escape them, she'd treated herself with just one trip to Cru. She'd put on a black dress and a couple of silver cuffs, took the subway into Manhattan, and parked herself at the bar amid the smell of wine and the clinking of glassware. The staff remembered her from her visit with her parents the year before, and by ten o'clock she was settled in, sipping an Austrian white that smelled faintly of grapefruit and having consumed two appetizers to justify her spot at the bar.

It became evident that the sommelier kept swooping in to impress the man on the stool beside her. The man was old but not elderly, balding, with a large Roman nose and eyes that kept roving all over the room. She could tell he knew she was eavesdropping. When he gestured for the sommelier to pour her some of the Sardinian Carignane he was drinking, she accepted the subsequent conversation as the price of voyeurism.

But she couldn't hide her surprise at the taste of that red: it was juicy and zippy, full of bright red berry and maybe a hint of orange peel. It was just so happy. "What do you think?" the man asked, and she said, "That was the most fun I've had since I moved to New York."

He laughed, held out a hand. "Lionel Garrett." When she'd said her own last name, he'd tipped his head to one side.

"Nice to meet you, Thessaly," he'd said. There was a break in their conversation while he turned to greet the latest of several people who'd come by and grabbed the shoulder of his expensive suit, pumped his hand, and asked what he was drinking. When he turned back to Thessaly, he said, "Sorry about that." He looked thoroughly pleased with himself, however, as though each exchange gave him another jolt of life. "Anyway, tell me about you. Are you just visiting New York before you take over for your parents? Or do you have other plans?"

She'd had enough wine to let her guard down, and she would never see this man again. So she said, "I'm not a farmer at heart. I'm planning on making my own wine."

"Ahh," Lionel said, raising his brows. "What kind of wine?"

Here she faltered. "Well, I'm still researching," she said, gesturing at the two empty glasses before her on the bar. "There's no point in making what's already overexposed. I just know there are varietals no one drinks and I think the market might be ready one day. I'm trying to learn what I can and play the long game."

He looked at her inscrutably. "Why not apprentice with one of the producers your family works with?" he asked innocently, sipping at his glass. "Go be a cellar rat, get started."

She felt her face flush deeply. Because she had to just keep learning, she thought. Because she was unready. "I definitely could," she said instead. "What if I'd do better learning more about other parts of the industry? Like chefs that *stage* at other restaurants or work the front of the house so they can open their own place someday." It sounded good, so she committed to the idea that this had been her plan all along.

"Like working in importing?" he asked. Still that innocent tone, as if he might just be fucking with her.

"Precisely," she declared. "I don't suppose you have a job you're trying to fill."

"As a matter of fact," Lionel said, "I do."

He had an entry-level opening and Thessaly said yes on the spot. She figured she had to, even if she'd never planned on working for an importer. She reported the next week as a low-level customer service rep, and there she was, in the machine.

The only problem was that she wished she'd never told Lionel about her hopes of making wine. She'd told herself he would never remember it, because he'd been drinking too, and because who cared what some underling spouted off at a bar one night? But she'd underestimated Lionel. He never forgot what she'd said, and every now and then he seemed to enjoy asking her about it. They'd all be at one of their tastings, or he'd sidle up to her at an event and say something like, "And what do you think? How would you make this differently, do you suppose?" Every time it made her almost sick with nerves, reminding her that she was terrified when she tried to imagine learning how to make it. Because maybe her father was right. The more time passed, the more delusional her early hopes seemed.

But she knew better than to show Lionel a shred of this. She'd say something like, "I'd have kept it out of the barrels for a little longer, myself," or "When I have my tasting room I'm going to make something like this and serve it for breakfast." And Lionel would let it go, but not before giving her a look that said he saw right through her.

All that day, through visits to three producers plus the last-minute stop at Duvillier, through sixty pours and sixty spits, her teeth more catastrophically alert with each harsh young wine that touched them, through fifty cheek kisses with a dozen distant, formal French winemakers, and through another long boozy dinner at another two-star Michelin restaurant, Thessaly got more frustrated with herself. She'd alienated someone she now wished she hadn't, because she'd failed to remember who she was talking to—Sales 101.

If Wren was aware of her consternation, it didn't show. She didn't ignore Thessaly; she just barely registered her existence. She remained mostly smooth-faced and chilly even when Jonathan placed a teeny, just-barely-not-insulting order at Duvillier. Thessaly wished she could pull Wren aside to say she wished Jonathan had stuck to his guns and ordered nothing because the Duvillier wines were unremarkable, but she'd caught a flash of satisfaction in Wren's expression when Jonathan ordered, so maybe Wren's commercial instincts really did lean more toward the mainstream. Thessaly was surprised to find herself disappointed.

The other oddity she would have liked to discuss was that Gavin had announced he was joining them in Germany the next day. "Just for a day," he said. "I'm realizing I ought to meet the great man while I can. You said Hermann hasn't been well."

Jonathan seemed more perplexed than affronted. "No," he said after a beat. "He hasn't. Wasn't it troublesome to move your Spain visits around?"

"Piece of cake," Gavin said brightly. "I really appreciate you letting me tag along."

Classic Gavin, brassily thanking someone for the very thing he'd forced them to do. Even Wren looked faintly admiring before her face fell, as it sank in that she had another twenty-four hours in close quarters with Gavin.

The whole night had ended on this peculiar, perplexed note, which was why Thessaly was caught off guard when Wren knocked on her hotel door later. Thessaly opened it to find her colleague standing there with a paper bag. "Are you ready to admit your teeth hurt?" Wren said.

Thessaly thought she might cry. "They're fucking killing me," she said. "I *did* the Sensodyne thing." This was one of the first things all of them were told before these trips: start using Sensodyne at least three weeks before. (Jonathan always sent out an all-caps email.)

"This stuff is a lot better," Wren said. She handed her the bag, inside of which was a white flip-top bottle with a prescription label on it. "*Don't* swallow it, though. I don't know what'll happen, but they make a big deal about it on the bottle. Try slathering it all over your teeth and leave it on there for a while."

Thessaly took the bottle, uncertain how to interpret this offering. It didn't quite seem like a friendly overture. All she wanted was to slam the door and squeeze a cupful of this stuff onto her nerve-shattered teeth, but then she remembered her manners. "How are yours? Are you going to need this back?"

Wren lifted her chin and bared her teeth, which were straight and white and strong. "Keep it," she said. "I have teeth like tusks."

· CHAPTER 4 ·

Dear god, Wren was glad to be eating German food after a week in France. She knew it was as rich as French food, but it was so much less demanding, with an invigorating bite. The night before they visited Jonathan's most important producer, Hermann Fuchs, they feasted on a dinner of shatteringly crisp schnitzel and chewy butter-seared spaetzle. How revelatory that enriching fat tasted after a cold damp day, what pleasure the lance of onion and vinegar and hops provided after so many ethereal wines.

Yes, the half meters of sausage would kill her if she did this much longer, and no, neither she nor anyone else had had a bowel movement in many days. No one discussed it outright, but everyone was prone to sudden fugue states in which they reckoned privately with this condition. But on these luxuriously taxing trips, the elements of pleasure, the warmth of a fire, the looseness among colleagues, took on a hypersaturated intensity. She tried to luxuriate in it, because whatever happened next—Lionel appointing Gavin or someone somehow worse than Gavin to run the company—she still got to feel this feeling.

She'd been so immersed in the visits and tasting that most of the time she thought only of what was before her. Then Wren would remember that maybe Lionel's endless growth plans were not about leaving them all better off but selling the whole joint, and then her stomach clenched all over. Or maybe it was just her latest schnitzel.

Tonight Jonathan was drinking one of the fruit-tinged mahogany ales he preferred, while everyone else sipped miniature snifters of cloudy, staggeringly alcoholic beer. Thessaly, Wren noticed, had an impressive tolerance, even for their industry. Her eyes often darted toward, and then away from, Wren's still-full glass.

"Tomorrow's the highlight of my whole trip," Jonathan was saying. "Hermann's the center of the industry around here. People don't look at some big commercial producer for what to do—they look to Hermann, because he has found the way to produce a lot but never compromise. Ever. It's remarkable, honestly."

Wren listened to this speech, which seemed to be aimed at Thessaly, the only one who might not know all of it already, with a squirm of embarrassment. Jonathan seemed to have gotten some of his mojo back in the wake of the Duvillier experience. Yes, he'd placed an order he only nominally wanted, but now they were back in his territory. Gavin was no expert in German wine, and he apparently had no more hidden producers he was going to spring on Jonathan. And, as he listened to Jonathan reminding them all that the most powerful winemaker in the region was in Jonathan's pocket, Gavin had a strange expression on his face: frustrated, long-suffering, patient.

"And kind of known for his temper, right?" Wren prodded, just to see if it would annoy Gavin. Because Gavin might be able to intimidate a bunch of guys as if he were an older brother home from college, but he was no match in economic, social, or physical power for a massive Teutonic farmer.

Jonathan gave an unseemly cackle. "He once overturned a *fuder* of wine after an apprentice let it get oxygenated. Just poured it all out. Well, he was younger then."

They said nothing for a moment. Gavin took a breath and then apparently decided to ignore everything Jonathan had just said. "Lionel certainly thinks highly of him," he said.

"Of course he does!" cried Jonathan. "Lionel knows damn well Hermann is one of the cornerstones of our business."

"Mm-hm," said Gavin. "His daughter too. When I told him I was staying to meet Hermann, he got passionate about how women like her ought to run more of the wine world. Shake things up for the men. Why, I don't know."

Thessaly glanced over at Wren. "Maybe Lionel's looking ahead," she said. "I think he's right. More companies need at *least* one woman at the top."

Gavin and Jonathan both nodded vigorously. "Definitely," Jonathan said. "It's not like it used to be when we first started." But Wren could see in the way both men looked so blandly pleased by the vague notion of women running the wine world that it never occurred to them Thessaly might be talking about their own company. They thought it sounded great for other companies. They didn't consider that at Lionel Garrett, men per se were in charge—they, Lionel and Jonathan and Gavin, were in charge. And that was different.

"I read Elke's going to be making more of her own wine," Gavin said. "Speaking of women in charge."

Thessaly perked up. "Exactly," she said. "I'd love to see the Old World producers just, like, modernized by the next generation of women."

"Well," said Gavin, "of course you think so. Didn't Lionel say once you had a little dream of making wine yourself?"

"Do you?" asked Wren. "What do you want to make? What are you doing here, then?" She meant it jokingly, but Thessaly stopped her with a poisonous look.

"Learning," she said shortly. "You forget I've seen all the people who run out to Napa and Sonoma certain they're the next big winemaker and they wind up broke and finished because they didn't take the time to educate themselves about the business."

"I agree," Jonathan said magnanimously. Anything to remind Gavin he was out of place here. "Thessaly, talk to Elke. She might be just what you need."

Jonathan had told Wren numerous times that Hermann Fuchs was the first winemaker he'd ever imported. At the time, Fuchs was young and taciturn, farming two hectares. Now he was in his late seventies and one of the largest producers in the country.

The tasting rooms in Germany were not regal, but instead modest rooms attached to the houses where the winemakers lived. The farmers themselves in their leather vests truly felt like farmers, not grand vignerons. They spoke little and watched their visitors closely.

Hermann, according to Jonathan, had once been a strapping tree of a man, and in the years Wren had been coming to Germany, she'd been able to see the ghost of that man. But this year Hermann looked frail, still tall but stooped, moving with an odd jerking gait.

Before they got out of the car to join Gavin and Jonathan with Hermann, Thessaly turned to Wren and said, "I guess he really isn't well. Maybe Gavin had a good reason to kiss the ring while he still can."

"No," Wren said, nonsensically. "I'm sure it's just a bad day." She was nervous about this visit, which held such weight for the company and for Jonathan, and with so much suddenly up in the air in her work life, she didn't want to contemplate the loss of such a central figure.

"Wren," Hermann said when she approached. "Welcome, my dear." He shook Thessaly's hand and nodded briefly to Gavin, as if he had no idea who he was.

Hermann made his way somewhat painfully toward a door in the great glass building. Jonathan took a few long steps to catch up with him, finding a way to place his shoulder right where it would need to be for Hermann to stabilize himself with one hand.

Elke met them inside, a middle-aged woman with green eyes and a rather forbidding nose. Thessaly darted forward to shake her hand too passionately—too Americanly—and Elke seemed briefly startled but recovered.

They toured the new public tasting room and the crisply clinical rooms containing the great tanks of fermenting juice, then a massive underground room stocked with *fuder* after *fuder*, massive oak barrels holding a thousand liters apiece. Elke walked beside her father, speaking little, until Hermann seemed to tire. At that point, she stepped smoothly forward and they resumed the tour as if she had been their guide all along.

Gavin was probably fifteen years younger than Elke, but as they walked together, they looked like companions. When their profiles turned toward each other to speak, Wren noticed they even looked oddly similar: the same firm chin and neat jawline. His manner showed none of his jabbing wit or the filial frustration he often displayed toward Jonathan. With Elke, he displayed an easy professional intimacy, of the sort Wren would have to learn to cultivate—and maybe even enjoy—herself.

The tasting was epic. She would never stop being amazed at how one grape varietal could be so varied according to its elevation, its exposure, its soil. They were all Riesling, but some were sprightly and effervescent and ephemeral, some floral and reserved, some picked young enough to show lime and Meyer lemon, hints of white rind.

They tasted with focus and certainty for a long time, the only sounds those of Thessaly's pen on the yellows and the tinny ring of the spittoon.

Hermann watched them with a hawk's focus, which made Wren concentrate harder. She liked being able to do one important job, not think ahead to the next bon mot (though she'd have to get better at that). Hermann did not gesture dramatically at the land outside and remind them who he was. He just watched. When asked a question, Hermann considered carefully before answering.

About halfway through the tasting, something happened. The wines shifted, though at first Wren wasn't sure what was different. It was as if the background music had changed. The wines began to feel less friendly, more restricted and sterile. Was Hermann fermenting differently? This dry, piercing style was fashionable now, but it wasn't typical of him.

Across the table, Thessaly looked dismayed. Jonathan was swirling his glass with a frown. Hermann had not spoken in some time. Should they ask if he was all right to continue, or would that be disrespectful? His face was sagging and his eyes at half-mast, his skin a mottled pink. He seemed to have relinquished the table altogether—it was Elke who poured each new taste, who directed them to the papers before them for the parcels and vintages and names.

The word Jonathan would use for these wines was *masochistic*. He liked some weird shit in wines—funk and charcuterie and petrol were all fine by him—but he also liked a wine to have some life. You couldn't have a conversation with these.

But Gavin was nodding. "So focused! So elegant and stern."

"I'm finding them a touch lean," Jonathan said softly. Elke turned her lovely green gaze in his direction and Wren saw that for once someone besides Gavin was uncharmed by Jonathan's thoughtfulness, his Poet's poise. It was startling. "Hermann," he said. "Tell me your thoughts."

But Hermann simply shook his head and gestured toward his daughter. Jonathan sat back in his seat, looking slightly hurt, until he covered it so smoothly with his professional face that Wren thought only she had seen it.

"These are, of course, different for us," Elke said proudly, "even a touch austere. As they open up, they take on a very modern, very forward-looking kind of lightness."

Wren would have believed her, if she hadn't been drinking the actual product. But she'd *felt* it, the moment the lovely balance had fled Hermann's wines.

Before they left, they opened one final bottle. "You had that Spätlese last year that was so gorgeous," Jonathan said to Hermann. "Long gone from our warehouse, of course. I don't suppose any is still lurking about?"

This was simply not done. Jonathan never asked to taste some random wine—they were here to experience the winemaker's work. Elke sent an underling to fetch it, and no one spoke while they waited. Wren tried not to look at Hermann, fearing they had sucked the life out of this man.

But when the bottle was brought in—a long, narrow brown bottle like any other German Riesling—and Elke opened it, the whole room changed. The wine filled the air with citrus, a faint shadow of violet and petrol.

Hermann had tasted very little all morning, but as Elke poured a glass for him, he raised his head and smiled at his daughter. His posture changed; his eyes lightened. He looked like the man she'd been expecting, the man Jonathan must have known for years.

"This was a lovely one, wasn't it?" Hermann said.

Jonathan smiled. "No one else gets quite the same finesse and *lushness* out of this varietal, Hermann. You can age this another fifteen years, I'll bet." Wren peered at the bottle and realized why this wine was so different—it was a 1998, far older than what they'd been tasting.

Hermann began to tell them about the year he'd made this wine. Elke had been living in Berlin, he said, smiling. His wife had still been alive. "This was a warm season," he said to Elke, "but not too rainy." He took a sip, content and melancholy. "Elke, do you remember what your mother said when we tasted the first bottling?"

Elke's flinty green eyes had softened. For a moment Thessaly thought she might cry. "She told you to double the price."

Hermann and Jonathan laughed. "She also said it was an honor, that this was the last new vintage she would taste," Hermann said. His smile dimmed only a touch.

Then it was time for business. Jonathan reserved three-quarters of what he usually did, and it was weighted heavily toward the first group of wines. Only one or two of the second.

"I think we should do more of the Kabinetts from the second batch," Gavin announced.

Jonathan swiftly turned to look at him. "You usually push for something less challenging," he said mildly. But in his eyes there was a clear rebuke.

"I know it's new and different, but I'd rather be first in than last." Gavin gave Elke a dazzling smile, his white teeth gleaming in the frame of his silky dark beard.

"We'll stick with what I ordered for now," Jonathan said shortly. He got up from the table and so did everyone else, commencing the farewell process. They had no choice but to follow along, and if Wren had not known better, she might have missed the edge in Gavin's voice, the pointed manner in which he clasped Elke's hand in his farewell.

Back at the car, Jonathan was either pretending not to notice or else he didn't care that Gavin, his shoulders practically at his ears, radiated frustration. Jonathan didn't look much happier.

"I'll drive, Gavin," he said. "You look distracted."

Wren had never seen Gavin so upset. He shook his head as if in disbelief, but slid behind the wheel, completely ignoring Jonathan. "Elke's wines are going to get reserved by other people," he said to Jonathan as they turned down the driveway, "and then we've missed our chance. Thessaly, what did you think? She'll probably be your winemaking colleague one day, you must have ideas."

Wren could see that Gavin was barely even thinking about Thessaly—he was needling her because he was angry with Jonathan, and he didn't really care what she thought of Elke's wines. Thessaly had been silent for the last half hour, and now she turned away from the window she'd been staring out and said, "Those wines were empty and mean."

Wren was astonished. She'd witnessed Thessaly tease Gavin, in a little-sister kind of way, but she'd never simply contradicted him, and certainly not when Gavin was making it clear he expected agreement. Gavin never allowed dissent in the sales team unless they were among themselves.

Gavin looked at her in the rearview mirror. "You'd do better, I suppose."

"Maybe I could," Thessaly said. "Maybe I'd make something much worse. I don't know."

"Well," Gavin said lightly, "maybe try it and then judge."

For some reason this was the thing that sent Wren over the edge. Or maybe it was everything: Jonathan seeming like half the person he'd been a week ago, Thessaly's genuinely pathetic disappointment in Elke's wines, the way Gavin fed off all of it and just got pissier.

"It's our job to judge," Wren said. "And Thessaly has as good a palate as any of us." She paused, gathering her thoughts. "You made such a big deal about how we need commercial wines," she said eventually. She was careful to make her tone curious, offhand. "We even went out of our way to Duvillier because you said it was so important to Lionel. But if that's Lionel's focus, why advocate for these wines that are going to be so much harder to sell?"

Peripherally, she saw Thessaly's eyes widen. Even Jonathan turned to look at her.

"Oh, Wren," Gavin said after a beat. "I always forget you're here, for some reason. And I manage thousands of SKUs, so forgive me if I don't walk you through my thought process for each one."

"Well, just *one*, really," said Wren, and this time Jonathan cut in.

"Would all of you please control yourselves?" Jonathan said. "I don't know what the problem is, and frankly I don't care. That was an old friend of mine, not thriving, you may have noticed."

The car was dead silent for a long beat. Jonathan turned around to look from one person to the other.

"Gavin?" he said. "You weren't even supposed to be on this visit."

Gavin rolled his neck in one direction and then the other. He looked at Wren in the mirror. "Sorry."

"Accepted," said Wren. Because she had to. But of course she didn't mean it.

They drove in silence to their dinner reservation, but when everyone got out of the car, Jonathan said, "Why don't we split up? Gavin and I need to have a little chat."

To his credit, Gavin looked nervous, but he tried to play it off as a fine idea he'd already had. The four of them were seated across the dining room from each other, and from their banquette Wren and Thessaly tried to pretend they weren't watching.

Wren said, "Is this what the next few months will be, just dick-swinging contests while they try to take over for Lionel?"

"It will be if Lionel doesn't get his act together and make a public plan," said Thessaly. "We're like those shark embryos that eat one another. It's ridiculous."

"Right?" said Wren. She was feeling much warmer toward Thessaly than she usually did. "The man dropped one little speculative hint, ten days ago, and look what's happened."

Thessaly took a sip of her beer, watching Wren over the rim of the glass. "And don't you think that's what he meant to do?" she said. "It's Lionel we're talking about. This is exactly what he knew would happen—he wants to see who distinguishes themselves."

Wren stared at her. "Come on," she said. "Isn't that a little melodramatic?"

Thessaly laughed, sounding unexpectedly merry. "These guys are the biggest drama queens I've ever met," she said. "My dad would laugh so hard he'd break a femur at all this stuff. You and I are the ones keeping calm, you know. They should be looking to us for pointers. But Gavin will never admit that sales should work with anyone outside of sales. He thinks we have to silo ourselves off or we'll lose everything."

Wren examined her colleague as she set about attacking a schnitzel that was a quarter inch thick and wider than her dinner plate. Thessaly's messy chocolate hair trembled as she sawed away with her knife, the fine silver rings on her hands gleaming in the dim light of the room. For the first time Thessaly seemed approachable, a little vulnerable, maybe not a rock star, or not *all* rock star. When she seemed like just a person, with disappointments and hopes and uncertainties, instead of Gavin's henchman and Lionel's golden girl, she was quite appealing. Wren felt an insane and probably foolhardy desire to just trust Thessaly or be trusted by her. This was such a tough business. And Wren would maim anyone who tried to kick her out of it, but sometimes, every now and then, you really did benefit from an alliance.

"What?" Thessaly asked, not looking up. "You've had thirty plates of schnitzel too, you know."

"Nothing," said Wren. "But listen. Tell me about this wine you want to make."

PART 2

the great men

· CHAPTER 5 ·

A few weeks later, everyone had staggered back to New York from their respective continents, falling into their familiar routines. Thessaly was back to her old self, at once revved up and tired, ready to have a few drinks and call it professional development, even though the whites of her eyes were slightly greener than before, and even though she began most days thinking she would surely have no urge at all to imbibe that night.

Tonight she was headed to a Japanese restaurant on St. Mark's Place for plates of octopus, spinach and bonito, fried shrimp, and skewers of chicken heart, duck, and scallion. It was the first fine day of spring, the air warm and gentle, and she had spent the afternoon walking around her sales beat with Wren.

"You're coming, right?" Thessaly said as they left the last account, a restaurant on Stanton Street. When Wren hesitated, she added, "That was rhetorical. There's no point in learning if no one knows you're learning."

"Impressively cynical," said Wren, but she nodded resolutely. "Yeah, I'm coming."

"Think of it as exposure therapy to Gavin and Greg," Thessaly said. "And Legs isn't terrifying once you get to know him. Though he does have a lot of stories about jumping people. Or being jumped; I've begun to tune them out." She was babbling, nervous that the sales crew, which was a driven team underneath all the partying, might trample Wren underfoot.

"Oh, I learned years ago you can't take Legs seriously," Wren said. "He's just messing with you."

They were cautiously attempting to learn from each other, she and Wren. This was an uncertain arrangement, given that they would wind up in competition with each other too—except that neither believed there was a genuine contest afoot. Lionel and Jonathan had begun asking people to exploratory lunches, which suggested they were indeed vetting successors. Then Gavin began to join these lunches, which suggested they were looking to see who might replace Gavin once he moved up into a director role. Still, even the charade of competition was a good motivator and had reminded Thessaly that she enjoyed striving. She'd gotten into a bit of a lull, which had begun to feel lazy once she realized how much Wren was doing: a French class, the notebooks full of tasting notes, the endless files on her computer of producers to watch. The least Thessaly could do was learn more about the various regulations and import practices that Wren understood so thoroughly. So they met for weekend coffee and Wren walked her through as much as she could. There was a reason Thessaly had avoided studying these arcane rules and processes, she discovered: it was mind-numbing. But she suspected she minded tariffs and transport issues less than Wren dreaded sales calls.

"How'd I do today?" Wren said, as if reading her mind. "I know my patter's a little shaky."

"It's not patter," Thessaly corrected her. "It's about listening. Only shitty salespeople go in there and try to sell whatever they need to sell instead of what someone needs to buy. For your first time, not bad."

She listed a few points to work on, but the basic accoutrements were simple enough: Manhattan reps walked and took the subway everywhere, which was why Thessaly wore chic flats, never heels, that were ridiculously expensive but could be worn to walk sixty blocks without requiring medical intervention. In her purse, she always carried blotting papers, lipstick, and mascara, because she'd learned the hard way that by lunchtime women who didn't do repairs resembled Janice the Muppet after a light microwaving. The last guy to have her territory had been pale and pointy, with faded black clothes and desperate purple bags beneath his eyes, but a professional woman couldn't wander around looking like Nosferatu. Not even downtown.

She loved the Lower East Side, the bistros and chic little booze boutiques and the decrepit brick buildings. Grand wines felt newly invigorated in such a setting, cheap wines felt cool and ironic, offbeat wines comfortable among the flea-market plates stacked with oysters. New restaurants opened every single day, and people were cranky about hipsters coming in and cranky about the old socialists refusing to leave. But Thessaly was right at home with cranky people.

When they arrived at the restaurant, Thessaly briefly regretted making Wren join them: Gavin and Greg both looked at her as if someone's maiden aunt had tagged along. But when Legs greeted Wren warmly—even standing up from their cramped table to kiss her cheek, which no one had ever seen him do—the new info rippled visibly through the rest of the crew. Gavin looked thoughtful; Greg looked wounded; Amit looked relieved to have someone who might take the night's hazing for uptightness that was usually directed at him.

Gavin used dinners like tonight's as another tool to keep them all engaged. The people with the best numbers would be pelted with backhanded praise ("You really have a handle on the *right* kind of cheap for that part of Jersey," he'd once said to Greg), while the ones with the worst numbers would be treated to the kind of gaslighting remonstration you went crazy putting your finger on: barely perceptible pauses after jokes, the sensation of eyes sliding past you too slowly or too quickly. Thessaly had gotten a taste of this years earlier, in her first few months in sales, when Gavin made a point of letting it slip that Greg had gone on full commission in less time than she had, despite being several years younger and hired straight out of college. The worst part was it worked. It was so galling she'd worked like a dog until she'd left Greg's numbers in the toilet by comparison.

Wren looked flushed but steady; she ordered the same big stein of beer everyone else had, and shrewdly added an order of duck heart skewers to what Legs had already requested. Legs ordered for the table tonight, whether they liked it or not. You couldn't hold court at the same table as Legs when he decided it was his night, not with that beanpole frame and weathered face, his piercing bloodshot gaze and scratchy voice. He would always wrench back the focus with some grotesque story about an errant Ramone, and it was easier just to cede the territory.

Thessaly was relieved to see this was not going to be a total fiasco. She began to settle in, knocked back her beer faster than she'd meant to because she felt so good, and helped herself to an octopus fritter.

The restaurant had a big square bar and Formica tables filled with people eating butter spinach with bonito flakes and skewers of scallion and chicken thigh. Their group of six was crammed in to a four-top, beside another crew of the same number. Thessaly kept noticing them without knowing why. Four men and two women, matching her table dish for dish, which was saying something. Everyone at Lionel Garrett had Balzacian appetites, except Legs. They'd made a bad hire if someone stopped after two ounces of pasta or balked at eating bone marrow.

The group at the next table was raucous but not drunk. They were all in jeans and loose shirts, not suits, so not lawyers on their way uptown. (She'd fallen into the salesperson's habit of constant categorizing.) They seemed to be in their late twenties, and all had a similar look of dishevelment. The men were unshaven, a rime of beard down their necks, their hair rumpled and untrimmed. The women wore ponytails and no makeup. All were regularly seized by fits of mirth and Sapporo. They had the intense, slightly crazed look of line cooks and chefs, but no tattoos; also, groups of chefs didn't appear in dining rooms until after one a.m.

She was busy trying to taxonomize them when she caught the eye of one of the men. He didn't smile. He was talking to someone else; she couldn't hear what he was saying. She watched his mouth move, his eyes—light-colored, with a dark rim of lashes—locked on her.

She turned away, to serve herself some fried squid with spicy mayonnaise and to decide what she thought of the guy looking her way. Greg, who was sitting beside her, handed her a bottle of furikake and returned to telling the table about his latest exploits in Hoboken. Thessaly focused on him, not the table beside them, trying not to let any tentacles hang out of her mouth.

"It was clear I was supposed to bribe him," Greg was saying. "He turned the credit card machine toward me and then pretended to polish glassware while facing the other way. I can work some samples magic 'cause it's Jersey, but come on."

"I should transfer," Amit exclaimed, taking the last grilled duck skewer. "It's so much easier in Jersey." This was just talk. Amit would quit before taking a Jersey territory. Everyone knew Manhattan had more cachet and higher numbers, and Amit was quite successful with his hot-nerd approach. Tonight he somehow made horn-rimmed glasses and a tight button-down shirt seem inviting. Or maybe Thessaly was just feeling restless. But she worked hard and she was one of the best in the sales force. Did she not deserve a good time?

"If you *don't* do some side-dealing they look at you funny," Greg said. "I think it might have something to do with the Mafia."

"You're adorable," Legs observed.

"I'll pretend I didn't hear any of that," said Gavin. "Anyway," he added to Amit, his dark eyes alighting on Thessaly for a moment, "you'll be too busy now to be jealous of Jersey."

Amit nodded but said nothing, which Thessaly found odd. Usually, if Amit had anything to crow about, he found several ways to do it.

"What'll you be busy with?" Wren asked. "Is Midtown West doing something exciting?" This was another benefit of having her here: If Thessaly started quizzing them, her motives were clear. Wren could ask because she was not in sales.

"We haven't hired a replacement for the Chelsea rep yet," Gavin said, "so I'm giving Amit some of those accounts that can't go unattended. And one or two to Greg to see how he does on this side of the river."

"Oh, cool," Wren said. In five years, Thessaly had never heard her say, "Oh, cool." "Did you guys decide it at lunch with Jonathan and Lionel? You had one this week, right?" She directed this last part at Greg.

But Greg was still an amateur at this. He said, "No, that was more about the future. This was already decided."

Amit was suddenly profoundly occupied with a dish of chicken skin.

Thessaly turned to Gavin. "What happens when you hire someone and half the plum accounts are being handled by Midtown and Hoboken?"

Gavin shrugged. "We'll figure it out. Maybe move people around."

Thessaly served herself some shrimp, trying to put her finger on what felt so unsettling. Salespeople moved around. She had moved into the Lower East Side, after all, and she wasn't looking to take on someone's old Chelsea accounts. So why did she feel like the only person who hadn't gotten passed a note at recess? Even Legs looked awkward, showily raising a finger to catch the waiter's eye.

"When did all this get decided?" she said finally.

"It's been in play," Gavin said. "We hashed the rest of it out one night last week."

Her eyes met Wren's and slid away; the last thing they needed was for a table full of their male colleagues to notice the women noticing them. But Thessaly understood now, and she suspected Wren did too. She knew from office chitchat that they'd gotten together the previous week to watch the French Open, the sort of post-work hangout that differed from unofficial work like tonight. The men in their office were obsessed with tennis, kept abreast of

European soccer, engaged with baseball if the Mets were having a particularly poetic season, but eschewed football as clunky and lumpen. Even Legs, who would never be caught dead breaking a sweat, occasionally revealed a deep working knowledge of lacrosse. Thessaly had never cared, because she had no interest in sports, but now she saw the drawback of that approach. In between hollering at Rafael Nadal, business moves had been made.

Gavin handed her a dish. There was no slick way to pursue the subject, certainly not to say, "Hey, can I come watch tennis with you if you're going to divvy up territories while you do it?"

So she helped herself to the chicken skin, which sounded disgusting but was crisp and delicious, and listened to Gavin tell a story about a buyer they all knew whose debauchery was legendary. Gavin could be pure charm when he wanted. He'd cut you dead and have you laughing a minute later, and she had to make a choice about whether to hold on to her frustration or enjoy the night. She chose the latter, because Gavin *was* being hilarious, because her colleagues were friendly and laughing, and she wanted to have some fun.

Legs's plate held only two skewers that had once been spiked with grilled prawns, the empty heads of which he was now slurping. He watched idly as people stepped over his long denimed legs and clunky boots stretched out into the aisle. The boots looked like Doc Martens but were Louboutins that Thessaly had seen at Barney's for something like eight hundred bucks. An enigma, Legs.

They paid the check and prepared to decamp to the bar on the same floor. As they made their way there, Thessaly slowed down beside Wren. "That tennis thing was some bullshit, right?" Wren said.

"It was," Thessaly said with a pleasant smile, in case anyone was glancing over their shoulders. "Maybe once Gavin takes over for Lionel he'll be too busy for all that secret socializing."

"He'll make time," Wren said, but Thessaly was already distracted. She'd caught a glimpse of the group from the other table headed their way, and realized they were all going to the same place.

That was all she needed to remind herself who she was. She was not Gavin's lapdog. She had better numbers than anyone else at that table, and the only reason Gavin propped up Greg was because his territory needed it. She did not need it. She was a wine person to the very core; she'd known more at twelve years old than Greg had labored to learn for a decade.

Sometimes Thessaly had to stifle her fears and insecurities and look herself in the face: she was so goddamn successful and magnanimous that she wasn't threatened by others, especially other women. Unlike Sabrina—who'd blunted her professional impact by dealing with violin lessons and tutors instead of these dinners—Thessaly was in the mix, out every night, where no one could forget her. Wren, who was now strolling toward the bar ahead of her and seeming a lot more at ease than Thessaly had expected, had turned out to be more impressive than Thessaly had realized, but deep down Thessaly knew she could beat her too. She wouldn't say as much, of course, because she had come to like her, but the unassailable truth was that what Wren knew, Thessaly could learn. What Thessaly could do was not teachable.

She strode into the bar on a fresh wave of confidence, ready to tear apart the rest of this night.

"You want a cocktail?" she asked Wren. "I'm getting a Manhattan." But Wren declined.

The group who'd been beside them in the restaurant was here too, and the dark-haired guy she'd been looking at stepped aside to make space for Thessaly at the bar. Among his group he'd seemed the most reserved; the rest were being uproarious. Grad students—or publishing? As she waited for her drink, Thessaly overheard a conversation of a particular incomprehensibility that could mean only one thing. Doctors! Either residents or interns; they were all young and exhausted.

When she got her drink and turned to join her table, two of the guys were blocking the way, their backs to her. "Excuse me," she said.

The blond one made a show of looking startled, but the dark-haired, light-eyed one just moved to the side to let her pass. He was exactly her height, his eyes, up close, a luminous green. Other than that, he was fairly ordinary-looking, but he had a way of looking her right in the eye that made her realize no one did that, not like this.

"You'll have to excuse us," the blond one said. "We're blowing off some steam."

"Uh-huh," Thessaly said, turning to go.

"If there's blood on me, don't worry, it isn't mine," the blond guy called after her.

"He's trying to get you to ask about his job," the dark-haired one said.

Thessaly turned back. She looked only at the dark-haired guy, didn't bother pretending otherwise. "Let me guess," she said. "You're vet techs. Things almost went cockeyed with a diabetic chinchilla today and no one will ever be the same."

"It was a fire skink," the blond one said merrily.

The dark-haired guy extended his hand. "Nick."

She was thirty years old, an age she was now convinced was the hottest age of them all, she was selling the shit out of a territory containing some of the coolest and most interesting restaurants in the city, and in spite or because of a buzz that was edging toward too much, she could have sworn this guy looked at her and saw every bit of that.

"We're emergency medicine residents at NYU," Nick said. "We just finished a twenty-four-hour shift, there probably *is* blood on Robby somewhere, and we're all extremely tired and proud of ourselves. Can I buy you a drink?"

· CHAPTER 6 ·

Two days later, Nick waited for her outside a Thai restaurant in the basement of a narrow side street in Chinatown. As she approached, she had a moment's hesitation. Then he came to the end of the block to meet her. "I thought Thai food might free you from the obligation to impress me with wine," he said, looking at the two bottles sticking out of her bag.

"Brace yourself, I'm going to impress you even more," she said. "Not only can you drink wine with Thai food, but if they're Pinot Blancs and Gewürztraminers, it's your obligation."

"Well, thank you. It's more than we'll even drink," he said. Thessaly laughed, and he gave her a quizzical look, and she realized he was serious. Every now and then she was reminded that other people were not professionally obliged to drink the way she did. The other night he'd barely finished his drink and drank water while she finished her wine.

She didn't want him to think she was a total degenerate, so she said, "I just couldn't decide, so I brought you a choice."

In truth, Thessaly should have been out with Gavin, Greg, and Legs tonight. They'd headed out to Battery Park for banh mi and wine in paper bags, and Thessaly had seriously considered canceling on Nick in order to make sure she was there. That had been Wren's vote: cancel on Nick, keep her face time with their colleagues, and who cared if Nick fell by the wayside. But Thessaly suspected Wren was not the right person from whom to take romantic cues. She'd never heard Wren mention any dates, though surely she must have had relationships. Wren might be scarily uptight and reserved to the point of inanimate, but she was, objectively, cute.

And Thessaly had not encountered a guy she really wanted to see again in quite some time. So that afternoon she'd told Greg she was expected somewhere in Chinatown, which was true, and that she hoped to meet up with them, which was not.

"Chinatown?" Greg had said, as if perhaps she had misspoken. He'd been poking through the employee refrigerator, opening up cartons, sniffing them thoughtfully, and putting them back. "Why not Flushing?" he asked pointedly, gazing at her over an open carton of falafel.

"I know, I know," Thessaly said. "But I don't have time to ride the subway out to Queens for an hour each way. Are you going to eat any of that or just contaminate it?"

Greg shrugged. "Someone ate my mom's leftover risotto last week. This is payback." Thessaly rolled her eyes. Greg maintained the fiction that his parents were not the providers of his designer sneakers, cashmere sweaters knitted by virgins and saints, and Nantucket-red trousers. But he admitted his mom made stellar risotto.

"You choose," Nick was saying, as they went down the stairs to the dining room. "I grew up with whiskey people. Tell me about Sonoma." He found her exotic, a species of plant that didn't grow in New England, and she enjoyed this so much she played it up, exaggerating stories about the harvest and telling him about the tasting room her sister ran now. No need to exaggerate anything about her father.

"It's gorgeous. And harsh and difficult. But I'll go back some-day. It's the family business, so it's bred into me."

"Ours is insurance," Nick said.

"See, your family has its own sense of romance."

He laughed. "Why are you here, if you're going back to Sonoma someday?"

"Oh," she said, "I came out here to learn all about the rest of the business. So one day I could maybe make wine myself. The trouble is, there's no end to what you can learn. I could keep doing this job for another decade and still feel I was scratching the surface."

"Medicine's like that," he said. "Though medicine kicks you up to the next level, or out, at regular intervals."

He served her another portion of curry. She watched him take a sip of the Gewürztraminer and consider it. "Never would've guessed, right?" she said. She filled her own glass and topped his off, though he'd barely touched his.

At first she found his calm discomfiting: She realized she had gotten used to operating with a high level of chatter that no one expected you to listen to. Nick didn't do chatter. He did frowning, carefully considered observations. She couldn't imagine him strolling into a room and filling the air with talk, which made her realize she'd spent the last five years immersed in the glib empti-ness of the men she worked with, the drunken spring break versions of themselves so many clients plunged into on work trips. (Twice, in Spain and in Tuscany, clients had knocked on her hotel room door, after midnight, in their underwear.)

Sometimes she feared that in all the drinking and conversation and dining out, she had gone soft. That one day she'd try to conduct the impossible labor of harvesting with her dad, or making wine as she wanted to, and she would discover she had lost her endurance and her knowledge, replacing important things with restaurant addresses. She drank more Gewürztraminer to stop worrying.

He was quiet, so she was not. She got to be the one who told a long story about the Portland wine store owners Lionel had taken to Portugal, who got so drunk after the very first day of eight hours of wine tasting that one climbed onto the other's shoulders to attempt a race, fell on the cobblestone path, and knocked out a front tooth. She got to be the one who made him laugh when they realized he'd spent undergrad taking premed classes at Princeton, while she had spent a slightly embarrassing amount of time at her demanding liberal arts college focusing on puppetry.

"Don't be embarrassed," he said. "I admire it when someone brings that Montessori preschool touch to their rigorous, criminally expensive education."

Nick, she realized, laughing, made jokes only when he had a good one. "Stop sounding so shocked I made you laugh," he said, laughing back at her. "You'll give me a complex and drive me into stand-up. Now, what does a man have to do to taste the Pinot Blanc?"

"You realize," she said, reaching for the second bottle, "we can't nip at it for days on end like the whiskeys of your childhood. We should just finish this."

He came up to her apartment after dinner that night, probably because she'd goaded him into an extra glass of wine and he was vulnerable to such things. For two years she'd occupied a walk-up cube five stories in the air above East Seventy-ninth Street, though she had no particular love for the Upper East Side beyond a certain level of zoological attention to the sinewy blond matrons on Madison Avenue and the kids in their crested private school blazers. Mixed in were the regular people like Thessaly, who had come here because it lacked the individuality and charm that made other places more popular and less affordable. It was crafty, really, that some of the city's richest people had deflected interest in their own neighborhood by making it so boring.

Thessaly yearned for a place in the East Village (Legs's territory; she thought of neighborhoods in terms of who sold to them), which was the home of most of her favorite restaurants and bars, but she was over-stretching enough to live alone here. She had no financial business doing this. Her parents had been appalled by the cost of her rent, even though she'd lied and lowered it by three hundred dollars.

When they got to her apartment, Nick strolled around the perimeter with an inscrutable expression, taking in the touches she was so proud of accruing: the wide cream-and-blue-flecked bowl on the table, the white rippled sixties mod pendant lamp above her tiny teak dining table. He paused beside a chair over which was thrown a dress she'd gotten at one of those flash sales where everyone crowded into an empty storefront and stripped unconcealed to try on the clothes.

He turned around and saw her looking at him. "I kind of forgot people can make their surroundings pleasant to be in," he said. "All I do is scurry in and out of my rathole. I'm suddenly feeling self-conscious about it."

"Don't," she said, handing him a glass, which he set down with barely a sip. "Is your rathole really that bad?"

"You'll see," he said, reaching for her hand.

She moved a step closer. "No," she said. "I'm proud of my little cube. And when I get promoted I'll move to a bigger cube. You can come to me."

"I like your confidence," he said.

"Good."

She slept with him that night not out of a gust of desire—not at first—but because he felt so far out of her orbit as to be an offhand experiment. She thought this even as he kissed her: Why not? Who the hell was this guy, that she should even pause to worry over whether she wanted to sleep with him? She planned to toy with him like a cat, but their first time stunned her. His body was wiry and beautifully made, flat planks of muscles in his thighs, long hands, a tantalizing scatter of dark curly hair over his chest. Standing in her living room, kissing him, his knees and hip bones and mouth all perfectly even with hers, had felt strangely and heatedly androgynous. All his reserve had vanished; she reached a hand beneath his shirt to the silky skin over his hip bone and felt a lurch of pleasure at being the one to have banished it. The feeling was so unexpected that a sound escaped her mouth before she'd known she was making it. By the time they got to her bed she was liquid and giddy, desire cresting through her. They'd rolled around and around, her hands in his hair, his cupping her jaw, until he pushed her back against the headboard and slid down between her legs and did something that made her spine melt. That refrain came back to her, but differently—who the hell *was* this guy?—and she gave herself over to it. This random guy she'd met almost out of boredom and idleness turned out to be a revelation. She forgot whether the windows were open; she forgot she had neighbors. Everything, everything was hers.

Nick was not her type in any way. She had a history of attachments to rangy, life-of-the-party types, the guys who were intoxicating until their flashes of meanness or unreliability or drunkenness reached critical mass. But Nick was exactly what he had appeared to be that first night: watchful but engaged, reserved but not silent. It wasn't that he had nothing to say—he had quite a lot to say, she soon discovered—but he liked hearing what other people said too. That, like the way he looked so frankly and appreciatively at her, was rarer than she'd realized.

He was not especially handsome. There would later be moments she thought he was beautiful—those light green eyes in a dark bar, his finely made hands around a bottle of beer—but the next time she saw him after that first encounter, he was more ordinary than she'd remembered, pale, a small pad of flesh beneath his chin, his otherworldly eyes bloodshot and swollen with fatigue. Somehow even this was part of the appeal. The younger Thessaly would have been insecure about it. She would have thought maybe he wasn't as hot as she'd thought, maybe she was deluded. But the woman she was now knew that she could see past the surface and the obvious, that she had an eye not only for rare wines and the vulnerabilities of surly restaurant owners, but an eye for people. She told him all about life at Lionel Garrett, how she'd just gotten home from Europe, and how her whole workplace was in an uproar competing for something that hadn't even been named yet, and he listened, rapt, just as she thought he would.

Nick also knew of a whole score of cheap, delicious places, which were gold among her colleagues, the sort of joints that let you occupy a table of twelve and bring in two dozen bottles. Over the next two months, he took her to Center Street for pho and plates of something called "hollow vegetable," to East Fifth for tonkotsu ramen with broth so clouded with pork fat it was practically solid, to Flushing (she made sure to mention this to Greg) for fried duck tongues and dumplings in a fiery, oily brownish red chili sauce. Every time he took her to another great place, she passed it on to Wren, whose wine portfolio was delicious with so many different kinds of food—low-alcohol Rieslings with the spicy foods, Chasselas with shrimp, Champagne with everything. Now that Wren was forcing herself to go out with the sales team more often, it only helped them both to have a deep roster of suggestions.

Some places did not make the list—there was a fine line between exciting and off-putting. One sweltering night in June they tried a place on Grand Street that was supposed to be a hidden gem of hand-pulled noodles and broth, and which turned out to be sweaty and hostile, serving grim metal bowls filled with knobs and knuckles, shreds of tissue clinging to the bones. "Well," Nick said, "this has been cartilaginous. Let's get some gelato and call it a night."

"Let's at least finish the bottle first," she said.

"I love your passion, but I can't deal with any more wine," he said.

"I know, sometimes I just need a beer. Let's get sushi. That goes well with beer."

He laughed. "No, I mean I need to detox. And you're not taking me out. This was my night to treat and I chose this nice little gulag. I have to at least buy you a slice of pizza."

He'd heard of all these places because residents made so little money; he had three roommates in a Brooklyn basement apartment and regarded it as holding up his end of the deal to find the most interesting holes-in-the-wall in the city. He never, ever failed to thank her for dinner.

He knew nothing about wine but liked hearing about the pleasures and perks of her work. He was too serene in the worth of his own career to feel a need to denigrate anyone else's. She suspected she made at least twice what he did, and the truth was, she loved that. She loved treating him to dinner at Lupa, not caring if he ordered a twenty-two-dollar ramekin of pasta. It made her feel expansive and generous, powerful and sexy. For the first time she was experiencing the luxury and the pleasure of being the one who was known for giving, the one who invited and offered and tempted and rewarded. Even her through-the-roof credit card bills did not bother her. During the day she just smiled wider and sold more, because now her goals were so clear: she wanted that promotion and she wanted the look on Nick's face that said she had surprised and pleased him, yet again.

She wondered if she would have taken such pleasure in this arrangement if it weren't fleeting. She wasn't in love with him (was she?) and their schedules were too demanding to think beyond their next date—which meant each date could be a seduction. "You don't have to buy me every wine on the menu," Nick said sometimes, and Thessaly would answer, only half joking, "But what else do I have to offer you?"

· CHAPTER 7 ·

Going out with the salespeople was not exactly fun, but it was instructive. Wren had come home after the Japanese restaurant on St. Mark's with a new sense of resolve: the salespeople all hung out with their boss. They had endless opportunities—too many, you might say—to influence Gavin and lobby for support and drop ideas in his ear. So what if Gavin probably didn't listen to or care about any of their efforts? They still got the face time. And she—who had worked for Jonathan for years, who was known to be his right hand—barely had a turkey sandwich with her boss.

And lunches were starting to seem important. By now Greg, Legs, and Sabrina had received invitations for one-on-ones with Lionel, Jonathan, and Gavin and not-so-subtly disseminated this information to the rest of the company. Legs had shrugged and called it exploratory surgery. Sabrina had returned looking satiated and smug, raving about the sear on the salmon as if to imply everyone else would be taken to more mediocre restaurants, forcing Wren and Thessaly to recalibrate their belief that Sabrina was no threat. Was it possible that you could move up in this company without going out boozing every night? Maybe so. Sabrina's expensive eyewear and matronly but well-cut trousers suddenly seemed reassuringly sane and predictable in a way Lionel never was. She'd even started dressing the part: her dark brown hair was a richer shade of mahogany; her pearl studs swelled a few millimeters; she began to squire around several chic, intimidating handbags. And suddenly she was dining out with them all at least once a week, telling hilarious stories of Jonathan's early years when he would show up at the same restaurants for weeks on end to persuade sommeliers that German wine was more than Liebfraumilch, and of Lionel going into towering debt to throw a blowout tasting for the top restaurants in the city. "I thought he was crazy," Sabrina said one evening, leaning forward at the table over her plate of bresaola. "These people had no idea who Lionel was. I mean, he was just a kid too, an assistant, basically. Don't tell Lionel, but after that tasting was such a hit, I had to call the other job I'd accepted and rescind."

It all pointed in the same direction: Wren had to ask Jonathan to lunch. He barely seemed to hear her, but he still said yes. Lately he had seemed especially distracted, by the lunches, the meetings, the impromptu conferences with Lionel that often took up half a morning. But he showed up when he'd said he would, and they set out for an Austrian place in the Village.

"So," she said, when they'd ordered. Faced with Jonathan across a table, she got nervous. It was tempting to pepper him with questions, but she liked to think she'd learned a thing or two from the sales team: that silence could be your ally, that blushing could be stopped if you convinced yourself you were not really frantic, that sometimes a statement of intent put the other person on the hot seat instead of you.

"I wanted to debrief about this whole succession plan," Wren said. "What do I need to do to be considered?"

"Just keep doing what you do," Jonathan said. "It'll all work out in the end."

Wren did not dignify this with a direct reply. "I know he wants everyone's numbers up. I can look at my sales sheets and see what angles we can play with the sales reps, but if we need serious growth, we need new producers. Fuchs is big and consistent, but they can't do everything."

Jonathan leaned back and sniffed at his wine. "The sales reps are the ones who'll feel that heat the most. If they give us the orders, we'll find them the wine."

"Well, no, we won't," said Wren. "That's what I'm saying. A lot of our growers are small farmers or estates. We can't double our orders to them because they wouldn't be able to fill it." She pulled out a file from the folder she'd retrieved from her desk, one copy for her and one for him, and set it before him. "Here are some producers I've been thinking about. My best picks are at the top."

Jonathan skimmed the sheet, which contained ten new producers for every country they covered, winemakers whose reputations she had checked out with their neighbors. She had another list as well but suspected if she kicked off this process with too many names, it would be too easy for Jonathan to set them all aside. "They're decent wines," he said, "and this is good research. Thank you. But we've tasted a lot of these before, and they were never quite the quality we need. There's a reason we aren't already carrying them."

"I know," Wren said. "But that was then. I think it's time to revisit the portfolio. We've been growing, but that doesn't mean we're maxing out our potential. We need to think bigger."

Jonathan nodded, but he was already closing the cover sheet on her report. "There's a difference between big and important," he said. "Having our portfolio associated with Lionel Garrett makes it possible for him to sell things like Big Sky without losing credibility. This is excellent work, but remember, I have a say in . . . who moves forward in consideration. And if I advocate for you, you'll be considered seriously."

Wren frowned. A part of her was flattered that he considered her a shoo-in. Then again, why was he being so obtuse? Being on a short list because Jonathan said so was not the same as getting a promotion because no one could deny she'd earned it.

"I have been paying attention to these places for a long time," she said, "and I really think they're worth a look."

Jonathan rubbed his eyes as if he had never met someone so exhausting.

"Wren," he said, in a tone she had not heard before, "I'm on it. You've made your case, more than once. I hear you."

She sat there for another moment. Only a few weeks earlier, before the prospect of this whole shake-up, she would not have hesitated to argue with him, because she had earned a degree of frankness. But with succession in play, it was suddenly wise to remember that Jonathan was not just her boss but everyone's, and she shouldn't risk antagonizing him when he was about to make a decision that could have so much impact. Dimly she wondered if this was all part of Lionel's social experiment: He was fine! He wasn't going anywhere! He'd just realized that when you dangled a carrot instead of a stick, everyone got tunnel vision for that distant orange blur. But she was only human, and it worked on her too.

What would Thessaly say? Something knowing and pointed but somehow not off-putting, a balance Wren had yet to master. She wanted to reset, but the only thing that came to mind was Lionel. "How's Lionel?" she heard herself say.

Jonathan blinked. "Oh," he said, "you know. The usual. Why, have you noticed anything concerning?"

Maybe she wasn't so off base to think there was something going on with Lionel's health. But she had not observed anything herself. He might be a little thinner than usual, but he did like to try the occasional fad diet.

"No, nothing," she said. "But you must know everyone is talking about him retiring. I thought maybe, away from all the gossip, you and I could have a real conversation about the future."

Jonathan was nodding slightly too enthusiastically. "Yes, yes, naturally. I don't know why he felt the need to bring it up the way he did, but I suppose you may as well know. He *is* thinking about when to step down." Wren waited. This was like Jonathan confiding that they were sitting in an establishment that exchanged food for money.

When it became clear he was not going to say more, she tried again. "I've been wondering what his plan might be. Would he ever sell? Or sell his part? Or keep his shares and appoint someone to do what he does?"

The waiter appeared with a basket of bread. Jonathan grabbed a piece and began to eat it hungrily, as if the faster he ate, the sooner he could end this questioning. What was the matter with him? She was not a reporter, for god's sake.

Jonathan touched his napkin to his lips and cleared his throat. "You realize this is all very unofficial," he said. "And it could change anytime; he has not made any hard-and-fast decisions. But if I were to guess, I'd say he won't sell. He'll keep his shares and appoint someone, provided I agree on whom, of course. Naturally that would necessitate some other, ah, shake-ups."

Wren took some time salting her food. Finally she said, "It looks like you already know who, though. Right?" Then a terrible idea struck her. "You don't mean shake-ups as in layoffs or downsizing, do you?"

"Oh no," Jonathan said. "No, no. If anything, we're expanding. And even if layoffs came, Wren, you must know you'd have nothing to worry about."

Wren's heart was thudding. She knew nothing of the sort. Nothing in her life had suggested she had nothing to worry about. If anything, she was always hyperaware of how many people moved about their lives with what was, to her, a shocking lack of appropriate, cautionary terror. Wren was so unnerved by the conversation that she did another thing she had never done. She asked him for reassurance.

"Jonathan." She set down her fork. "I wouldn't ask you to tell me anything you can't. But after all this time we've worked together, in which I've been nothing but completely trustworthy, can you just . . . tell me a little about what's going on? It'll stay with me. I swear."

For a beat they stared at each other uncomfortably. Wren was realizing she and Jonathan did not do this—they chatted and strategized and tasted and discussed, swirling wines and pointing at spreadsheets, but they did not lock eyes and take each other's measure. She thought he must see in hers the panic she was trying very hard to mute. She knew in theory she could get another job. But what was happening inside her was not theoretical or logical. Her body was following an old chemical footprint, and she felt that if nothing else, he had to see that, had to care enough for her in his distant uncle way that he would want to alleviate it. That she had earned that consideration.

She looked in Jonathan's eyes, the same chilly blue they always were, the same pale lashes and the tired pouches beneath. He lifted one hand from the tabletop and moved it an inch or so in her direction—but then he laid it back down. In his gaze, she saw the moment it happened, when he went from empathetic and concerned for her to closing the shutters. "There really is nothing to tell," he said. "Not yet. I'll tell you when there is."

She waited to see if silence would change anything; it didn't. Then she did what she always did for him: She followed his lead. It was so deeply ingrained in her by now that she was barely aware of it happening as she picked up her fork and nodded briskly. After all, who was she to ask? Jonathan was the one who had mentored her for years and one of the main reasons Wren had forced her way out of customer service and further up the ladder. She had spent five years watching him for cues, and that was what she did now too.

A few minutes later, he said, "How did I never know about this place? This rabbit is lovely."

"It's brand-new," Wren said.

And then he cleared his throat and asked, "Has Hermann been in touch with you?"

At this Wren did look up. Since they'd come home from Germany, Hermann had called once to ask when he should send out a shipping container that had already arrived, but was then impossible to reach. Only Elke kept returning their calls, which had never been the case before.

"No," Wren admitted, "but I spoke to Elke. She's glad about her wines selling better than we thought."

"Yes, well, I think they're getting an extraordinary push from the sales force." And this was true. Thessaly had told her as much, though she appeared to think little of it. Just another one of Gavin's sudden inexplicable directives, which they both believed he might exert just to see if he could.

"But why?" Wren said, and Jonathan shrugged one shoulder.

"To prove a point, perhaps. Did she say anything else?"

"I don't think so. Just made sure the shipping container mix-up was handled and thanked us for the visit." It struck her that there had been one note in that conversation Wren had not known what to make of: Elke had mentioned how lovely they were to work with, how responsive Wren was, how Jonathan understood their wines so well, how gracious and plentiful Gavin's notes and phone calls were. At the time she'd thought little of it, but now, realizing those wines probably *were* selling thanks to Gavin's push, she recalled thinking that Gavin and Elke had just met, so how much time had they had to be in touch? Maybe an office romance. And why not? Gavin's romantic tastes were little-known but fun to speculate about. The consensus right now was that Gavin was a romancer of corporate raiders, sculptors of international renown, and the occasional mythical dragon.

Jonathan was busy considering the Riesling he'd ordered with his rabbit and spaetzle. He didn't even notice her hesitation, so Wren decided not to mention any of it. So what if Gavin was networking with Elke?

Sometimes she wondered if Jonathan was the right boss for her, but she could never get around the fact that he had so much prestige, such a brilliant and discerning palate, and in a cutthroat world, he had integrity. Jonathan wasn't perfect, but he never lied, never yelled (at her), never did anything remotely unethical. He could have treated her more like a colleague and less like a niece, but she still didn't think anyone else could teach her more. He'd brought her this far, after all. It made sense to see if they would get further.

"I do think Hermann seemed a lot weaker this year," she said softly. "I wasn't surprised he got mixed up about the container."

Jonathan stopped chewing for a moment. Then he said, "Remember that bread and broth?"

For the first time in this lunch, Wren relaxed. One of her fondest memories of the many hours she had spent in Germany was of the very first time she visited Fuchs, years earlier, an endless tasting at one in the afternoon on a drizzling, bone-cold, pewter kind of day. She'd been particularly tired and hungry, and during a pause in the conversation her stomach had growled insistently. Jonathan, fully inured to the hunger of his colleagues, didn't notice. But Hermann had insisted they come from the tasting room into the less formal family part of the house, where he'd served them the simplest lunch of her life, simpler even than the bologna sandwiches and tomato soup of her childhood: a bowl of steaming broth, a plate of thick-cut bread, and a dish of butter. Even Jonathan would never dream of refusing.

She still thought about that lunch sometimes: the yeasty, porous crumb of the bread and the sweet butter that she was convinced had been made from the milk of some enchanted German dairy cow but probably had just come from the grocery store; the way the warmth and yellow light in the dim room were entirely concentrated over the wooden table where the three of them had sat, drinking limpid golden broth that was not discernibly poultry or beef but some greater alchemy of all that was savory in both, warming her body with a slow radiance.

"It's funny," she said. "We go to these incredible places, and yet that's one of my top five food moments." Jonathan nodded, but the look on his face was rather distant and melancholy, too private to break through.

Perhaps Jonathan told Lionel he was going to have to address the rumors, because the very next day Lionel called them all into the conference room. He stood at his customary spot at the head of the table, while twenty pairs of eyes roved over his face for signs of weakness.

"It's been a stunning couple of years," Lionel said. "It showed me what you're capable of."

The sound of everyone bracing themselves was nearly audible. They all knew what this meant: Another impossible/compulsory goal was coming. While this would be hardest on the salespeople who had to meet some elevated numbers, it would be no picnic for people like Wren, who had to find the necessary quantities of wines Lionel so blithely threw around. Just as she'd warned Jonathan at lunch, too often their producers simply did not make enough, which meant a full-court press to expand and to find those magic wines that sold commercial numbers but didn't undermine their luxury brand.

She sneaked a look at Thessaly, whose head was tilted to one side as if she were thinking deeply—except when an expression crossed her face of distraction and satisfaction. Then she stifled herself into looking like a professional and not someone who was thinking in filthy detail about her hot doctor. Ever since that night on St. Mark's Place, Thessaly had been on a high. She was less inclined to ponder their professional future or to follow through on the things they'd agreed on. Wren was still taking French, still trying to master the sales pitch, but Thessaly kept forgetting to bone up on the basics of how their product got from one place to another. Like a true salesperson, she just asked for what she needed and assumed it would arrive.

Also, Wren was quite jealous of her for having a hot doctor. Wren's recent relationships had barely earned the title—they were more like tentative dining partners. After a few meals together, the prospect of another date often drew weariness instead of anticipation. It had been a while since she'd felt even a hint of what Thessaly—currently allowing a private smile to lift one corner of her mouth—seemed to be experiencing twenty-four hours a day. Wren considered that her systematic dating life was yet another thing that needed an overhaul: perhaps approaching love as if it were studying for the LSAT was working against her.

But that was not important right now.

"I know we usually take a company trip of some kind around August," Lionel was saying, "and I'll be organizing one this year as well. But it won't be a typical trip." He paused to let them wonder what this meant. "It's going to be a smaller group this year," Lionel continued. "A self-selecting group, you might say."

"Well," Jonathan began uneasily.

"What I mean is, it's a merit-based trip," Lionel said quickly. "Of course, they all are. But I'd like to see what happens when everyone has the right incentive. Say, a trip to Italy. Verona, specifically."

"How are you making the decision?" Sabrina asked.

"We'll see whose sales are highest, whose customers are happiest, whose department is the most profitable. I'd like to have every department represented. But of course," he said, smiling, "that's up to you. I have to think about the future of this company and I want to get to know all of my top people. You guys have two months to show me who that is. And I'm not looking for conventional wisdom. I might decide this position is best split between two people, who can drive each other to be better than they'd each be solo. Maybe I want someone fresh and untested, who hasn't learned a lot of bad habits yet. We haven't had women in management yet. That feels worth examining too. Everything is on the table."

Suddenly the vague and possible were immediate and real. He really was going to step down. Jonathan's face was fixed in stern agreement. Sabrina cast a significant look at Oliver, the Upper East Side rep. They did a lot of that because the two of them were the oldest and most experienced of the salespeople and were known to consider everyone else an upstart. Gavin, to Wren's surprise, looked oddly distracted, as if this were all unrelated to him. And maybe it was. Maybe he didn't even need to go to Verona; his fate was fixed.

Thessaly was staring straight at Wren, her dark eyes blazing. She also looked a little tired and baggy-eyed, which on her looked rather alluring.

Wren wasn't even back to her desk when a text came through from Thessaly about meeting that night. She agreed and headed to the office kitchen for a coffee. Gavin came strolling in behind her. "So what'd you think in there?" he asked, rather chummily. He pulled open a cupboard. Empty. "No clean cups?"

"People just dump them," Wren said, gesturing to the sink. She wondered if Gavin was hoping she'd offer to wash a dirty mug for him. He would never ask her directly, too overtly sexist, but as he stood there, coffeeless, she hated the part of her that itched to clean those dishes. She couldn't live in a mess the way men could, and they knew it. Resisting the urge, she headed toward the fridge for milk.

"Lionel and I have been thinking," Gavin said casually. He began poking through the cabinets. "We could stand to goose our Alsace sales. I've always thought Persand et Fils makes a wine that'd translate in the U.S. or Flunard or Laurent. So many potential producers in that region. Maybe Alsace needs a visit."

He wasn't looking at her as he spoke, so he didn't see Wren swallow hard, trying not to make it audible. She was alight with nerves. Gavin had just named the top three producers she'd had on the list she'd unsuccessfully pitched to Jonathan.

They weren't obscure producers. Gavin and Lionel would know of them. But why bring them up to her now? Why not acknowledge that they were her ideas? Or had Jonathan mentioned them without saying they were her ideas? Was Gavin offering something, giving her a sign? Or was this just a coincidence?

"Those are all very good," she said finally, neutrally. "Jonathan and I were just discussing them the other day." There. Transparency. "And"—she couldn't stop herself—"there are so many other opportunities there too."

Gavin nodded. "Oh, definitely," he said. "Lot more autonomy for you too, if you move up. Portfolio director, maybe. Hang in there."

Suddenly she was hit with paranoia. What if Jonathan walked by and heard them strategizing with his territory? Gavin might just be setting her up. "I hope so," she said. "But I can't think of a better mentor than Jonathan."

Gavin paused at the door to the break room. "Very loyal," he said. "Good for you. You never said what you thought about the trip, though."

"I think it's a great opportunity," she said, pouring milk into her coffee.

"It will be," he said, leaving "for someone" unspoken. "I think that milk's bad." Then he left the kitchen. She waited till she was out of his line of vision to sniff it—he was right.

As she walked back to her desk, she wondered what was going on. Maybe they wanted to push Jonathan out. Maybe they wanted to force him to expand his offerings. She imagined a map: she saw the countries she and Jonathan had spent the last few years exploring, the undulating rivers and the green hills and the dots where Jonathan had already made his mark, the places he had chosen as an expression of no one's taste but his. And she saw a sort of ghost map laid right over it, patterned like a lace overlay. It could be the map of her palate instead. She could fill in all those empty places.

· CHAPTER 8 ·

Thessaly told Wren to meet her at a bar in the West Forties so they could discuss the upcoming trip. She told Nick to meet her there too. She wanted to see him and knew he'd bring a posse of doctors, so she could easily take Wren aside to figure out what was going on with Lionel.

The bar was a boxers' hangout, full of leather and dark wood and photos of men in various states of beatings, and populated mostly by middle-aged men hunched over beer, plus a few young people drawn to the ambience. Thessaly picked it because no one hit on you and they often handed you a shot with your beer for free, if they liked the look of you. Plus, she was worried she was running out of interesting places to take Nick, so she'd begun hitting up her colleagues for new ideas. Naturally, this place was Legs's choice, but her colleagues had plenty of other suggestions. Oliver had spent twenty minutes telling her about a place where he was reasonably sure you might be able to eat ortolan if you paid several hundred dollars for it, but then made one phone call and said no, it was just quail. Amit was excited about a place that used beakers and thermometers and dry ice, which was too much like what Nick did all day. Wren told her about a place in the Bronx that was basically an off-the-books restaurant: you made a reservation to eat in the living room of a woman who made nothing but fufu and Ghanaian fish stew. Thessaly decided she'd rather be with boxers, which might have a certain aura of virility at least, rather than trying to look sexy in a stranger's living room.

She was right—the boxing bar was unassuming, but it had the air of a place that was exactly what it wanted to be, a subculture that felt just foreign enough to be a different world. It smelled of leather and rubber tennis shoes and the bartenders all had cauliflower ears or noses smeared to one side of their faces: honestly, it reminded her of home, where work also carried a degree of physical risk. She ordered a shot to go with her beer and greeted Nick and his friends when they showed up. She listened to their war stories, getting a contact high from hearing about their days. She loved it that Nick had his own magic knowledge, his own secrets and rituals.

Thessaly thought she might be hitting a new stride. It had gathered steam since she'd met Nick, but it was not because of Nick: It felt like she was getting better, better at her job, better at socializing, better at being in the world. Lionel's announcement about the Verona trip might as well be an invitation straight to her. Tonight she could see every thread in the weave of Nick's linen shirt, the weight of someone else's heavy silver watch, that burst of navy blue at the center of Wren's clear gray eyes, and the dark gold curls that gathered around her forehead in the heat of the bar. This must be how adulthood felt, when you excelled at work and sex and friendship. She was either reaching the height of her powers or routinely getting a secondhand high from ambient weed on the streets.

"So did you notice the most important thing Lionel said today?" Wren was saying. She'd barely touched her beer, which for some reason irritated Thessaly.

"What?" she said. "Italy seemed like enough to me."

"Two people," Wren said. "Women at the top. Maybe not an actual promise, but I think it really was a signal. Gavin looked like he hardly even cared, though, so maybe it was all hot air anyway."

"Probably." Thessaly threw back the last of her shot and looked toward the bar where Nick and his friends were still clustered. "All we have to do is get on that trip and be undeniable. How hard can it be?"

Wren laughed at this, but Thessaly was serious. She truly felt she could do anything she wanted to. They were out and about in one of the great cities of the world. They could go anywhere they liked.

"Okay, I can see we'll have to save any real strategizing for when you're not two drinks in," Wren said. Thessaly nodded even though she was far more than two drinks in.

Wren stood and picked up her purse. "Stay," Thessaly said. "Have a little fun, for once."

Wren paused. "This was supposed to be work, not fun," she said finally, and Thessaly was, unaccountably, hurt.

"Stop being such a little house sparrow," she said.

Wren's face dropped. "Forget it," she said. "I'll go to Italy myself." Then she turned and left.

Thessaly hadn't meant to hurt her, exactly—she just did not want to talk about work all night, and Wren never seemed to think about anything else. What did she even do on the weekends? Did she date? That was why she was being such a downer, she was envious. Thessaly told herself this as she went to join Nick standing at the bar.

Standing there waiting for a chance to talk, Nick's hand warm on the small of her back, Thessaly realized that lately there had been no avoiding the residents. Nick couldn't possibly be avoiding being alone with her, so maybe residents always traveled in packs, the same way they entered the bowels of Bellevue or Langone in the morning and exited days later to sleep and eat, only to stream back in in a clump.

They were not normal people. None of *them* had taken two semesters of advanced puppetry. They'd taken biochemistry at Yale and Princeton and Harvard, they churned through stunning amounts of information every day and looked quizzical at the idea of a skipped class or a bad grade. They were towering adrenaline junkies who struggled to sit for long periods. That was why they were in emergency medicine, which would kill the doctors who couldn't handle stress.

One of the things she liked about Nick was that he seemed able to compartmentalize the need for chaos in his work and then achieve a Buddhist calm the rest of the time. The only time that frantic energy resurfaced was in bed.

Whitney, who'd been telling a lengthy, incomprehensible story that appeared to have had a happy ending, finished talking and noticed Thessaly standing there. Thessaly's stories of farmers and her clients' drunken sprees on wine tours couldn't compare with the crushed limbs and overdoses and car wrecks and codes they liked to discuss in their medical-pidgin-English. "Did Nick tell you about the baby?" Whitney said.

"No," Thessaly said warily, praying this was not going to ruin her night.

"I shocked a baby's heart back to life today," Nick admitted. "Which is incredible, because it doesn't work that often."

Thessaly felt the slick linoleum floor tilt beneath her boots. She didn't want to think about the times it didn't work. She didn't want to think about the way the bar suddenly smelled less of manhood and more of feet.

Maybe she was not as confident about getting to Italy as she'd thought. Maybe that last shot was a mistake.

"How was the baby when you left?" she asked Nick, suddenly desperate to confirm.

"That one was just fine," he said.

After they left the bar, he accompanied her upstairs and set an early alarm for work. She had a vague memory of him sitting on the couch for a long time that night, which couldn't be right, because he would surely have gone straight to bed. She woke up feeling hungover and bereft in the middle of the night. He'd already left. Suddenly all the bits of knowledge she'd gleaned from the doctors the night before through an admiring haze of alcohol was left in barren relief against the blank white ceiling: she knew the signs of a stroke and the window after which it was irreversible; she knew they often tried procedures they knew would never work; she knew that codes were not largely successful ministrations to the living, but brutal, and mostly futile, rituals performed on people who were already dead.

"Where'd you go last night?" she asked him on the phone the next day.

There was a pause. "I wanted to head home," Nick said. "I didn't think you'd notice."

"That feels pointed," Thessaly said. She had a headache, which she often did, but today was worse than usual. She prayed this wasn't the phenomenon everyone talked about, when you turned thirty and suddenly your hangovers went nuclear. She decided she'd just been drinking more, that was all.

"It was kind of pointed. I want to take you home and get you in bed, not take you home and poke around your kitchen for a bowl you can throw up in."

"Jesus, Nick. It was one night. It was a *boxing* bar. It just got the better of me."

"Is this your argument?" he said. "That you drank too much because you were confronted with evidence that the sport of boxing exists?" But she could hear amusement creeping into his voice.

"It won't happen again," she said, thinking of the pounding headache she would never admit she felt.

"Then let's stay out of boxing bars," he said. "Okay? I've gotta go, baby. They're paging me."

"Fine," she said. "I'll just get swept off to Italy on a sea of professional glory." But he was already gone.

She got up, dosed herself with Tylenol, water, coffee, and a dry bagel. She rode the subway to work and walked the endless avenue blocks toward the Hartnett-Klein Building and the West Side Highway, grateful for the journey because it gave her more time to work off her hangover.

She was thinking of the time she'd happened upon Lionel after they moved to the Manhattan offices. He was standing out before the building, his hands shoved into the pockets of his cashmere coat, gazing up at the curves of the building. The look on his face was one of gratification, satisfaction, solitude: it had made her think this was the look he must have during some private erotic moment, and she'd turned and walked straight back the other way so she didn't have to encounter him.

But now they were all used to being in this building; the triumph of the move had long worn off. She went inside and up in the elevator, and when she saw Wren standing at her desk, a thought flashed that Wren was still angry at her for the night before. She had the vague suspicion she had said something unkind, though she could not quite recall what it was. Wren turned to her, her eyes swimming, and Thessaly was amazed at the depth of her regret for making Wren feel so badly. What had she said?

"I'm sorry," she said, but Wren only looked confused.

"How did you know?" she asked, and now Thessaly was baffled.

"Know what?"

"That Hermann's dead," Wren said. "He died last night."

· CHAPTER 9 ·

Hermann Fuchs had always been such a dedicated farmer that Wren was surprised he'd died before the growing season was done. But he had: Elke had found her father, already cold in his bed, after he didn't come down for breakfast.

There was no particular reason Wren should feel as saddened as she did by his gentle, expected death. Jonathan, who'd known him longer and more intimately, was red-eyed and somber. She tried to comfort him by reminiscing, but Jonathan cleared his throat and excused himself.

When he came back to her office a while later, he was more composed.

"The funeral is on Friday," he said. "Would you please book three tickets?"

"Of course," she said. "For you, Lionel, and Gavin?"

"Not Gavin," Jonathan said. "I was asking you."

Wren felt tears spring to her eyes. She had not expected to be considered close enough to attend. She knew Jonathan would not have crossed the Atlantic for anyone other than Hermann—this was a generational business, and for a producer to die at an old age was no rare occurrence. Wren could think of two or three families off the top of her head where the younger generation was probably actively awaiting the handover. But it was different when it was your friend and partner of twenty years, who'd welcomed you into his home and his cellars when you were not a seasoned professional but just a messy-looking kid who liked his wine. It occurred to her that this applied to both her and Jonathan.

She went off to book tickets and attend to a hundred other tasks, but thirty minutes later she heard Jonathan's voice through the flimsy walls of his office.

"Are you fucking kidding me?" he said. She'd never heard him speak like this before. She stopped in the hallway. She couldn't hear much after that—Jonathan's voice dropped low. Then the sound of something being set down hard on a desk.

Jonathan appeared in her office doorway a moment later. "Let's get a drink," he said grimly.

"It's eleven-thirty," Wren said. He just looked at her. "Yeah, okay."

They walked without speaking over to Eleventh Avenue and into the kind of bar that was serving before noon, a dark place with walls of no particular color and a few regulars scattered along the brass-railed bar. Jonathan ordered a gin martini with extra vermouth and olives and a twist, the martini of someone who dislikes martinis. She had never seen him drink one before. She ordered a seltzer and a beer.

After the bartender moved away, Jonathan lifted his glass. "Well," he said, "to Hermann. This is the wrong drink to toast him with."

"We'll toast him with something more appropriate later."

He sipped and shook his head. A few minutes later, Jonathan said, "Lionel isn't going to the funeral. It shouldn't shock me, I suppose. But you'd think he'd want to show respect to one of the people he's worked with the longest."

"Ah," Wren said. "I see." She decided to let him talk.

"Hermann was one of the first producers I ever brought in. I ordered seventy-five cases from him and I had no idea how to sell them. I just knew I loved it. Lionel's the one who told me to do it in the first place. We were both working in wine stores and when I was about to go on yet another trip I'd scrimped to afford, Lionel said, 'You've been watching the business for years, why don't you get in the game?'"

He peered into his martini. "You need a hawk like Lionel sometimes. They keep us on our toes. But he might be getting myopic, now that he's thinking of stepping down. He's forgetting that a significant portion of our business flowed straight from Hermann." Jonathan looked hard at Wren, who by this point had finished her seltzer.

"Just don't learn the wrong lessons here, Wren," he said with sudden urgency. "This business is one hundred percent relationships. It's built on coming together, on conviviality, on being a goddamn human being. Lionel's losing that—he's lost it—and it breaks my heart."

Jonathan's phone buzzed and he sighed and picked it up. His face lightened. "Well. Looks like Gavin's volunteered to go. At least *someone* has some manners."

German funerals were not so different from Wisconsin ones. There was a church service, though in a far more beautiful, ornately carved and gilded church than the simple wooden chapels Wren had grown up in. A procession to a grave site, where Elke stood, her blond hair a crisp border against her black silk dress.

Everyone wore dark glasses, though it was not especially bright. It seemed to be a funerary custom, like the flowers everyone carried.

When Elke saw the three of them appear in the receiving line, her green eyes had swum with tears. Wren had already carefully practiced her condolences with Jonathan and Gavin, who turned out to have an unexpectedly fine German accent. After Elke finished speaking, the simple wooden coffin was lowered into the grave and she reached into a ceremonial receptacle of earth and tossed some dirt onto the coffin. Then she tossed in her own bouquet and the mourners lined up to do the same.

When it was Wren's turn to drop in her flowers and dirt, she paused. She'd never been to a funeral of someone with whom her relationship was limited yet deep. She and Hermann had never had intimate conversations of any kind. But they had sat together many times, around the same massive wooden table, and it was impossible not to have feelings about someone with whom you shared something one of you had made. The coffin itself looked smaller than she expected.

They did not attend the gathering afterward. Jonathan said it wouldn't be appropriate. "Close friends and family only," he said. "We've done our part." They all walked back to the car, where Gavin offered to drive and Jonathan accepted, waving Wren into the front seat. It was lunchtime, and no one was hungry yet.

"How about if we take a break," Gavin said, "and then meet for dinner around seven? I imagine we can all use some downtime."

Gavin had been surprisingly gentle this entire trip, treating Jonathan with a kind of deference she'd never seen before from him. Even the dinner suggestion was made offhandedly, and

Wren suspected that if either of them had wished to go drink coffee together or take a walk instead of splitting off, Gavin would have acquiesced just as easily. It was a side of Gavin she'd never seen before, and a part of her wondered if she'd judged him too harshly.

They were staying at an inn with a restaurant on the ground floor. Once there, they went off to their respective rooms, and Wren opened her laptop to catch up on some work. She had to make another series of presentations as soon as they got home, so the sales reps could sell as much of their wines as Lionel insisted and she could crow about it in Italy. And she hated to think this way, but the truth was, Hermann's wines would only be more valuable now. Plus, he had just handed them a great story, and stories sold wine: a story of succession, of the sun setting on a great man, and his final, limited-supply vintages. Terrible, maybe. But useful.

When she went downstairs to the restaurant, she found Gavin at a table by himself. He looked up and nodded. By the time she reached the table he had already poured her a glass of wine, rising briefly in greeting as she approached. Gavin had been looking rather pale and thin lately, lankier than ever, the lines of his cheekbones more visible above his dark beard. Even his eyes had dulled to a mossy brown.

"What are we drinking?" she asked. Gavin turned the bottle toward her. Of course: it was one of Hermann's, one of his older vintages, the ones Jonathan loved and Gavin tolerated.

"That was nice of you," she said. "Jonathan will appreciate the thought. I do too." She did not want to speak for Jonathan, to be merely his amanuensis. She too had had a relationship with Hermann, and she too was glad to drink his wine.

Gavin waved this away, but graciously, as if he were abashed to have been caught being thoughtful. "Being here makes me want to drink this," he said. "It drinks differently here."

"Like how wine at lunch never gets you drunk in France?"

He laughed. "Exactly."

"What's next?" Wren asked, swirling her glass and peering into its depths. "I assume Elke's taking over."

"I suppose so," Gavin said. "Who knows if she ever wanted to take over the winery? But she will. They don't have the succession questions we do in America, where most of the winemakers' kids went off and studied theater or something."

"Look at Thessaly," Wren agreed. "Her dad's in his sixties. Maybe she'll take over the farm and finally start making wine."

"Do you really think so?" Gavin said. "I've heard about this wine dream for years."

"She's just preparing. Speaking of succession: How's Lionel?" Wren said. She didn't want to insult Thessaly the way he seemed to be inviting her to.

"Lionel?" Gavin said, stalling for time. He was turning faintly pink around the cheekbones.

She enjoyed the squirming. "I mean, that's what we've all been talking about for the last month or two. I thought if anyone knew, it would be you."

She didn't enjoy flattering Gavin, but it was worth it to see what he might tell her. Besides, it was just the two of them, far from home, drinking wine, feeling like intimates and even, almost, friends.

Gavin swallowed some wine. "I still have a hard time picturing Lionel loosening his grip in any way." Which might be true but was not really an answer.

"Are you going on the trip?" she asked recklessly. "To Italy?"

"Are you?" he asked. "You must have your eye on something too."

"If there's a prize, I want to try for it," she said. But she didn't like the sound of it, on the very day they'd buried Jonathan's friend.

Gavin shook his head and said, "Don't pretend you don't have a plan. It doesn't become you."

"I'm not pretending anything," she said. She was still that girl from Madison who wanted to be part of something magnificent, ephemeral, something with significance and beauty alike. Sales numbers and trips to Verona were only tools to accomplish that. "It's just, I'm in a world I love and I want to be amazing in it," she said.

"You know I'm not in the habit of being nice," Gavin said, topping off her glass. "But it's a compliment when I say the look in your eyes scares the tar out of me sometimes."

"True. You're not in the habit of being nice," she said.

He watched her steadily, but it didn't seem calculated. It seemed . . . open. A bit naked. Wren didn't know exactly what was happening.

"I should probably give you a lot more compliments, for a lot more reasons. Only some of them about work." He watched her to see if this landed.

It did. She felt a rush of blood creep up her chest and her scalp.

No one else was here, she thought. Jonathan might not even come to dinner. Here they were in another country, far from everything that mattered. There was an exciting shock to seeing a familiar person in a new light, and part of her wanted to see what that meant.

If only it were someone else, someone she didn't know so well.

Over Gavin's shoulder, she saw Jonathan appear in the entrance to the dining room. The moment broken, they both rose to greet him.

Jonathan seemed more himself now. Perhaps it was the relief of it being done. In the morning they would fly to JFK and then life would resume. But there was something warm and convivial about the three of them together in this white room, with its dark wood trim and murmurs of German conversation.

Jonathan had not looked at the bottle before he took a sip of his wine. As he drank, his brow furrowed and then he smiled, almost involuntarily. Gavin was pretending to read his menu. Jonathan took another deep inhalation, another sip. He looked up with a brilliant smile that lanced Wren right in the sternum. "It's Hermann's," he said, "the 1998 Spätlese. Where in the world did you get it? Nobody has it now."

Gavin looked so pleased and proud, Wren felt almost maternal for him. "Just made a few calls," he said gruffly. "I thought you might enjoy it."

Jonathan's eyes welled, and to Wren's exasperation, so did hers. She'd recognized the general wine, but not that exact vintage. She would not have expected Gavin to remember how Hermann had so recently drunk that wine and come back to life. Gavin didn't care about emotional moments like that. That he not only remembered but had clearly gone to some lengths to obtain this bottle for Jonathan—for Wren herself had attempted to source that vintage a few times for a knowledgeable sommelier and had struck out—made her wonder, once again, if she'd gotten Gavin wrong.

Everything in her wanted to joke, speculate on what he must have done to get his hands on this bottle. Instead she said, "That was a lovely thing to do," and forced herself to stop there.

Jonathan was drinking the wine with that same pleased and mournful expression, and Gavin wore an odd look of his own, a mixture of tenderness and brusqueness and mourning, as if he were vexed at them for making him feel this way. Wren wondered suddenly if he was much older than she'd thought—*something* had certainly aged him and softened him, if briefly. Death, maybe. It did that to everyone.

· CHAPTER 10 ·

Thessaly found herself relieved Wren had left for Hermann's funeral. She still felt embarrassed and ashamed of being drunk and bitchy to her. Worse, she had been half-assing her professional development goals ever since she'd met Nick. She'd ducked out of a German class and kept procrastinating on the studying she'd sworn to do about various regulations she'd had no reason to learn about before. And the more she thought about it, the more she wondered if any of this would help her. She didn't want to be an operations wonk like Wren. She didn't want to know how much it cost to ship wine to Massachusetts. This was not her forever job. This was just the stopgap. Sometimes she thought it was time to pull the trigger on that too, just apply to a wine program somewhere, but she never got around to that either. Who wanted to go home and gather applications when there was dinner to be had, drinks to be drunk, Nick to be Nicked?

On Friday she went out with Legs and Amit to an East Village bar Legs chose and made the mistake of texting Nick to join her after she'd been in the bar for two hours, playing pool and doing shots, trying to see if Legs ever really got drunk or if his body was no longer capable of it. Nick showed up after a shift, exhausted and unshaven, and he looked at her in a way Thessaly immediately wished she hadn't seen. She'd tried to play it off, but he'd made excuses about getting up early and went home without her.

The next morning she knew it was time for damage control. She made herself feel as human as she could, put on a short dress, and called Nick to lure him into going up to Arthur Avenue with her later that day. She was hoping if they got great ingredients and ate dinner at home, she'd keep a lid on things and they'd have a better night. She just needed that first glass of wine to take away the headache the ibuprofen wasn't touching. And obviously she had to wait until a reasonable hour.

"You don't know this about me," Thessaly said to Nick on the D train up to the Bronx, "but I cook. Well, I bake. And not just brownies, either." She was still viciously hungover and trying not to show it. Didn't doctors ever drink too much? Apparently not, but being hungover was such a typical state of affairs in her world that Thessaly bought Tylenol and Alka-Seltzer as regularly as she bought coffee and bread; mornings, and sometimes afternoons, being reliably grisly was an occupational hazard. She didn't see a way around it. This was the thing Nick didn't understand. If wine was just a commodity to you like soda, you didn't care if you let it go flat and poured it down the drain. But when you knew what had gone into making it, when you knew how little might be left in the world, you showed it respect and you drank that wine. She considered trying to tell him this now, except last night they'd drunk vodka in a gritty bar, so her argument didn't hold up.

Now he looked her over. "There's a difference between baking and cooking?"

"Definitely. You can get all creative and silly when you cook. Like tonight I'll put a bunch of things together and I don't even know what they are yet. But if I'm making pastry I have to plan and weigh things. It's no joke."

"I thought we were getting stuff to make pasta," he said.

She eyed him, trying to tell how annoyed he was with her today. Maybe this was a good time to break out some puff pastry.

"We'll see how the afternoon goes," she allowed. "Besides, the place I'm taking you makes me feel like I can cook. So brace yourself for that no matter what."

He looked up at the map, which showed they would get out a solid half mile from their destination on East 187th Street. "Are you sure you can walk that far?"

"Of course," she said. "I'm in great shape."

"Yeah? You seem under the weather," he said neutrally.

"Well, I'm not," she said.

What had once been a sprawling Italian neighborhood now occupied no more than three or four blocks of Italian stores and restaurants. The restaurants were pizza and red sauce and veal parm joints; they weren't the draw. The draw was the mozzarella made every day and still warm from the brine, a fleshy, creamy orb she'd learned never to refrigerate or it lost its sweet freshness. Or the pasta from the place that charged an extra thirty cents a pound for special cuts like pappardelle, which she always ordered while the octogenarian nonna who ran the pasta store gazed balefully at Thessaly, seeing all her sins as clear as day. There were a dozen shops she liked to go to up here, buying a different item at each one. She loved this neighborhood, which felt like the remains of a city she had assumed she'd missed out on. Also, she suspected she needed new material. She might have already taken Nick through some of her best stuff.

They got off the subway and walked for fifteen blazing minutes past unpromising clothing stores and apartment buildings until they got to the right street, a pool of Italian colors and memorabilia in the middle of the borough. "You see?" she said happily, relieved it was as good as she remembered it, relieved he seemed pleased too. Even her head pounded more softly.

They went from place to place and bought one or two things at each, soft ripe figs in the indoor market; cupfuls of capers in salt; fat-streaked, chile-flecked slabs of house-cured pancetta. He stopped at the raw bar on the street and ate six clams; Thessaly refused to admit that when she felt the way she did today, such an act was hostile. None of the countermen would speak to Nick, but to her they were courtly and avuncular. She showed him the sausage store, where the entire room smelled like the powdery cured skin on a prosciutto. They paused over the windows filled with rabbits and sheeps' heads and pig faces labeled "pork snoots," considered the shining purple-gray livers and brains. Even seeing literal trays of organs in her delicate state could not dim her mood: She had the weekend before her, Nick had all night before he'd leave for work at four a.m. In a month she'd be in Italy on the company trip. She was going to spend less money this fall, too. That was why they were up here shopping to eat at home instead of trying some exciting new place. She wasn't so abstemious that she couldn't still show off. She wasn't taking him to Key Foods for a box of spaghetti. She had a spell to maintain. It might be time to make puff pastry *and* baguettes. Also, the faster they got to her house for a glass of cold white wine, the faster this headache would go away. She was wondering if she could persuade him to get a drink here in the neighborhood, under the guise of research, but had a feeling it wouldn't work.

126

"Did I tell you how Wren found this place?" she said chattily, breathing deeply to forget those glistening purple organs, those fucking raw clam and oyster bars they were passing on the street. "She read in the *Times* about some place you could buy great olive oil for like twenty-five bucks a gallon. She's the only person I know who'll devote a whole weekend day to getting cheap olive oil, but that's how we found out there's basically a second Little Italy up here. But an actual real Little Italy, not the tourist trap."

"Yes," Nick said, "you mentioned that. Couple times." Fuck. She was so thrown off by this, by being the tedious repetitive blowhard she must have already become without realizing it, that she stopped cold on the sidewalk. For a moment she just stood there, trying unsuccessfully to summon the kind of sexy repartee the first month or two of her time with Nick had been so filled with. Then she realized she was right across the street from the store that sold Wren's favorite olive oil. She could get him one of those greenish-yellow gallon tins, possibly two, and remind him she was the knowledgeable urban dweller, the one who knew where to go and what to buy and why it was better than the rest. Relieved, she started across the street.

Time, in the seconds after she stepped off the sidewalk, seemed to crumple into itself. She was turning to speak to Nick, she was holding a bag filled with cheese and boxes of pastry. There was a screeching of brakes and several wordless shouts, the kind of exclamations people gave when they were too shocked to use language. Then she was moving without having planned to. There'd been a great thumping noise and impact on her body, a shove so hard it sent her flying, then she was sitting in the street amid a confusion of spilled food and torn bags. Nick was looming over her. Her leg was bleeding. She watched her hand reach out to touch the glossy red skin, as if to be sure it was hers.

The people who surrounded her had that concerned, angry look New Yorkers got when you forced them to attend to you. She expected it from them. She hadn't expected it from Nick.

"Jesus," he was saying. "Thessaly, look at me, please. Are you okay? It's important you look at me. Right now." She was aware of the grille of an old, rusty orange car, the one that had knocked into her, and which had stopped only a foot or so away from where she'd landed. She thought distantly that that car could never pass inspection. She followed Nick's finger with her eyes and turned her head back and forth and up and down and tested her limbs and blotted at the wound on her leg, which turned out to be an ugly but superficial scrape. Someone gathered all the things she'd lost in the street and gave them back to her and she peered into the bag—they'd gotten her a new one—at the dented pasta box and the slightly rumpled cheese packages, wondering if it was bad form to take them with her. Was it frivolous to care about cheese even after being hit by a car?

"Come on," Nick said. He was calm now, businesslike. "We'll get a cab home."

"There are no cabs up here," she said, but she looked gamely around for one. Nick walked up the block and flagged down one of the livery cars that ran throughout the Bronx and which you were never supposed to flag down, but somehow trudging bleeding to the subway with their bags felt more impossible than climbing into an unmarked car.

"Do I need to go to the ER?" she said finally, once they were settled in the back of a black Buick.

"I'll be your ER," Nick said. He kept examining her, his eyes roving clinically over her. "You just stepped right out in front of a car," he said eventually. "The only reason you're not dead is he'd barely started up. You could have gotten seriously injured back there. Killed. What were you looking at? What were you thinking?"

"I was looking at something for you," she said. She thought it might appease him, but he looked appalled. He said nothing else until they pulled up to her place. She certainly wasn't going to admit she'd been thinking about a glass of cold white wine. She tried to pay the exorbitant fare, but Nick handed over two twenties without looking at her.

"I wish you had an elevator," he said. "Can you make it up the stairs?"

"Yeah," she said. "I'm okay."

"You might be," he said. He wrapped her arm over his shoulders and his arm around her waist and they went slowly up the stairs.

When they made it into her apartment, Nick sighed and cleared the laundry bags off her couch so she could sit down while he brought her a bowl of ice and a kitchen towel, which he filled efficiently and laid over her knee. It was bruising but not very swollen. She was home in her cube, feeling dazed, and Nick was putting things into the refrigerator and then carefully washing her leg with a soapy, stinging cloth. "You don't have big bandages, I bet," he said.

"Neither do you," she said. "Who keeps giant bandages around?"

Thessaly was suddenly exhausted. All the adrenaline had left her and she felt tremulous and empty. She felt rather affronted, because she hadn't been drunk like he clearly thought she was; she'd been brutally hungover like a good little martyr when everyone knew she should have had a quick drink in the morning, or at least at lunch, and felt better in a snap.

Nick was woundingly businesslike as he wrapped up her leg. But at least by then she'd started to get her bearings back. "So, your bedside manner," she ventured. "Kind of grim."

"I'm sorry," he said. He stood up and looked around her tiny apartment as if for something to do. "At work they come to me already injured. I don't usually have to watch it happen. It felt a lot scarier than you think it will."

"It was an accident," she said, and here he turned on her.

"You realize if you walk around either drunk or hungover most of the time, you're going to get hurt one way or another. You can't walk around this city like you own it. You can't just assume cars'll stop and you'll be fine."

"I wasn't hungover. It could've happened to anyone." Oh, a lie, of course it was a lie, but now she was dug in and she would suffer all night with this headache and this scraped bruised leg before allowing herself to drink a drop of wine in front of him. She was enraged to find tears stinging her eyes. Her father was a lot like this, she thought suddenly; when someone got hurt on their farm he yelled at them the whole time he was helping them. "You act like I'm such a degenerate, but I swear, Nick, I'm in fucking AA compared to the people I work with."

"Soon enough," he said, and that was the last straw.

"I can't believe you're being such a dick when I could have gotten hurt!"

"That's my point," Nick hollered. "If you did, it would have been your own fault! Jesus, Thessaly, you're incredible. But it seems like all you want to do is get drunk and shoot the shit about Spain and France and all your idiot clients. Seeing you was my escape, but now it's just watching you get soused and walk into traffic."

There was a long silence. Thessaly turned this over in her head. She was thinking of all the times she'd felt so erudite around him, when she'd shown him all she'd learned over the years, the things that mattered immensely to her. That the deeply animal flavor of foie gras was sublime not with red wine but sweet whites, that every fig contained the tiny wasp that had fertilized it, that you could drink Champagne for no reason at all. Things that felt like concrete clues leading into a richer, more sensuous world. At some point, when she still thought she was opening door after door for him, offering him gift after gift, he just saw a drunk.

"I didn't realize I was just a diversion," she said.

"You're not a diversion," he said. "You know damn well that isn't what I said." None of the talents she had begun to wield so richly and easily in her own world had any value in his. That was the part that hurt. She wasn't his equal in his eyes, she understood now, and he was angry at her not because he adored her and feared any harm coming to her, but because she'd broken the spell, like the lights coming on during a movie.

"Why don't you go," she said.

"Come on," he said. "I'm sorry I was a dick, but you need someone here. The only reason I didn't take you to the ER was because I was planning to be here. I have to stay overnight. Somebody has to be with you."

For the first time, Thessaly wished Wren were not in Germany at Hermann's funeral. She had never thought of Wren as an actual friend, someone she could ask something from, but she knew at once that she could have called, and Wren would have come straight over.

She wanted to get Nick out of her apartment so she could stop pretending she was cool and unfazed—she felt sick with shame and disbelief. That they were inside this tiny studio where they'd fucked on every surface only made it worse. There was no neutral place where she could go and sit and cry and drink and not see him. But she could tell he was dug in. He sat down at the other end of the couch and passed her the remote without looking at her and took out his phone to check for messages. He was staying all night, Thessaly realized. That son of a bitch was going to show her one last time what a great doctor he was, what a great boyfriend he would have been, for some better girl.

· CHAPTER 11 ·

On a Monday in July, a couple of weeks after Hermann had died, Wren came into the office to find most of the team toiling away. Even the salespeople were there, which was unusual. They'd come in for a sales meeting, then stayed—first to bitch about Gavin calling in sick, and then to catch up on admin on a day when most restaurants were closed. Traditionally a dead zone for wine, summer had picked up the last few years. Americans had finally started to appreciate dry rosé, the ultimate summer wine, and all the pink wine they'd sold several months ago was already in need of reorders.

Legs had his feet propped on a chair and was taking notes with a chewed Bic he'd probably found on the subway. Oliver was trying fruitlessly to get a restaurant reservation, and Greg was emailing frantically, trying to keep up with Jersey in all its lawlessness. Thessaly, who had been industrious during the day and a holy terror out at night ever since she and Nick had broken up, was at her desk with what looked like a rabid hangover, drinking Gatorade, chewing some remedy.

Wren was still trying to decide if she knew Thessaly well enough to say anything about the increasing quantity of her hangovers.

133

She had just steeled herself to ask her to meet up after work for that purpose when Lionel came tearing out of his office, looking deranged. His collar was pulled to one side and his hair was wild. He stopped in the center of the room and looked around without focusing on anyone. "I need a box," he boomed. "Someone bring a fucking box to Gavin's office."

No one moved for a moment. Did Gavin have some secret stash in his office that Lionel had just discovered? Wren and Thessaly looked at each other. Thessaly raised her eyebrows and nodded encouragingly, but Wren shook her head.

Sabrina charged to the tasting room, which had towers of empty cases of wine, and disappeared into Gavin's office. A series of thumps and bangs emitted from the open door. Lionel swore. Sabrina murmured soothingly.

All of it was too tantalizing not to investigate. Finally, Wren got up and strolled by Gavin's door. His office was a strange den of ambition and self-regard, pictures of Gavin with various winemakers, obscure maps with the words "Here Be Dragons" penciled at the edges, books that had nothing to do with wine but which he wished to make it known he'd read. (Back when he was trying to educate Wren, earlier in her career, he'd once gestured in the direction of the shelves and said, "Heidegger makes my point for me.") Sabrina was backed into a corner of the office, clutching a jar of pens for some reason, watching Lionel tear the maps off Gavin's walls, the books off his desk and shelves. He tossed them all into the box. Not tossed. He threw them with force. All of Sabrina's maternal and professional sangfroid had fled.

Wren paused long enough to hear Lionel say to Sabrina, "I need another one." His voice was full of fury and—Wren was almost certain about this—tears. Sabrina saw Wren in the doorway and shook her head almost imperceptibly.

She'd go to Jonathan. Jonathan would tell her everything. But Jonathan was sitting at his desk, unmoving. His eyes were fixed on a map of Germany that hung on his wall. When Wren paused in the doorway, he pretended not to see her.

After that, she didn't know what to do. What in the world had Gavin done? Maybe he was dead. She went slowly back to her desk and sat down, shrugging subtly in Thessaly's direction, and tried to look busy while she listened to the ongoing thumps. They'd know if he was dead, she decided. Someone would have gotten a call.

Eventually Lionel emerged. He exhaled a great puff of air and looked at no one. He set the box in the hallway outside Gavin's door and stalked down the hall toward Jonathan's office.

Everyone just sat there. They were accustomed to hollering, which could be effusive or outraged, and they were accustomed to bursts of rage over the details of shipping, taxation, tariffs, or supply. But that sort of commotion felt different, controlled. This had a feeling of genuine chaos. No one knew what Lionel was going to do. It wasn't clear that he knew either.

Across the room, Legs set down his gnarled Bic. Wren watched him as he started walking toward the door—she assumed he was on his way to the elevator, or to throw himself into the mix with Jonathan and Lionel. But as he passed Wren's desk, he tapped a finger on her desktop. "Come downstairs," he said softly. He didn't wait for her.

Outside, they took a right toward the West Side Highway, where no one would follow them. The humid wind whipping off the Hudson brought tears to her eyes.

"What's going on?" Wren said.

"Gavin quit," Legs said. "He's forming his own company and Lionel just found out."

She took a surprised breath. Maybe Gavin had been so decent in Germany because he wanted to depart on good terms.

"The quitting isn't so bad," Legs said. "Gavin took Fuchs with him. Gavin and Elke Fuchs are import partners now."

Wren felt her face go blank. "You're kidding" was all she could say.

Legs gave her a pitying look. "Do you need a cigarette or something?" he asked, patting his jacket pockets. "I probably have a pack in this jacket somewhere."

"That little shit," she said almost admiringly. "He went to the funeral to lock it down, I bet. Or to get the next steps started. And he was so nice! He knew how Jonathan felt about Hermann. There was no one else Gavin could've started a company with?"

Legs shrugged. "I always knew I couldn't trust him. When he's being nice, he wants something. Now Jonathan's lost his biggest producer. That might have ramifications for other people."

Hearing this from Legs made it worse. She and Thessaly had speculated endlessly about what was going to happen, but it had always felt reassuringly private. Now she felt exposed.

Legs said, "I may not trust Gavin, but I listen when he tries to impress me. We hit a few clubs once or twice. The reason Lionel's so pissed is that obviously this ruins the whole plan. Gavin won't take over now, and Gavin was supposed to be the one who would run this place the way Lionel wants it run. Less boutique wines like Jonathan's, more Big Sky. Gavin wasn't supposed to take Fuchs, he was supposed to take over the region."

"But Jonathan's an owner. It's his region."

"Barely an owner. He was always too busy pondering wine to buy more shares of the company and get some power to balance Lionel's. Lionel can do what he wants, sell what he wants, dilute

Jonathan's shares, and wait till Jonathan gets sick of it and asks for a buyout. It's kind of impressive, when you think about it, outfoxing Lionel so thoroughly."

Wren found herself nodding. "Gavin was sort of testing the waters with me too, I think. I thought he was just goading me about trying to get a promotion he already had locked up."

Legs looked uncomfortable. "He was testing. But if Gavin had stayed, he wasn't going to keep you. He thought you were too aligned with Jonathan. Either you'd have to go if Jonathan did, or he could get rid of you to *make* Jonathan want to quit. Either way: clean house."

Wren felt every inch of her skin, inside her clothing and against the hot summer air, prickling with betrayal and disbelief. What was all that complimenting and eye contact in Germany? The follicles of her hair lifted with pure rage.

"They think they'd do better without me?" she said. "That fucking beard-stroking weasel. When did he say all this? Why didn't you tell me?"

"I didn't know if they were going to do anything at all," said Legs. "What if I got you all riled up and then they changed the plan? I mean, that *is* what happened. If they'd seemed like they were about to move, I'd have let you know."

She tried to get her breath back under control. If Jonathan got pushed out now, did he take her with him? Did everyone see them as a package deal? Or what if they did, but he didn't? Suddenly she was terrified she'd apprenticed herself to someone who was about to be put out to pasture—and it was too late to separate her career from his. She hated to think this way about Jonathan, who had taught her so much and whom she still admired greatly—but she hadn't been ready for this. "Maybe nothing'll happen right away," she said, panicking.

Legs had finally found a cigarette pack in an interior pocket of his jacket—it was lined in beautiful silk, she noticed, a venomous shade of green—and he offered her the crumpled pack of Camels, but she shook her head. "I don't know what a wounded Lionel does, but I wouldn't count on empathy and generosity," he said.

"I guess he isn't exactly a give-you-the-shirt-off-his-back kind of guy," Wren said.

"No," Legs said, magically lighting a cigarette despite the wind. "More like, 'a chill is imminent, give me yours.'"

Wren took the cigarette from him after all, because she wasn't sure what else to do. She told Legs to go back inside while she walked and smoked and realized she hated smoking. She tried to recall details of the funeral that she'd missed the first time. She thought about Gavin tracking down that rare wine for Jonathan, why he'd made such a generous gesture, and then she understood where he'd gotten it: straight from Elke. Had Gavin spoken at greater length with Elke than the rest of them? Had he betrayed some hint of intimacy with her, something that would explain how both Wren and Jonathan could have missed his plans? She came up with nothing.

She searched her memory for evidence of some hidden motive, something he might have let slip. But she didn't think there was one. Despite everything else she knew now, Wren was certain that in that moment in the restaurant, if no other time she'd known him, he had been sincere.

That night Wren did something she hadn't done since her early years in New York. She stopped at the grocery store, and not the nice one where she treated herself to a wedge of cheese or a bright orange slice of bottarga. She went to the Circle K near her subway stop, a depressingly fluorescent-lit store in which a mouse had once darted playfully across the cereal aisle just as Wren was reaching for granola. She wanted the cheapest kind of pasta, the sort you could buy for a dollar a box if you bought ten. She bought ten. She considered buying twenty but didn't want to carry it all home. Then she stocked up on dried beans: cannellini, garbanzo, turtle, lima, lentils. Twenty pounds of food to lug six blocks to her apartment.

When she got home, sweaty and sore, she lined everything up in her cabinets and did the math. If a pound of pasta was four servings, ten pounds of pasta was forty servings. She calculated how long she could live off what she'd just bought. Looking at the neat rows of food calmed her down. This was maybe a month of food, if she made sure she had some butter and onions. Which was a better buy, olive oil or butter? Once she would have known. She was out of practice.

She didn't eat any of it. It wasn't for dinner. It was food for the apocalypse. She thought she had graduated from this feeling, which she remembered well from childhood, but now it came roaring back to her. The constant counting. The calculation of noodles, tomatoes, and milk, the feeling of dread every time you checked your bank account. As a child, at the end of the month, she used to make meals of things she'd found in the kitchen, trying unsuccessfully to believe it was inventive and festive to eat pretzels with the last of the cream cheese. At least now she had some control over this. She was more skilled at feeding herself than she was when she was ten. If she wound up destitute, she knew how to stay alive eating beans.

•

The mood at the office became spiky and odd, with an underbelly of unseemly excitement. With Gavin gone, suddenly the whole company felt up for grabs. Everyone stopped angling to replace Gavin and began to think bigger. Thessaly thought if auras had been visible, they would all have been hazard-yellow.

No official announcement was made about Gavin. His office door was simply closed until it was decided who would take over the position of the national sales director. For a while they waited to see if he would come in to retrieve his things, but Thessaly had peered in one day and realized that none of Gavin's most prized possessions were there. He'd planned ahead and removed everything he cared about without anyone noticing. "I almost admire that son of a bitch," Wren admitted to Thessaly.

Lionel kept calling various employees into his office to watch him nod and listen to him think aloud before they were invited to answer questions about loyalty. No one admitted that they were keeping a close eye on Gavin's new company, but they all examined its website, poring over the photos of Elke and Gavin (sunlit, professional; Gavin's beard oiled to a minky gleam) and the copy (pristine, with none of the usual translation and punctuation issues) and the list of producers (small but wisely chosen). Wren pointed out what Thessaly hadn't noticed at first: that several of the producers she'd been pushing on Jonathan were among the ones Gavin was now importing.

Lionel's lunches became haphazard, repetitive. Greg said they'd mostly talked about numbers: Was pricing too high, too low? Oliver discussed supply-side economics, for which he was eminently unqualified. Amit, confounded, admitted they'd talked of nothing but Chilean Cab Franc for ninety minutes. At every single lunch, they all agreed, Lionel at some point turned to his companion and said, "Where would you take this company in a year? In six months? In three?" It was hard to know if they should be thrilled or frightened, because no one knew any more than Lionel did what he was going to do. They just kept gamely disappearing with Lionel midday and returning confused and slightly drunk.

The night after Thessaly's lunch, Wren asked her over to her place in Astoria, where she was making pasta. Thessaly took a quick walk around the little place, which was slightly larger than her cube, but not as well appointed. Wren had a quality couch, two rickety side chairs, and a sharp-edged, shin-level coffee table. But her kitchen was warm and welcoming, with pale yellow walls and dishes of peaches and zucchini on the tiny countertop.

Thessaly waited for Wren to offer her a glass of wine, but all she seemed to have was herbal tea and seltzer. So she sat and drank glasses of seltzer while Wren sautéed garlic.

"So how was it?" Wren asked. "What do I have to look forward to?"

Thessaly sighed. She'd gone over her best sales strategies, made notes on underrepresented regions and varietals. Against everything she dreamed of, she came up with ideas for new Big Sky SKUs. "It was weird. Possibly helpful. He kept saying stuff about how I too must have experienced betrayal, a lovely young woman like me. Does he think I was sleeping with Gavin or something? Or does everyone know about me getting dumped?" She said this lightly, but in fact Thessaly felt a deep pool of shame and embarrassment every time she thought of her colleagues watching her with Nick, watching him look at her like she was just another fuckup.

Wren laughed. "I don't think Lionel got filled in on your romantic struggles."

"Good. Anyway, every time I tried to talk about actual business, or ideas, or marketing, or whatever, he'd nod like he was barely listening." She paused. She'd been debating whether to say this next part or not. But she decided she and Wren were in this together. Gavin was gone, Lionel might very well restructure the whole place in a way that would serve them both, or he might do nothing of the kind. "He did say he has a few nibbles on selling the company," she said. "And he seemed kind of relieved about it."

Wren turned and looked at her, olive oil dripping off the spoon she was holding. "How seriously?" she asked. "How relieved?"

Thessaly sighed. "I don't know. I asked if he was still doing the August trip and he said, 'Oh sure, why not?'"

She waited for Wren to speak, but Wren was just standing there, brows knit.

"When's yours?" Thessaly prompted her.

"Hmm? Oh. Thursday," Wren said. "I think he made me wait because he and Jonathan aren't talking much right now. They both think Gavin leaving is the other person's fault."

"It kind of is," Thessaly said.

"Whatever. I just don't want to get stuck working for some giant behemoth. I could have done that years ago, if I wanted to."

"I don't think we can stop him if he wants to sell," Thessaly said. She opened the freezer for some ice and paused. It was stuffed with bricks of frozen spinach and bags of mixed veggies and peas. "Good god, Sparrow, do you even have room for ice in here?"

Wren's face froze when she saw Thessaly before the stuffed freezer.

"Are you stockpiling," Thessaly joked, "or is it always like this?"

Wren tossed her head as if she were trying to get her bangs out of her face. Her neck was turning red. Thessaly realized she had hit a nerve.

"I'm sorry," she said, closing the freezer door. "I keep saying dumb things to you."

Wren turned to look at her. "You do," she said. "You should stop. But also, that reminds me. I want to discuss something with you."

Thessaly swallowed some water. It felt quite pointed now, that that was all she'd been offered.

Wren turned the flame down under the pan and leaned back against the counter to face her. "I don't want to seem evil," she said, "but Lionel being such a mess can work to our advantage. He's flailing, and yeah, he might just decide it's easier to sell the whole thing and be done. But he also might be so wounded and off balance that he would rather show up Gavin by making Lionel Garrett better than ever, thriving more than ever, in the same space Gavin wants to. This is as close to malleable as Lionel will ever be, so maybe we just need to make it easy for him. Make it so abundantly clear he has an easy way forward, a team who's incredible at operations *and* sales, a deep bench behind us, and then it's all so simple, right? He keeps making money, his name is still on the door, yadda yadda."

"Okay," Thessaly said slowly. "I think you're overestimating our powers of persuasion, but I'm game to try."

"I probably am," Wren said. "But I'm not going to sulk until he sells and all we do is shill jugs of wine. Which is what I want to talk to you about. Do you want to try and present that kind of team with me? Because I can go in there and make the argument that that's what we can do."

"Sure," Thessaly said. She was so relieved that Wren's serious expression was only about work that her voice was louder than necessary. "Do it!"

"I'm not doing it if you can't get your shit together."

Thessaly felt as if she might throw up. She couldn't stand to look at Wren for a beat, and when she did Wren was not smiling, not even a touch.

"It's pretty clear why you and Nick broke up. And why you got hurt. And since then, holy shit, Thessaly. Do you have a real problem, or do you just have no idea how to cope with garden-variety heartbreak?"

"Wow," Thessaly said. "Fuck you."

Wren didn't even blink. "I mean it," she said. "I am not going to go in there and yoke myself to you if you can't get your drinking under control. We all know how this goes if you can't. How many times have we seen it? You lost someone because of it, what's next?"

"Nick was never even that into me," Thessaly said. "He just got bored."

"He was wild about you," Wren said softly. "I barely hung out with you and I could see it. So what happened?"

Thessaly shook her head. "Look," she said, "I'm not some alcoholic who's insisting I don't have a problem. I just had a bad stretch. It looks worse to you because you barely drink."

Wren shrugged. "You know why I barely drink, though, right?"

"No, why? A drunk in your family? Maybe it's genetic. But no one in my family has issues, if that makes you feel any better."

"Not especially. My dad was a total mess, and when you grow up with someone who's always trying to get sober and trying AA and trying rehab, you do learn a few things. You don't have to have a gene that activates the first time you have a sip of alcohol.

You can just drink so much for so long that you change your brain chemistry and turn into the same thing."

"How's your dad now?" Thessaly asked.

Wren shrugged. "I have no idea," she said. "I haven't talked to him since I was about eighteen. I was working at this fancy restaurant, really proud of it. I wanted to make some dish I'd learned to cook and I remember him looking me straight in the eye and making a plan for my next day off. He even wrote it down. I mean, I knew it was all bullshit. I believed him one hundred percent and I also knew whatever he promised me was never going to happen. Something about watching him commit to the pretense of writing it down was just it for me." She stopped talking, as if just realizing how much she had said.

"Anyway," she said, "the point is I don't screw around with untrustworthy people, and I need to be sure you're not one of them."

Thessaly said nothing for a moment. Wren was unnervingly on point in so many ways. Thessaly had indeed been thinking that if no one else was an alcoholic in her family, she'd be fine too. She could reel it in whenever she was ready. And she'd been thinking that one mix-up was not much to sever a relationship over—until you saw it in terms of basic character.

"I know I've been drinking too much," she said eventually. "But I can change it."

"So change it," Wren said. "Let's quit half learning from each other and half competing, let's really *do* this."

Thessaly was caught in a mix of terror and opportunism. Of course she wanted to do this. Of course she didn't want to be a drunk. Of course she knew she'd ruined a good thing with Nick. She waited for Wren to say more, expecting a rant full of examples of her behavior in order to drive home the point. But Wren's head was tilted and her gaze was perfectly calm. She would do whatever she needed to do if Thessaly failed. She'd find a new job, she'd let Thessaly languish in a lower position, but she would not do it with any real animosity. She was making a simple offer, and Thessaly had started to understand that Wren did not go around inviting people into her life and her professional goals. A simple offer from her was a marriage proposal from someone else.

"I'm a little scared," Thessaly admitted. "What if I try and it turns out I really need to drink?"

"Well, then you get help," Wren said. "It won't be any easier if you wait."

Thessaly smiled. "You're not big on bedside manner, are you?" she said, and for the first time Wren laughed, really laughed, and Thessaly noticed that she was rather beautiful when she let herself be.

"My mom works in the NICU," Wren said, "and she always told me she used up all the sweetness at work. I guess I do the same."

"Except you're not sweet at work either," Thessaly said, and Wren just smiled.

•

Wren thought she must be the last of these lunches. The Italy trip was only a few weeks away, so Lionel was going to have to decide sooner rather than later.

At a restaurant in Chelsea, they sat at a booth, ordered halibut and pasta, and then stared silently at each other. Wren concentrated on remembering to blink. He was probably testing her.

Lionel took a deep swallow of water.

"Funny thing is," he said, as if they were mid-conversation, "I haven't wanted wine lately. Isn't that crazy? It depresses me right now."

"What are you drinking instead?" Wren asked.

"Oh, beer. Martinis. You want something?"

"We have a lot to talk about. I'm fine."

Lionel leaned forward, hands folded. "Well," he said. "What would you like to talk about?"

Wren paused, sipping her water to hide her response. Was it possible Lionel was just winging all of this? She had assumed he was playing some Machiavellian game at least part of the time, amplifying his confusion and distress at Gavin's betrayal. But it was worse than she'd thought.

"Lionel," she said—and realized she had never once called the man by name to his face. It seemed to startle both of them. "I've been giving a lot of thought to what we do now. We're looking at such a big shift, but I don't want our core values to change with a successor—"

Lionel turned his face to the plate the waiter was placing before him. "I thought Gavin was my successor," he informed the halibut.

Wren was losing patience. It was as if he could hear her only if she talked about his feelings. "Well," she said, "you were wrong."

They took bites and chewed, trying to find the next thing to say. It was clear to her that the only way she'd get to talk business with Lionel today was if she forced it.

"I thought I could trust him," Lionel said.

He was seeking some source of comfort and reassurance, as if she were his therapist or an unlucky seatmate at a dinner party.

He wasn't even drunk—an excuse she'd made in the past for the great men who wanted to tell her about their divorces or their midlife crises.

"Lionel," she said. "I'm here to discuss the future. What you said about a team of people the other day got me thinking. I've been working a lot more closely with Thessaly lately, and you realize she's your top salesperson."

"Don't forget about Bob." Lionel perked up a touch as he said this. She was glad to see the old Lionel, ready to debate and critique. Anything was an improvement over the sad sack.

"I didn't, but Bob is never coming to the city and he's certainly not interested in management. But I am. Thessaly is. Let me lay out what we're thinking."

She spent the rest of the lunch explaining a shared position, a vision for the future, all the things they could do together that no one else could. And it seemed to work; Lionel was nodding and listening, asking questions designed to shake her, just as she'd expected him to do. It felt good, it felt right, it felt a hell of a lot better than validating Lionel's emotions. She was so busy talking she forgot to eat. She and Lionel went back to the office, shook hands at the elevator, and split off to work. Wren could feel the eyes following her as she returned to her desk. She realized with a jolt that she was hungrier than ever.

· CHAPTER 12 ·

On Friday, the day after Wren's meeting with Lionel, the names were announced for the Italy trip: Thessaly, Wren, Sabrina, Greg, and a guy named Elijah who coordinated the warehouses and shipping.

"Are we there as a team, you think?" Thessaly asked Wren. They were in a bathroom on a different floor but whispering anyway.

"Yeah. We need to show him what that'll look like. Make it impossible to picture anyone else."

"That shouldn't be too hard with some of them. Greg, come on."

"Lionel loves him because they both have the same taste in books and wine," Thessaly said. "I seriously think he just wants to hang with him in Italy. Greg's numbers aren't even that good."

"Elijah doesn't have enough presence to run the place. A lot of people aren't sure who he is. I think Sabrina's the one to watch," Wren said. "If it's not us, it should be her. She's been here the longest, Lionel respects her, and I think he's noticed she's not leaving early for school plays anymore. She's pretty formidable when she goes all in at work."

In the weeks before they left for Italy, the staff tried to address the other hole left by Gavin's departure: the social power vacuum.

Gavin had been not only their boss, but also the alpha in after-work plans. One by one, staff members stepped forward with a plan, trying to assert themselves as the new official ringleader. Even the ones who were not going to Italy got into it; they might not be in the running for a management position, but they could still direct the social calendar. Every week, someone chose a restaurant that demonstrated their culinary knowledge and eye for the market, their ability to direct conversation at the table to serve their goals. Every week, someone discovered that Gavin had made this look a lot easier than it was.

Legs seemed like a lock, until his dinner revealed the truth of the man in black: Deep down, Legs was really very nice. He ordered too much food, and his attempts at Gavin-style back-handed compliments came out simply as compliments. Ever since Greg had learned he'd be going to Italy, he'd been walking taller, clearly feeling like the heir apparent, but at dinner he fumbled, doing little more than grilling people about their sales numbers without any insight into their actual strengths and failings, which was the reason to bring up the numbers in the first place. Oliver held forth on a little-known region called Costières de Nîmes but forgot to elicit the demonstrations of ignorance that were the whole point, and Amit took them to an old-fashioned, wildly expensive steakhouse and talked too long about his mother's superior creamed spinach. Too little a leader, everyone thought, too much a son.

Two days after the steakhouse, Sabrina invited them all to a terrifying Russian bar in the Theater District that served dumplings and borscht alongside beakers of house-infused vodka. She ordered a vial of every flavor for the table—garlic-and-dill vodka, horseradish vodka, celery, gooseberry, pomegranate—and dominated the conversation with a subtle, wounding jujitsu that Gavin could only dream of. She dropped artful cultural refer- cnces that reminded Greg he was an infant, wheedled out of Legs that he had gone to Andover, suggested that Wren should apply to college someday, and reminded Thessaly that she'd gotten her job by virtue of her family.

Her masterstroke was knowing that every single one of them would regard the tasting of two dozen infused vodkas as a chal- lenge to their knowledge and their honor. After two hours they all careened out of the place in a woozy clump and dispersed rag- gedly into the night. The next day Sabrina was fresh and energetic—Wren was convinced she'd fit in a facial before work— while the rest of them peered out of flabby oyster faces and potato-slit eyes and nibbled saltines all morning to calm their stomachs.

Wren and Thessaly planned their dinner together. They chose a serene Japanese restaurant that made its own soba, the kind of place that said refinement and confidence and calm. But their masterstroke was to invite Lionel and Jonathan. No one else had thought, or dared, to do this. Thessaly had had to persuade Wren, which reminded her why they needed each other. Wren was full of confidence and strategy on her own turf, but she tended to avoid contact with Lionel to make sure she didn't screw it up. Thessaly, who'd grown up treating farming and wine drinking like a contact sport, had no such trouble.

Grudgingly, Thessaly had set drinking rules in place and forced herself to follow them, hoping they would become a habit. No more than three drinks a night, at least three nights a week without any drinking at all. She hated limiting something that had always been about joy and abandon, but she needed a system. And it was working: Mornings were so lovely when you didn't drink, no linger-ing chemical dread, no panicked mental scan for that wrong thing you'd said or done. She felt clean and light every time she woke up, and happy, except for the fact that her bed was empty.

She was nervous about maintaining in Italy, but the thought of Wren ditching her would have to be enough to keep her on the path. Last year she would have had gel packs for swollen eyes and ibuprofen for headaches and a shot of something alcoholic most mornings, the only way you could get back on the horse after the excesses of the night before. (Legs had often spoken longingly of the cocaine of years past.) This year she would have coffee, water, and the tedious satisfaction of restraint.

The night of their dinner, they got to the restaurant before everyone else and made sure everything was on point. They'd told no one that Lionel and Jonathan were coming, and instead let everyone eye the two empty seats at the table and fall silent when the door opened. Then Thessaly stood up and poured them each a glass of sake like the consummate hostess she could suddenly imagine herself being. All through dinner she could feel eyes upon them both, people palpably reevaluating her and Wren. For the evening, Wren had replaced her usual nondescript black sep-arates with charcoal-gray cashmere and chic denim. She wore her blond curls in a twist that revealed her long neck and minus-cule earrings, expensive silver disks from a boutique in Brooklyn. Her jewelry drew all its effect from barely existing: the fairy-like twists of gold on a middle finger, the faint glint of a necklace on a collarbone.

For two hours, they all conversed and joked and eyed one another over buckwheat noodles, earthy and slippery on their bamboo mats. The dipping sauce was so limpid and saline with kelp that the rings of crisp green scallion crackled like a shot across the palate. The pearly grains of rice had the faintest hint of tanginess from vinegar, the raw fish was firm and sweet and reserved. Every other restaurant suddenly seemed loutish and strenuous. By the time Wren had ordered one final bottle of nearly impossible-to-find sake that wafted over their palates in a vapor of rice and underripe Asian fruit, the whole table was looking at them with new appreciation.

Even Lionel was impressed. "Thank you for an illuminating evening," he said. He raised one last glass of sake in their honor and the table followed suit, but then there was a pause, in which Lionel gazed in the direction of his own hand, holding a glass with a last sip of rice wine, and seemed to forget what he'd intended to do. For a beat, he was no longer their leader and conqueror but a man who was older than they'd realized, distracted by things he did not tell them. Then he returned to himself and flashed a proud grin at Wren and Thessaly. "The two of you are a truly formidable team," he continued. "We may have to get used to taking direction from you."

Thessaly called upon the mighty will that had kept her from calling Nick or faking injury just to see him in the ER or drinking more than a whiff of sake and managed not to look around the table for reactions. But she could feel the tension surge as they tapped glasses, the glances that zigzagged around the table in consternation. Beneath the table Wren pressed a leg against hers, but her face remained serene.

In the cab on the way home, they leaned back in the seat and looked at each other. Wren exhaled a huge gust of air, looking relieved and victorious. "Well done," she said as they hurtled across town. "Now we do the same thing in Verona, and we're there."

"It doesn't seem like such a long shot anymore, does it?" Thessaly said.

"I never thought it was," said Wren.

· CHAPTER 13 ·

Even the soothing, muted color palette of Italy could not make Wren less anxious. It was all the same: the mountains and hills a gentle, slightly desiccated green, the fluted ocher roofs, the bricks of the churches cream-colored or an ancient smudgy gray. And yet this was not a normal trip. Instead of a big group taking up two or three tables, renting out vans and populating tasting rooms, they were fewer than ten: Jonathan and Lionel and the candidates. She could almost see the moments when Lionel realized he was still projecting for a bigger crowd and had to modulate his voice. Jonathan had no such struggles; he was always too soft-spoken for their group and so, for once, the two men felt like the equals they almost were.

The brightest colors in Verona were the tall stucco apartments with the exterior walls painted tangerine or sunny yellow. A first-century amphitheater sat right in the center of town. They had seen *Aida* there their second night, perched high on the steep stone benches, overlooking the stage. Jonathan and Lionel were genuinely captivated, but the rest of them had what they needed by the end of the first act. All they had to do was capture an impression—the smell in the air, the ancient crumbling stonework—and mention an anecdote or two for the sales sheets and conversation. It was all about one or two details that buyers wanted to experience vicariously by drinking this wine. Another year they would have started to filter out early, but this year everyone sat straight and attentive as schoolchildren waiting out a church service.

They'd visited producers, they'd dined out, they'd all done their best to sparkle in a businesslike way. Wren never stopped thinking, How would a partner do this? When would a successful partner let Thessaly charm the winemakers, when would that partner step forward herself? They hadn't gotten it right every time—once or twice she'd hesitated, and Greg, of all people, stepped into the pause with hearty handshakes and a put-on Italian accent. The next time Wren didn't let that happen; she stepped right in front of him just for good measure.

Now they were on their final day, and Wren was dismayed to realize she could make a decent argument for most of her colleagues to get the job she wanted. Elijah was an old hand at finessing trucking unions and warehouse workers and could move product around the region as if by magic. Sabrina knew almost as much as Lionel and Jonathan did about the company's history and had contacts in several countries. With her children and husband on another continent she blossomed into a mix of grand dame and older sister, effortlessly occupying the right-hand seat beside Lionel and offering magnanimous, unthreatened compliments to the others. The only one Wren didn't take as seriously was Greg, who seemed even younger than he was and whose bravado seemed to irritate all of them, if their habit of averting their eyes were any indication. But even he was better here than at home. When Greg wasn't following Gavin's orders of emulating Legs as if he were Greg's corrugated, cooler older cousin, Greg sometimes just listened to people, or let pass an opportunity to make a joke at someone else's expense. And Thessaly, to her credit, had been serious about changing her drinking. She drank the way Wren drank now, a few glasses tops, except for the most special rare wines, along with so much water the Italian waiters must have wondered if they each had a kidney issue.

On the last night, Wren waited for Thessaly in the lobby of the hotel to walk over to dinner. They were determined to end on the right note.

"We're early," said Thessaly. "You want to walk a little first?"

They went out into the narrow cobblestone streets and wended their way toward the address Lionel had given them, detouring down streets and pausing before windows. Periodically, chic Italian matrons zipped past them on Vespas. They would have stopped for a glass of wine in another country, but Italians had strong feelings about drinking wine without food. They'd lose all credibility.

They were strolling along when Wren found herself looking at two men half a block away, standing in the window of a bar. One was old and one was young, but both were short and broad, with the same posture, shoulders thrown back, chins up a quarter inch more than needed. Then she realized she knew them.

Wren said, "That's Greg and Lionel."

Two colleagues grabbing an aperitif was not notable. Wren and Thessaly were out together too, and there was nothing odd about that. But it was the way the men were talking, heads together, nodding, like a father and son, that caught their attention.

They were just outside the bar when Greg looked at them. For a beat, his face barely changed, as if he'd never met them. Then he turned away.

Wren and Thessaly kept walking past them. It would've been odd not to.

Lionel disappeared from the window, and a moment later he exited the café and strode in the opposite direction. He never acknowledged them.

"Did he see us?" Thessaly said. "I thought Greg was staring right at us." He'd left the window now too, probably waiting until they were gone.

"He saw us," Wren said, "but he's just too scared to share face time with Lionel. He probably asked him to meet up." She frowned. "Shit, maybe we should have."

"Nope," Thessaly said. "I can see what you're doing and we're not going to freak out now. We have one more night to be amazing, which we will. Don't forget we were the first ones to realize we could even invite Lionel and Jonathan out to anything. Greg's playing catch-up."

Wren nodded. She had begun to realize something unexpected over the last few weeks, as she and Thessaly planned their dinner and their trips and their overall strategy. It was that a partner was not solely a burden to manage or an observer to impress at close range. A partner could see things she didn't. A partner could be calming. As if she knew exactly what Wren was thinking, Thessaly gave her a sisterly pat on the shoulder.

•

Italy was an odd place to be thinking about Nick. It was barely midnight. Italian desserts were scattered around the table, ignored. They had all gorged themselves on risotto with baccalà or vitello tonnato or plump chestnut-colored guinea hens, and Thessaly was allowing a tiny pour of Amarone in her glass when she realized she'd been thinking of him all night.

But why? He wasn't Italian, they'd never entertained ideas of traveling here together. Yet Thessaly was feeling good, feeling powerful, and she was filled with regret that here she was, exactly the woman he'd thought her to be when they'd met, the woman who deep down she really was—but it didn't matter anymore.

She found herself thinking of a night when Nick had leaned over during one of his friends' endless hospital stories and she'd braced herself for some volcanically hot proposition. Instead he'd whispered that he'd forgotten his underwear at the hospital, and she'd burst out laughing.

Something tightened inside her chest. She lifted her glass, but then she set it down without drinking. She turned to Elijah beside her. Greg was telling a lengthy story about a soccer match in Lisbon, while Sabrina's head was tilted toward Jonathan's, her face grave. Wren and Lionel had been deep in conversation all night.

"How was the guinea hen?" Thessaly asked Elijah. He had a shaggy beard and a permanently rosy face; rumor had it he'd once been in a biker gang, but he struck Thessaly as being too sweet-natured for that.

"Fantastic," he said. "Best chicken you ever tasted. My wife would love it."

Somewhere Nick was probably seducing some brilliant ER resident, swapping incomprehensible medical terms over ramen. They would walk back to his rathole slowly, deliciously, letting their bodies simmer. And then—

"I thought you and Wren made some pretty good points about the marketing," Elijah was saying. "Probably shouldn't tell you that, since we're competing. But it's out of our hands now."

It was true, but hearing it aloud only made Thessaly nervous. What was she going to do if they didn't get this promotion? Would she have to quit just to make the point? Or could she just keep doing what she was doing, just working, and pretend it hadn't happened? Because she knew what people would say if she quit this job and took another sales job. They'd say, "Now's a good time to go apprentice yourself, Thessaly. Go do what you've been talking about for ten years."

She felt a little short of breath. What would her father say if she admitted she'd made a play for the big job and failed? "Keep learning about that" too? What would Wren say?

She took a long sip of water and eyed her would-be partner, who was raising one shoulder artfully as she said something that made Lionel laugh. Wren, Thessaly decided, was a lot more helpful than her father had been. Wren would tell her to figure out the next steps and do them. Earlier that spring, when Thessaly told her about that fantasy of her oddball, nonexistent wines, in just fifteen minutes Wren had helped her feel clearer on her future in winemaking.

She realized that that had frightened her. How Wren made that pipe dream feel scarily and reassuringly possible. It really *could* be done; there were steps one could take to do it. And Thessaly was running out of reasons to say she could not.

•

Wren made certain to sit beside Lionel, because she had one last shot at conversing with him the way she wanted to. It was not easy. Lionel rarely asked questions, and when he did, it was always a leading statement-question, like, "Something odd is going on with Piemonte this year," and you couldn't tell if you were supposed to agree or argue. Over polenta, he'd uttered a note about Berlusconi, and as he awaited a response—from her? from the cosmos?—he'd fixed his eyes just to the left of hers, at a colleague, the window, a passing waiter.

The feeling, Wren had understood just now, was completely familiar. It was like talking to her father: There but not there, listening but not. They both made Wren suspect that they were there, but *she* wasn't. This realization infuriated her. She didn't need some middle-aged man dumping declarations in her lap, letting her make sense of them. Even if she was trying to make one of them promote her.

By now she'd had a fair amount of wine, for her. "Of course, no one can ever tell what Berlusconi is thinking," she said. "*You* understand." Lionel gazed at her, and she stared back calmly. Let Lionel figure it out.

Astonishingly, it seemed to work. Lionel offered his own thoughts on Berlusconi's intentions, and as far as Wren could tell they were sane. "Exactly" was all she said to Lionel. She glanced at the bottles on the table, which were almost empty. She had to finish this off. She turned to Lionel, looked in his fathomless dark eyes, and said, "This has been an incredible trip, Lionel. Whatever happens, thank you."

Lionel looked taken aback, pleased. "Well, good," he said. "I'm always shocked at just how much difference they make on the bottom line. You ever compare the sales for a region we've visited, a winery we've visited, to the ones we haven't?"

"I have," Wren said. "It feels like maybe the one time capitalism is working in my favor."

Lionel laughed, loudly enough that several colleagues glanced their way, looking peevish. Emboldened, Wren said, "So have you gotten what you needed out of this trip?" It was as close as she dared to asking if he had made a decision.

Lionel paused. Then he said, "I think so. So much of this job is the conversation, the hospitality, and I always need to feel we have a face for the company that can connect with people, wherever we are. So it's been useful to focus on you all a little more closely."

Wren nodded. She could not tell if he was saying that this was something true of her or that it was not and that was why she would not get the job. Then again, maybe she was not the most convivial—but Thessaly was. Look around, she told herself: Greg's a competitive boy-child, Elijah too shy, and in spite of her recent showing, Sabrina will inevitably disappear again because what Lionel wants isn't sustainable. But even as Wren ticked off each competitor in her head, she did not do it with animosity—she was one of them too. The company might be a bunch of sharks, but it was also a tribe, her tribe.

I am here too, Wren thought. I am sitting right here at the table. She had clung to this job when it was the only road out of her old life, but for the first time she looked around and understood Lionel Garrett might not be the sole avenue in front of her. She had created options for herself. She took a bite of cake for the pleasure of its taste; she wasn't hungry. She needed nothing at all. Whatever she didn't already know, she would figure out. She leaned forward to join the conversation, curious to see what would happen.

· CHAPTER 14 ·

Thessaly had had the notion that Italy would change her at a cellular level. She would fly to Europe, eat and drink and transform her professional life, and come home refreshed and freed of all that had plagued her: her embarrassment and sadness and disbelief that her breakup was final and that her faint slurring memories of Nick looking at her coldly were accurate. But when she got off her plane at JFK and took a cab to her cube, it was all exactly the same. She'd been gone only a few days.

Saturday morning, she got up and went for a run along the East River. Technically, she went for a walk, forced herself to break into a jog, and felt leaden and exhausted immediately. This was why Italians didn't jog. In the profound life choice between salumi and fitness, they had chosen salumi, and she had too. So she stopped pretending and began to walk.

She walked all the way from the Upper East Side to Battery Park, then started working her way north through the Financial District, Chinatown, and SoHo. She was sweating and messy, her hair sticking to the back of her neck, her vital organs probably halfway to being cured into prosciutto, but she was not hungover. And not once in Italy had she been hungover either. This was a shocking sea change for her, a state of affairs she had never even realized was possible, and she was walking along and mulling over this triumph when she saw him.

Nick was coming out of a bookstore on Broadway, looking at his phone as he walked. Even this—his presence in a bookstore where he had apparently bought nothing—was a sharp cut, because she had no idea what he'd gone in there looking for. He never had time to read; had he finally found some? He was wearing a loose white linen button-down she knew all too well; they used to call it his island shirt. And his attention was focused on his phone, so she was able to stare at him for a moment. His hair was shaggy; his jawline was dark with stubble; an expression of annoyance crossed his face right before he looked up. He was painfully the same and painfully different. She had not spoken to him for a month.

She never adjusted her pace, just kept walking up the sidewalk to him until he felt her presence. His face, always so unreadable to her, was suddenly terribly transparent. She saw his flash of pleasure at seeing her, then the wariness, then the reluctance. She saw the moment he decided to speak to her.

"You out for a run?" he asked, as if they ran into each other every day.

"I was," she said. They stood there, people eddying around them, and then Nick seemed to remember himself and leaned forward to kiss her in a jerky motion that scraped his stubble uncomfortably across her cheek. He smelled the same, of clean laundry and soap, he was standing as close to her as he'd stood when they were still together, back when she could still touch him.

"How are you?" she asked finally.

"I'm good," he said. "Nothing too new. You?"

"I went to Italy," she said.

He took another step toward her, even closer. "For work? Or did you whisk some guy over for a long weekend?"

She knew he was trying to make a joke at his own expense instead of hers. He was admitting she would be the one doing the whisking, and he wasn't acting like she had been weeping over the loss of him. She understood all of this, but she was unable to do anything playful or sophisticated with it. She just said, "For work. Kind of a final challenge to see who gets the big promotion."

"Well," he said, "I hope it's you."

"You look tired," she blurted. "I mean, you look good, but a little tired."

He gave her a crooked smile. "It's pretty permanent at this point. But you look great. You look *bright*."

Thessaly felt a rush of words leave her mouth before she knew what they were. "I cut way back," she heard herself say. "Wren and I had a big talk about it, and I thought about what you said and I thought about my job, and I made changes, Nick, like a lot of changes, well, just the one, but it was a big change. And I feel a lot better. You were right." Even as she spoke she saw what was happening, how he stepped back to put more distance between them, but she couldn't stop talking until he reached out and picked up her hand.

They just stood there, him holding her hand as if he'd found it somewhere and had no idea what to do with it. She found it impossible to believe that there was a time she could have touched him anywhere, any way she wanted to. Not even necessarily sexually—she could have reached out and touched the velvety skin of his neck, she could have tucked a finger through his belt loop and tugged, she could have taken his ear in her teeth and bitten down. Now she just had to stand here.

"You want to get lunch?" she asked. "Coffee? Bubble tea?"

Nick hesitated, his eyes moving over her face. Then he seemed to make a decision. "I don't think I can," he said. But he didn't sound entirely certain. "Even if I thought it was a good idea."

"People screw up," she said. "You have to let people change, Nick."

"I know," he said. "I can tell—you seem different." He seemed to consider something, and Thessaly did not move, did not even breathe or blink, because surely this was it: she would get what she wanted; this was not a dream. Nick flashed a strange little grimace, as if he were doubting what he was about to say. "It's good to see you," he said, still holding her hand. "You look beautiful."

Did it not happen this way sometimes? When you might have stayed apart until a chance meeting reminded you of someone there was no denying?

But then she realized he was still speaking. "I'm not going to make up excuses," he was saying. "I just know I don't want to try and do this again only to admit that it's different."

"Different isn't all bad," Thessaly said, but she knew by the plummeting in her body that it was no use.

Nick's hand squeezed hers a shade too hard. "You can feel it already, right," he said, "that it's not coming back?"

Thessaly was glad she wasn't crying. She was relieved to feel only numbness, because she didn't want to leave him with an image of tears streaming down her face, unable to believe that you could kill something just by screwing up a little, *just a few times*, and discover there was no reviving it.

"Sure," she heard herself say. She retrieved her hand. "I miss you."

"I know," he said. "I miss you too." And then he walked away.

•

Wren was having her favorite kind of Saturday, particularly after a trip: she was in leggings and a tank top with her hair in a bun, sweatily cleaning her apartment and listening to music and thinking of eating a salad the size of a bathtub for dinner. She had just gotten out of the shower when her phone rang.

She could see it was Thessaly but at first she thought it must be a butt dial, because all she heard was a wordless sound like traffic rushing by. "Hey," she said, "where are you?" That was when she realized what the sound was. Not traffic, not the wind, just the kind of crying when a person could not stop, or talk, or breathe, or explain that they were standing on the street below Wren's apartment, hoping to be let up.

Thessaly was a kind of fucked up Wren had not witnessed in some time. She looked smeary and blotchy and confused, and when Wren said, "Come on, you're coming up," she didn't bother to answer, just trudged up the stairs behind her. Upstairs, Wren sat her on the couch and went into the kitchen for bread or water or something to soak up some of the booze in her system, but when she came back with supplies, she could see that Thessaly was not, perhaps, quite as drunk as she had first thought. She was definitely drunk, but she was, more than that, bereft. She had refused to admit even the slightest sadness over losing Nick, and Wren had chosen to believe her, because, honestly, it was easier. And why should Thessaly feel that bad about one intense but brief relationship coming to a screeching halt? Sure, Wren might feel terrible in such a situation, but Thessaly had her pick. There was always someone else out there for her.

"I fucked up something that can't be unfucked," Thessaly said, and it was the first time in their entire acquaintance that Wren could see Thessaly had hit a wall she'd never hit before. Wren had been there before as a child, and she had watched others hit it her whole life, the moment you understood there were things you'd live with but could not change.

It was a little late for Thessaly to be grasping this. But who was perfect?

Perhaps that was why Wren did not do what she would have done every single other time in her life when someone showed up wasted and sad, which was send them home or close the door on a spare room and ignore them until they sobered up. She just didn't have the heart.

She went to the kitchen and came back with a bottle of wine and a glass into which she poured a soda-sized serving.

"I don't think—" Thessaly said, sniffling, but Wren said, "It's not for you," and drank the whole glass in a few swallows. Then she filled it up again.

"What are you *doing*?" Thessaly said.

"I'm catching up." Wren shrugged. "You're the kind of wasted you really can't be by yourself." She felt her face heating up and the blood in her skull begin to pound. She wished she had vodka or something she could have knocked back faster, medicinally, because this was a rather nice Grüner, but it was what she had. She drank away, realizing as she did that she had never drunk this way in her entire life, but it felt necessary. Between letting Thessaly sit there with tears seeping down her face and her dirty-nailed hands—where exactly had she been all day?—wrapped around a glass of water and the hangover Wren knew was coming . . . the hangover was the lesser evil.

By the time the bottle was gone, Wren was feeling free, downright experimental. Why had she always fought this so hard? Because here was a brief interlude in which she felt like all things were possible. "Look," she said. Her vowels sounded longer than usual. "I know this feels terrible. But it could be worse, so, so much worse. Do you know who I dated right after I moved here?"

Thessaly was lying on one end of the couch, clutching a piece of bread to her stomach from which she remembered to take a bite every few minutes. She looked comfortable enough that Wren did the same on her end, squeezing her legs between Thessaly's and the back of the couch.

"You never tell me anything," Thessaly said around a mouthful of bread.

"Because it all sucks," Wren cried. She flung an arm out to make her point and watched it flail a few seconds longer than it should have. "The sommelier who told me I had to pass a tasting quiz before he bought me dinner. A guy who invited me to a picnic and brought a jar of peanut butter and a bag of Wonder bread. Some dickhead from Bayonne."

Thessaly offered her the bread and Wren took it. "At least this was worth it for a while," Wren said, chewing. "At least it was *some*thing."

"I feel so stupid," Thessaly said. "There was this time like a week before we broke up when I saw him looking at me and I was like, Oh, he loves me. He is so in love with me, I don't have to wonder anymore. And I was *right*. I know I was. How did I fuck that up?"

Wren gestured toward the empty wine bottle on the table, their crumb-covered torsos.

"Yeah, yeah," Thessaly said, in a tone of resignation. She closed her eyes and put the last piece of bread in her mouth. Wren watched her to be sure she didn't choke. When Thessaly had safely swallowed her bread and had turned over onto her side, Wren carefully and clumsily extricated herself and went to bed. She left the door open in case Thessaly needed her.

Wren awoke to a blazing headache and Thessaly sitting cross-legged at the end of her bed, looking recently exhumed. Wordlessly, she reached over to the nightstand and handed Wren a cup of coffee, heavy on the milk.

"I can't," Wren said.

"It's the only way," Thessaly said. "This, water, ibuprofen, something greasy for breakfast."

Wren managed to sit up. She sipped her coffee, hoping she would keep it down, watching Thessaly balefully over the rim of the mug.

"Thank you," Thessaly said.

Wren nodded. "Are we done with this shit now?" she said. She didn't mean Nick.

Thessaly knew what she meant. "Yeah," she said, and they turned toward the window to watch the sun finish coming up over the roofs of the buildings.

· CHAPTER 15 ·

The wine business made all its money in the last three months of the year: October, November, December, which everyone called OND. OND was the period when the market let loose. Restaurant goers and store customers all stopped feigning moderation, the world suffused with a collective feeling of high spirits and welcome. It was as if the customers were delighted to do the company's job for them: they offered and accepted wine, they tried new varietals and bought bottles instead of glasses and cases instead of bottles. Basically, the world briefly adopted the lifestyle Lionel Garrett employees lived all year-round.

September was now almost as big a month as the other three. The moment they got back from Verona, the market kicked in and Wren was briefly able to forget about the competition. It was a relief to feel it was out of her hands. Thessaly threw herself into selling, admitting that it helped her miss Nick less, and Wren got busy doing tastings of Jonathan's wines up and down the eastern seaboard.

No one forgot what they were waiting for, exactly, and everyone noticed that Lionel had taken several days off to work at home after Verona, which was not like him. When he returned, his cheeks seemed hollowed, his eyes shadowed. But his voice was as strong as ever, his pace as quick as ever, when he called them in for a Friday evening meeting.

They did not do Friday evening meetings. The company had never called one. Wren and Thessaly silently walked to the conference room, knowing this was it. Wren glanced down at the front of her sweater, to see if her heartbeat was visible. Thessaly pulled out a tube of expensive lip balm and swiped it on compulsively, the only sign of how nervous she was.

In the room they all found seats and waited for Lionel and Jonathan, at the head of the table, to speak. Finally, Jonathan nodded at Lionel. Lionel rose and began to give a preamble they all expected: the fierce competition, the impossible choice. Wren barely heard anything he said. She was waiting for a name and she didn't care what came out before that.

But she was not expecting to hear the name she heard.

"We've made an offer, which has been accepted," Lionel was saying. "Greg, stand up."

Wren watched Greg get slowly to his feet, and as he did, she wondered what Greg was supposed to do. She truly believed for a moment that he was getting up to hand Lionel an envelope with the name of the winner inside, or to walk around the table like a messenger or spokesmodel and signal who it was with a shake of his hand.

It took her longer than it should have to register that Greg was the new sales and operations director.

The moment was met with a stunned silence. Greg now stood conspicuously to Lionel's left, in a new shirt and fresh haircut and with the fake shy grin of a boy who never dreamed he'd win the spelling bee.

"Sometimes you have to trust your gut," Lionel mused to fill the dead air. "I started this company around Greg's age, and I can see a lot of myself in him."

Amit began furiously cleaning his glasses and Oliver just stared piercingly, caressing a cuff link as if he might pop open the top and tip poison into Greg's coffee. Elijah had the stricken look of a man who'd made a long trip in from the Jersey warehouse to learn he'd lost the job. Sabrina's face went white, then a frightening magenta.

This was the moment the wondering stopped. With a lurch Wren realized she had been wrong to think not knowing was the worst. All of a sudden they worked at a new company. With *Greg* in charge.

Wren had forgotten that Thessaly was sitting beside her until she felt a fingernail dig into her forearm under the table. She tried to see her without visibly looking; all she glimpsed was Thessaly flexing her hands, back and forth, as if trying to get the blood moving.

Someone's stomach gurgled; outside, a siren fled the avenue.

Legs was first to recover, clapping tentatively. Greg accepted the smattering of applause with a nod, his gaze focused politely on the table. Now everyone waited for the rest. There had to be more to say. Wren could feel her coworkers watching her, clearly believing she had already been fired, since she worked for Jonathan, the man who'd lost a major chunk of his business, and she'd lost out to Greg. But there was nothing more to say.

Jonathan congratulated Greg and talked about the timeline of the transition and how more would be revealed about the day-to-day shifts as Lionel moved on. He then mentioned some ideas they had—"ideas Wren had," he took care to note—to replace the lost business with Fuchs and rebuild the portfolio, plus some discussion of the plans for Big Sky that would make it that much bigger and about which absolutely no one cared.

Jonathan called after her as they were all leaving. "Wait downstairs for me," Wren said to Thessaly. Wren followed Jonathan to his office and closed the door, though they were the only ones left.

"I'm sorry about that," Jonathan said. "I pushed for you. I did. And I want you to know I was going to take care of you, no matter what Lionel decided. I spent the last year going to the mats for you with all this Gavin nonsense and I certainly won't stop now."

It took a beat for this to sink in. "So for a year," she said, her body on fire, "you've known they were considering getting rid of me? And you didn't tell me? Or tell me I had no shot at this?"

"Of course you had a shot at this. How could you not?"

"Because," Wren said, "apparently I either had a shot at a major promotion *or* I was about to get fired. What the hell is wrong with you people if these are the options?"

"Wren. If I worried you and you performed badly, or if you left the company, how would that help anyone?"

"It would've helped *me*," she said. "You could've told me to watch my back, to make myself indispensable. You could have told me to job-hunt, for Christ's sake. How far do you think unemployment goes in this city?"

Jonathan looked shocked. "I'm sorry," he said. "I can't even tell you how hard I lobbied for you and Thessaly. And I think Lionel almost went there, but—well, in the end it was his choice."

Wren stood up. Her jaw was doing something strange, shivering, as if the room were freezing. "I'm heading out," she said. "Thank you."

Jonathan looked puzzled, which was even more infuriating. She waited for more, for him to grasp what it meant to her that he'd just shrugged and let Lionel toy with her career like a cat.

"Please don't thank me," Jonathan said.

"I was being polite," Wren said, and left.

•

Thessaly watched Wren come out of the building with an expression on her face that suggested now was a time for arson. Wren didn't slow down when she got to Thessaly, just kept walking and assumed Thessaly would match her pace, which she did.

They walked all the way from Chelsea to Chinatown, and into a place at Bayard and Bowery that would never draw fellow wine people (unless they too were avoiding other wine people). Wren was walking so fast her whole body tipped forward as she stomped down the sidewalks.

"What did Jonathan say?" Thessaly asked at one point.

"Nothing that makes any difference," said Wren.

At the restaurant she polished off enough pork lo mein, roast duck, and flowering chives for a family of four. Wren seemed a lot calmer—a lot colder, it must be said—than Thessaly had expected. She pushed back her chair and slurped down a cup of green tea.

"You know what?" Wren said. "I think I'm finished discussing what happened today. I don't want to talk about Greg reminding Lionel of himself and whether any women could ever remind Lionel of himself, and I don't want to speculate on all the extremely relevant-to-me, significant-to-me shit Jonathan protects me from."

"Okay," said Thessaly. "I'll pretend we aren't discussing any of that." She sighed and set her napkin on the table.

"I'm going to go back in there on Monday and I'm going to make Greg look so terrible even he'll perceive it. I just want Lionel to spend every day from now on feeling like an idiot. Sabrina's going to quit, I'm sure of it."

"Definitely," Thessaly said. "I mean, fuck this, really. She's right." She didn't know until she said it that she believed this wholeheartedly. She felt like a bigger fool than anyone else, because not only had she misread this situation—she, a salesperson, a professional reader of people who'd failed catastrophically to read her boyfriend and failed to read her boss—but now she was stuck in this fiasco. It was her father all over again. And once again she thought she would rather go jump off something tall than spend every fucking day with people who thought so little of her, because what if they were right?

"Hey," Thessaly said, "how about if instead we talk about doing this on our own? You and me."

Wren looked at her. "Doing what?" she said.

Thessaly gestured, a little wildly, around the restaurant, before realizing a cheap noodle joint did not quite convey her vision. "Start our own business. Just get the fuck out of here. Not that I'm a big believer in Gavin, but if he did it, why not us?"

"I'm not doing it like Gavin," Wren said, and Thessaly waved this away.

"I don't mean we steal a major client, and I don't mean we run it like other people's livelihoods are a game for our amusement. Look, we know how to do this. We could make what Lionel Garrett used to be. Or could've been. I think we should do it together. We should start our own company."

"We don't have any money," Wren said thoughtfully. "We don't have any licenses, we don't have warehouses."

"Lionel didn't have any of that either."

"What about making wine? If you're making a change, isn't that the direction for you?"

Thessaly nodded impatiently, but she was so set on the idea of getting far away from all of this—all of these people, that stupid conference room, that building on the West Side Highway, all of it—that she believed everything she was saying even though, technically, Wren was right and she knew it. But she could not handle another failure, not at the thing that mattered most. "Doing this would get me closer. Winemakers run their own companies too, and I can learn how. You know I won't do it without you."

"True," Wren said. She examined Thessaly's face for a long moment. "You're probably not saying we quit tomorrow," Wren prompted, and Thessaly picked it up like the salesman she was.

"Of course not! We'll be smart. I'm saying let's start imagining. We can buy the wine we love. Mid-range stuff that sells. We have the palates and the connections."

Wren arranged her chopsticks on the edge of her plate.

"I have to admit it sounds tempting," she said. "Definitely more tempting than just working for a better person."

Thessaly sat back in her chair. She knew a win when she saw one. "The hell with working for a better person," she said, believing herself almost entirely. "You're sick of the great men. I am too. That doesn't mean we should go apprentice ourselves to some mediocre ones. It means, fuck it, let's do it ourselves."

PART 3

bottle shock

· CHAPTER 16 ·

Thessaly had failed to consider many possibilities in this new life: That the Midwest would seem so miniature compared to the West Coast; that Madison's pleasures would be so accessible it seemed churlish not to walk through the park near her apartment, jog by the lake, eat the morning bun from a sunlit shop. And that Wren would seem so different here.

She had noticed changes the moment they'd moved in January, more than two years after Greg inherited the throne: how Wren leaned back in the driver's seat and gestured out the window at this lake, that building, excited and hyper and yet somehow so much more at ease than she'd been in New York. Wren had found them two apartments in the same neighborhood on the near east side, flats in converted Victorian houses. Wren took the larger one with the home office, and gave Thessaly the smaller one a block away with a great view of a spacious park filled with old oaks and a gazebo. Thessaly assumed this was deliberate to make sure she'd last through the first winter.

Little stories of Wren's childhood popped up here and there, as if she were only now allowing herself to remember them. Sometimes they were personal—a description of walking out onto the frozen

181

lake, her mother bringing her to State Street—and other times they were bizarre cultural remnants, like a period when margarine had been outlawed and people went on jaunts over the border to smuggle it in. Another day, as they were walking past Wren's elementary school, she referred offhandedly to "milk break," as if everyone had those. It turned out all the Wisconsin children had stopped school in the morning to drink a carton of milk. Wren was shocked to realize no one else did, having never once considered the dairy industry held more sway in her home state than it did in others. Embarrassed, she'd said, "Are you telling me California doesn't have any propaganda like this? Seriously?"

"Oh no," said Thessaly, to make her feel better. "First-graders were the true drivers of Chardonnay break."

Wren was still noticeably self-conscious here, it was true—just in a different way. In New York, Wren had often stood to the side, figuring out how to break in or avoid standing out. Here she was self-conscious in the manner of someone who wanted to be sure she had exceeded expectations, her own and everyone else's. Everywhere she went, she was always slightly dressed up.

No wonder: It was terrifying, what they were doing and what they'd done. They'd planned to take one year to get their business off the ground before leaving Lionel Garrett, but it had taken them more than two. The paperwork was exhausting, but that was nothing, given the decisions that had to be made before they got that far. After considering New York, New Jersey, Chicago, the Northwest, Atlanta, Wren had surprised them both by making an ardent case for Madison. It was comparatively cheap but the market was there, a college town with professors and government people drinking inexpensively and the tech or health care execs and lawyers and doctors drinking pricily.

After two and a half years of saving and planning, they'd finally given notice in December, an announcement Jonathan met with unflattering surprise and Greg with a broad, avuncular goodwill that was off-putting from someone two years younger than both of them. "Well, I'm proud of you two," Greg had said when they faced him across an expensive mid-century modern desk, the polished surface of which he had been known to caress during meetings. "We'll throw a dinner. Send you out in style."

He'd done the same for Sabrina, when she left for a job with a huge importer and distributor soon after Greg's ascension. Now and then Thessaly looked her up to see what she was doing, and found that Sabrina was rising steadily through the ranks at her new company. Had the race for director of sales and operations lit a fire in Sabrina, or reminded her of something she'd set aside for a few years? Maybe her kids had gotten old enough. Thessaly knew only that she'd spent years dismissing Sabrina as a distracted mom type and still felt chastened by it.

Thessaly had to admit that Greg had said goodbye to them in style too. He'd overspent on grower Champagne and Burgundy and duck confit, while the rest of their colleagues alternated between effusive congratulations and searching questions about who they'd borrowed money from. (Themselves, mostly, but also a carefully vetted loan from Thessaly's family after Wren and Thessaly both flew out to Sonoma to face the gauntlet of her glowering father and her suddenly intimidating mother.) The only one they were both sorry to leave was Legs, who'd given them each a thoughtfully inscribed rare edition of a novel. "Why, Larry," Thessaly had said, clearing the threat of tears from her throat, "that Swiss finishing school taught you well."

"Fuck you," Legs said tenderly, and kissed her on the cheek.

Although so many of their daily tasks were familiar to both of them, Thessaly still felt as if they were playacting sometimes: Did anyone take them seriously when they signed a lease for warehouse space, when they applied for licenses to import and ship alcohol, when they put up a website and ordered business cards with their company name—Passerine Imports—and a simple, tasteful bird silhouette for the logo?

Apparently they did, because as they set about their duties they were greeted by warmth and welcome: Thessaly started systematically working her way around the Madison market, stopping in at restaurants and wine shops to see where their people were, while Wren attended to the endless administrative work of buying product, moving product, selling product. While Thessaly spent her days driving around town and frequently got stuck in traffic on the isthmus that connected one side of town to the other—she had received insufficient warning that a midsize midwestern city had so much traffic—Wren barely moved from the office she'd set up in her house, except to eat weird elderly lunches of sardines and crispbread, or lefse with butter and jam.

Their first buying trip, in March, they'd flown to Madrid, where Wren had fallen in love with the minerally, zesty whites in northern Spain. From there, they'd worked their way eastward for the fruity, elegant Tempranillos and Garnachas. Then it was on to Cava and Priorat over on the northern Mediterranean Sea. And finally to Italy, Le Marche, which was underrepresented in the American market because it was inconvenient to get there. They were gone for only three weeks, but it felt like much longer.

Days after they returned, Wren had insisted on having dinner at Heirloom, the restaurant where she'd gotten her first job and learned about wine. It was a triangular brick structure that stood at the apex of two downtown streets. Inside, it was narrow and warm and bustling, the staff sleek in dress shirts and skirts. Thessaly liked it immediately. High-end but friendly.

"They'd fit a lot more covers if they tightened up the dining room," Wren said, once they were seated.

"It'd be too cramped if they did," Thessaly said. "I don't want to eavesdrop on the people at the next table. I can do that on the Lower East Side."

Wren was counting everything these days: the warehouse's square footage, miles between accounts, pallets and containers. "True, true," she said. She looked at someone over Thessaly's shoulder and her face bloomed. "Nathan!"

The man, who must be the sommelier, Thessaly gathered, was approaching the table with a half bottle of Champagne. "From Jonathan," he said. "I mentioned you were coming in the other day." Wren got up to embrace him. Thessaly got up to shake hands too, marveling that she had never seen Wren allow herself to display such delight at anyone. She was a tiny bit jealous.

Pour after pour appeared with each course, a steady parade of old colleagues dropping by the table to say hello. As Wren was introducing her to the fortieth person of the night, not once failing to mention their new company and the wines they would be offering, Thessaly realized how strategic Wren had been by choosing this restaurant and this night: Thursdays were busy, but the staff wouldn't be too slammed to pay attention to them.

"Now, when you come back in to sell to them," Wren said, reading her mind, "it won't be like we're begging for an audience."

"Well played." They tapped their flutes and took a sip.

"I think I'm freaking out less," Wren said a while later, over the cheese course. "I have opinions again."

"Thank god," Thessaly said. This paralysis had struck them both at different times, but it stemmed from the same place: they no longer had the luxury of throwing around opinions and prognostications with Lionel's money. It was their money now, and as a result they questioned things they'd taken for granted. Was this bone-dry Cava unforgiving or focused? Was that Lachryma that smelled of lavender and saint's tears an exciting new option for a small market, or had they lost their minds thinking anyone wanted a glass of flowers and grief? Did people even drink as much wine as they needed to sell? What *was* wine, anyway?

They had learned to sneak each other signals if one was struck by this catastrophic palate failure in front of producers, so the other could take over. Luckily, like parents who balanced out each other's fears for their children, one of them was always calm while the other was gripped with panic.

"Right?" Wren was saying. She ate a slice of cheese. "I didn't want to tell you that I still freak out sometimes."

Wren had that hangdog look she got when she wanted Thessaly to reassure her. But they were sitting in Wren's hometown, in her home restaurant, and for the first time Thessaly did not feel able to go through the motions. "Sparrow," she said, "the time to get scared was months ago. *Years* ago. You agreed with me that this was the right road."

"So you're feeling no worries on your end," Wren said, an edge creeping into her voice. She glanced around to be sure no one could hear her.

"Oh, stop it." Thessaly sighed. "Obviously I'm petrified."

"Jesus," said Wren, "finally."

"But we can't show it," Thessaly added, raising her eyebrows at the tables crowded around them, the servers flying by.

Wren lowered her voice. "Never? Not even to each other?"

"Of course we can, to each other. Just don't wallow in it. Here's what I do: I tell myself there's nothing to fear. We're not going to die. Even if we fail, even if we have to get new jobs to pay my family back, we can do that. We might have to break a lease, I guess, but it's in Wisconsin so no one'll mind."

"I think you think Midwest real estate is a little friendlier than it really is," Wren said, but Thessaly waved this off.

"We'd still be able to say we did it," she went on, "even if we change our minds about the whole thing in five or ten years."

Wren nodded, but she seemed to be convincing herself. "Okay," she said uncertainly.

What if Wren was worried about something she, Thessaly, was doing? "Now might be a good time to check in," Thessaly said. "Do you have any feedback for me? Since I gave you some sales tips in Italy."

It worked: Wren began to focus on answering thoughtfully instead of continuing to worry. "I wish you'd be a little more organized with the paperwork and receipts," she said finally.

"Receipts," said Thessaly with an amused smile. "Okay."

"It's not going to seem so silly when we're trying to do our taxes and you've been shoving our rental agreements and hotel bills into your giant shoulder bag."

"Okay, I get it," Thessaly admitted, chastened. "If it's bothering you, I need to handle it."

Wren took a sip of the aged port that had appeared with their cheese plate. "That's very chill of you. I don't want anyone to notice me unless it's for something positive."

"Well, get used to being seen. You're the face of a company," Thessaly said. She'd meant it lightly, but Wren responded by rubbing her hands over her face, one desperate gesture before she remembered herself and sat up straight.

"Can I tell you something embarrassing?" It came out in a hiss. "All this time I didn't always mind being on the periphery. I looked down on people for not paying attention to me. Because I knew they weren't smart enough to know what I was capable of, but one day they would . . . But now if I fail, then they *did* know what I was capable of."

How did Wren find these ingenious ways to torture herself? Thessaly had met Wren's mother, Jeannie, only once, and she had never even seen Wren's father, but she felt a surge of anger at them both. "You realize," she said, "that you've managed to make the good things bad and the bad things good."

Wren tried to chuckle, but she looked as if she wanted to throw up or flee. "I know," she said. "I know it sounds dumb, but this is *the thing*, you know? The thing I have to stifle, just to accomplish— well, anything I've ever accomplished."

For a moment Thessaly didn't know what to say. Then she heard herself confess, in a great rush, "Sometimes I think I'm just hiding out. I know I'm supposed to be making wine myself, or farming with my dad, or figuring out how to take that over. And I worry I never *will* do any of that. I'll just move boxes around, like the postal service. Just bureaucracy."

"People need the postal service," Wren pointed out. She began folding and refolding her napkin. "Anyway, why did you bring it up in the first place, then, if our company's just getting in the way of things you care about more?"

Thessaly felt her face aflame—she had never admitted to Wren, barely to herself, that what had driven her to make such a confident proposal several years earlier had not been a clear, visionary idea, and it had not been because it was the logical next step for both of them. It had been a pure and simple desire to get the fuck out of a place of backstabbing and boozing and the way they had begun to resemble a human carnival to entertain Lionel's psyche.

"I *don't* care less about Passerine than other things," Thessaly said hastily. "I mean, every job has its downsides. I wanted to do this because when I do go off to make wine, I want to be older and more settled and feel ready for the challenge of a whole new thing. If I did it now I might do it all wrong—like pick the wrong place and varietals."

Wren looked skeptical. "Aren't you worried you won't want to start over at forty-five or fifty?"

"That's nothing, my family lives into their hundreds," Thessaly declared, hoping this convinced them both. She could see it had not, not yet, so she returned to the same thing she had for the last few years, whenever she was feeling squirrely: *What were they trying to do? What did they want to make?*

"I can't think about fifteen years from now," she said. "I'm thinking about now. I want to find things people haven't tried before and not have someone flogging me to sell twenty percent more of it every six months. And, sure, I want to learn how these winemakers do it, so I can do it too. But not until we're rich."

"So you're still in it?" Wren said. "For five, ten, fifteen years, you're really in it. With me. Because this is not a stepping stone for me."

"I'm in it," Thessaly replied, but even to her, her voice sounded shaky.

It felt as though they'd just gotten engaged. How different was this partnership from a marriage, anyway, except for sex? They had to share an office. They had to agree on finances and plans and values. They were traveling together and staying in the same rooms, and at least some of their money would be pooled just like spouses'. Wren was just going to have to trust her.

Wren stretched out one leg under the table and poked Thessaly in the shin with the toe of her shoe.

"What are you doing?" Thessaly said.

"Nothing," Wren said. "I'm just lightening the mood." She prodded Thessaly again, without any indication she was doing so. In her expression, which was gleeful and slightly unhinged, Thessaly had an inkling of what Wren might have looked like as a child, if she'd ever been the sort of child who felt safe enough to be mischievous, which Thessaly did not think she had.

"You're being a lunatic," Thessaly said, trying not laugh. "We're in a professional space. Cut it out."

"I want to, but I can't," Wren said, and now Thessaly did laugh, pushing away Wren's foot with her own, but gently.

She felt as if they had turned some corner she hadn't expected to encounter, not even an hour before. Thessaly picked up her glass and swirled it thoughtfully, noticing that across the table Wren was doing the same thing, almost perfectly in sync. Thessaly did not say it, but she knew what Wren had been telling her with that light kick: she had never been closer to anyone in her life.

•

A few days later, Wren had another welcome-home dinner, one she approached with less vigor. As she drove down Route 14 and into the suburbs, she lowered the window to breathe some of the brisk April breeze. A bottle of mass-market Pinot Grigio and a six-pack of beer were tucked beside her purse on the passenger seat. The six-pack was for Jeannie's boyfriend of the past two years,

Marcus. The wine was for her mother—not Wren's favorite, but she'd given up years ago on persuading her mother to try new wine. Honestly, she understood why people liked mass-market Pinot Grigio, so why not give her mother what she enjoyed?

Now that Wren lived close by, she knew she was supposed to call her mother more often, or her mother was supposed to call her more often. But Wren was her worst, most insecure and childish self with her mother and her mother's siblings and cousins, among whom she had never fit in and did not now. She always came away feeling unsettled, trying to pinpoint why she didn't feel good after seeing someone she loved, and who loved her. Was it as simple as the fact that they each associated the other with such bad memories? Her whole childhood was like the backyard grave of a pet they'd walk around for the rest of their lives.

When Wren arrived, Jeannie exclaimed over the wine. "I hope it didn't cost too much," she said, examining the label.

"We're doing well enough to spring for a bottle of Yellow Tail," Wren said.

They sat at the kitchen table to catch up while Marcus devoted himself to grilling chicken out on the patio. Jeannie gazed fondly through the sliding glass door at the back of his plaid shirt and cargo shorts, his high-and-tight haircut. He was perfect for Jeannie—he'd been a Marine in his youth, and his precision in hair, shoe-tying, and knife sharpening were a good match for her mother's brisk efficiency. The world could implode and these two would just go on about their day, exchanging affectionate pats on the hand and repairing the power grid.

"Your father," Jeannie said suddenly, "was very sweet before he got so sick. I'd hate to think you avoid dating just because of his bad luck." She let her gaze linger on Marcus as he came inside and set down a platter of chicken. She'd had a glass of wine.

Wren sighed. Love was making her mother introspective. It had also made her seek out some reassurance that she hadn't ruined Wren's love life. This only made the dinner, which was already punctuated by quick but unsettling kisses between Jeannie and Marcus, more uncomfortable: Wren wanted her mother to be happy and in love, but she did not have any desire to watch it flower. And she certainly did not want to hear any hint of the sensual riches Jeannie was now experiencing and appeared to want Wren to enjoy as well.

"I don't avoid dating," Wren said, which was true. She dated when she wanted to and made no specific effort not to. It was just that these things always followed the same pattern: She would start off optimistic about some man's looks or sense of humor or his way of placing a hand at the small of her back as they crossed the street, and she'd feel genuine enjoyment for a time. But next came the moment when all the electricity died and she looked at this man and could see only that he chewed loudly, brayed when he laughed, acted as if shaving his face were a crushing burden when most women shaved their whole bodies every single day, or he had some unfortunate, fixable dental issue that she became enraged he hadn't bothered to address. It was disheartening, the whole exercise, and she had found that the most freeing way to date was not to bother.

"Well, you don't want to look back someday when it's too late and wish you'd gotten married or had kids," her mother said. "That's why a quick lunch with your father might let you form a different image of him, you know?"

"I don't think I need a new image," Wren said. The chicken was suddenly all tendons and globules of fat. "I know you're feeling generous toward him, but he's just not in my life."

Marcus cleared his throat and then said, "I'll go get more bread."

"Thanks, sweetheart," Jeannie said to him. She turned back to Wren. "I'm not saying he deserves it. I'm saying it might do you good to see him sober. I do think he's sober now."

"I've heard that a lot over the years," Wren said, "from Dad and from you." She felt like a child, hurting her mother that way, but she meant it too.

"Wren," her mother said, hardening slightly, "you need a family. Thessaly is a friend and a business partner, but it's not like a sister. You need more people in your life."

Wren thought about her father as rarely as possible, because it was calmer and easier that way, and her few sweet memories only made her feel guilty. There was a time her father had taken her out for ice cream and they'd walked along a river, eating their cones and talking. She'd been too small to remember what they discussed, but the feeling had stayed with her, a sense of calm and pleasant attention, a sense of her own personal importance. And there was a time she'd gotten sick at school and he was the one to pick her up. He'd brought her a tray with a glass of 7UP and orange juice with a straw, a plate of crackers, and one cookie "as incentive," in case she felt well enough later. Then he'd sat at the other end of the couch, her feet on his leg, and watched *Sesame Street* with her.

No one understood that these moments only raised the question of why the man who evidently could be a caring, attentive father chose not to be. If Wren allowed herself to think about it, it was hard not to conclude that he simply didn't find her worth the trouble.

"Maybe I do need more people," she said to her mother. "But I get to pick them."

Two months later, just as summer was setting in, the light linger-ing into the evening and the neighborhood swarming with people out walking and bicycling, Wren came home to find Thessaly's car in the street in front of her house. This was nothing notable; she often stopped in to do paperwork or pick up samples.

But when Wren opened the front door, calling hello, Thessaly came out from the kitchen with an odd look on her face. She was holding her hands clasped in front of her, and she was blinking rapidly. "Hey," she said, with a strange kind of emphasis. "You have a guest. He's out back, smoking a cigarette."

"Who do we know who smokes?" Wren said. But she knew who it was.

"Maybe I should have told him to leave," said Thessaly. Her eyes were searching Wren's face. "I can do it now. But I just thought maybe your mom had a point?"

Wren was so overwhelmed and turned-around, she couldn't even answer. She marched through the kitchen and out to the back patio. And there was Barry, sitting in one of the rickety green chairs, wearing old jeans and work boots and a button-down shirt, his hair still shaggy at the bottom but thinner at the top, his face softened and more lined than she'd remembered. But his eyes were the thing she was looking for—his eyes always told her who she was dealing with, the inert mass or the human being. When he turned to look at her, she saw that they were alert and direct, that her father saw her very clearly.

•

Thessaly knew she'd done the wrong thing the moment she asked Wren's father to stay. She thought about how she would feel if

Wren forced her to reconcile with someone—she'd be annoyed but ultimately grateful, wouldn't she? But she knew that was not how Wren would feel. Not at all.

She watched out the window over the sink: Wren was standing, her father sitting, but they seemed to be speaking. It did not look warm, nor did it seem as tense as she'd feared.

She had imagined Barry as a hobo, or a slick, charming reptile. But the knock on the door had revealed a nervous-looking but kind-faced man with longish light brown hair and large gray eyes, Wren's eyes. Maybe that was why she'd been too nice to him—he reminded her of Wren. He also looked like any guy they might deal with at the warehouse, and Thessaly wondered if he'd once worked in one. Maybe he did now. Maybe he needed a job and they could get him hired.

People could change. Thessaly had changed. She thought she was steadier than she'd once been, calmer and wiser. Some of that was because Wren had pushed her to be less impetuous, and the truth was, Wren needed a loving push herself sometimes. Maybe this man was not the monster she believed.

"Hey," she said, opening the back door. "Why don't I make the three of us a bite to eat?" Barry looked bashful and pleased as he accepted; Wren's face did not move a muscle.

In Wren's kitchen, she unearthed linguine, tomatoes, shallot, and butter, and plucked a few leaves of basil from the plant beside the window.

They sat down by five-fifteen, about two hours before they normally would eat, but none of them had any idea how to pass those hours.

"Have some wine if you want it," Wren said.

"I'm good," Thessaly said, feeling virtuous.

"I hear you saw Mom," Wren said, turning to her father. Thessaly focused on dishing up the pasta.

Barry cleared his throat. "I ran into her at the grocery store a while back," he said. "She looks well."

"She's an RN now. In the NICU," said Wren. "And she's in love with a guy at the hospital. Marcus."

Barry nodded. "Yes," he said, "she told me all of that."

He twirled a few strands of linguine on his fork. He didn't hold his utensils like Wren did, but gripped the fork as if he were going to stab someone. Thessaly saw his gaze rest on Wren's hands, poised with exaggerated delicacy over her plate, as if Wren wanted him to notice.

"How's business?" Wren's father asked eventually.

"Excellent," Wren said. "I'd even say booming."

Both father and daughter turned to look at her and Thessaly nodded, her mouth full of pasta. Then she swallowed and said, "It's a numbers game; basically we bet on a shipping container full of the wine we think will sell, and then we need to sell it all to pay for the next one."

"We've surpassed all our projections so far," Wren put in. "And that's just Madison. We've barely touched Milwaukee yet."

"I'm not surprised you're doing so well," Barry said. "I always knew you'd do something."

"Did you," said Wren.

He nodded. "You know, I started a business myself around your age. You were still a baby."

Wren perked up. "I never knew that."

"It was a lawn care business," Barry said. "Bought a truck, painted it with a spiffy logo. It did well the first summer. Your mom and I treated ourselves to a little vacation, we saved some cash. But you need a lot of capital—all that equipment breaks down. Now I like not being in charge. I can just show up and do my job and go home."

Wren had a look on her face like she'd just remembered a pet she'd forgotten to feed for several days. "And where is home these days?" she asked.

"Oh," Barry said, "I share a place with a friend with better credit."

"There's a lot of ways to improve your credit," Thessaly said hopefully. She glanced at Wren, whose eyes were moving carefully over Barry's dirty fingernails, the fabric of his jeans. Thessaly didn't think it was snobbery that was driving her examination, but fear.

Wren began to clear the dishes, but her father insisted he wash them. In the living room, they could hear dishes being put into the dishwasher, but just faintly, under the sound of the Rolling Stones. "Do you want to step out front?" Thessaly murmured, but Wren shook her head, eyes fixed on the wall.

When Barry returned, he was more relaxed, as if that task in Wren's kitchen had helped him get to know something useful about who she'd become. His shirtsleeves were rolled up to his elbows. "Well," Thessaly said, "shall we have dessert? Take a walk?"

"Oh, no need," Barry said. He sat down and rested an ankle on one knee. He seemed more languid and Wren chilly, brittle, tense.

"Well," Thessaly ventured. "Thanks so much for letting me join in." She let her eyes drift to the clock above the TV.

But he only nodded sententiously. Thessaly glanced at Wren, a nervous tingle prickling all over her skin. It had only been, what, twenty minutes since dinner? What could he have done in that time that was loosening him up like this, making his eyes not quite meet hers? She had seen an endless number of drunk people in her day, but she'd never seen one like this, and she wasn't entirely sure what substance was causing it.

But she knew she was responsible.

"In Florida," Barry was saying slowly, "I worked in fishing a bit, plus some other factory work. Now I'm working at a cheese plant, on the production line. Lots of free samples." He sat up straight, seeming to recall something. "Oh, I forgot. I even brought you some, honey."

"I'm not hungry," Wren said, but her father was already up again and back in the kitchen.

He returned a couple of minutes later, holding two packages of plastic-wrapped cheese, which he placed on the coffee table with a flourish. "This one is aged two years," he said. "And *this* one's aged way more. Five? Six, maybe." He set his other hand on the other brick of cheese and then left them both there for a long minute, as if he were steadying himself.

Wren stood up with a jolt. She left the room without saying a word, went into the kitchen, and returned with three wineglasses and an opened sample bottle of Rhône blend they hadn't liked enough to order. "Oh, let's not—" Thessaly began to say, but Wren shot her a look of such coldness that she stopped.

Wren opened the bottle, expertly sliding the cork out to Barry's exclamations of admiration and reminders that he no longer drank, and then she poured a glass for each of them. She filled Barry's close to the brim.

"I know you're angry," he was saying, "but you don't have to get back at me." His words were coming more drowsily now, and as he spoke he studied the wineglass.

Wren didn't say a word. She picked up her glass and handed Thessaly hers, and clinked their glasses smartly. "I don't like this wine," she said. "But who fucking cares?"

"I would never drink in front of you," Barry declared.

"Then keep drinking in the kitchen," Wren said. "That flask of vodka is still right in your jacket pocket. If that runs dry, I have plenty to drink. I made a whole life out of it."

For several days, Thessaly waited for Wren to yell at her. She knew she deserved it: She could have asked Barry to leave. She could have just stayed in the kitchen and let Wren decide if she wanted him to stay for dinner—or not. But she hadn't.

The longer the silence lingered on the topic, the more Thessaly perseverated. Unlike in New York, when she'd been the drunk one or the brokenhearted one, and Wren got to be the grown-up, this was Thessaly trying to be the adult. The younger Thessaly would never have bothered. It was not her fault that Wren's father was a screwup. Maybe there was a better way for Wren herself to handle that rift, had Wren thought of that?

Then she noticed that the silence extended beyond the topic of Wren's father. Her phone got no texts from Wren unless they were about work. The one time she tried sending something funny, she received only a wan emoji in reply.

This was the kind of discomfort Thessaly rarely felt, the sort of rejection she had experienced only a few times and had always taken solace in knowing that it would never happen with Wren. It made her remember the way she and Wren had interacted years earlier, when they first met at work, and Wren had always looked at Thessaly with a cool disinterest. Wren now admitted she had been intimidated by Thessaly, and for years Thessaly had believed her. But in retrospect, it certainly felt a lot like disdain. And so did this.

By the end of the week, Thessaly couldn't take the silence. She finished a round of sales calls and went over to Wren's, where she found her, as always, on her computer. Thessaly pulled over the other chair and sat down. Wren just looked at her, waiting.

"I'm sorry about your dad," Thessaly said. "I thought I was helping, but I knew you didn't want to see him and I ignored you. I didn't understand what would happen."

"That he'd get drunk?" Wren said, cocking her head. "I'd think that's the one thing you—anyone, really—could foresee."

"No, how it affected you."

"That's because you're thinking of your family. Your father."

"You're right," Thessaly said. She scooted her chair closer to Wren's. Wren just watched her approach, as if she were wildlife. Thessaly decided to say nothing more. She didn't know what to say, and she was starting to get angry. That was a lot like her father too.

"Don't get pissed at *me*," Wren said. "Just because you did something crappy."

Thessaly closed her eyes for a second. "Okay, let's have some perspective," she said. "I didn't burn your house down. I tried to help you and your dad."

"Well, quit trying," Wren said. "Go help your own dad do whatever he needs to do—learn how to quit fighting with people, I guess."

Thessaly leaned back. "My dad loves you," she said. "Don't even." This was true. Wren had been afraid to speak in front of David the first several times they met. David, who found quiet people unnerving, needled and teased and joshed her until Wren lost patience and told him a winemaker he admired greatly now spent most of his time finding the right hat to wear in the vineyard. It was true, so they'd wound up bonding over it.

All of which made Thessaly bristle even further on her dad's behalf. She stood up and began to gather her things. "Forget it," she said. "You can give me the silent treatment all you want, but I have things to do."

"I'm not giving you the silent treatment!" Wren hollered. "I don't know what the fuck to say to you!"

Thessaly sat back down, her tote bag in her lap. Wren's face was flushed, but she didn't look away.

"Why wouldn't you know what to say to me?" she asked. The words filled her with a sizzle of unease as soon as she said them. What was Wren trying not to say? Was this going to be another time when Thessaly did one thing wrong and paid for it through the nose? Why did she surround herself with such judgmental, self-righteous people? She wanted to get up and leave, not even just the house but the state, their company. Why was she always trying to work with people when it was all easier alone? She could be off somewhere in Oregon or Washington or the Finger Lakes or at home in Sonoma, alone in a cellar making blends and listening to music and serving wine to people and then walking down the street to have dinner at the bar of some fancy little restaurant that served her wine. And she wasn't going to do any of that here in this little milk town. She had made a mistake.

"Because it's embarrassing," Wren said finally. "It's mortifying to have this drunk of a dad and for you to have experienced the whole range of that."

"You don't have to be embarrassed in front of me," Thessaly said. "Not when I've done it so many times."

"Well, that's you," said Wren, and Thessaly's anger flared up all over again. She was about to spout off when Wren shook her head and raised one hand to stop her.

"Are you *shushing* me?" Thessaly said.

"I'm shushing us both," Wren said. "Leave it till tomorrow. Just leave it."

•

That night Wren lay in bed, thinking of how they almost didn't do any of this. They'd had their dinner of lo mein and outrage after Greg's promotion, they'd thrown around some big ideas about what they could do better, but the truth was that once life settled back down, they were not obligated to follow through. It took a long time to save up the money and set up the paperwork; there was plenty of time to decide that life at the new Lionel Garrett was not so bad, or that there were easier ways to leave it—move to Chicago, get a new job, take up Pilates. Sometimes they would go weeks without talking about it, and sometimes Wren had watched Thessaly's demeanor during those fallow periods and wondered, did she regret bringing it up? Was she realizing that she could do all the things she wanted to do without Wren? Then she wondered what, precisely, were those things Thessaly wanted to do. She wondered if Thessaly was still serious about winemaking, if she ever had been, and how long she would be a partner before she lit out to do that.

But eventually one of them always brought it up again, and together they'd moved each chess piece forward, one at a time.

But as she lay there, eyes fixed on the crack in the ceiling above her bed, Wren considered that she had been the one to continually raise the topic. And she was the one who felt this gnawing desire to shore everything up, to make Passerine bigger and wider, brick by brick, until it could not be set aside or overlooked.

The trouble was, Thessaly didn't dream of a big corporate import business any more than she dreamed of making

202

grocery-store wine. But Thessaly was also the one who'd made Wren look at her father when she did not want to. It was, after all, Thessaly who'd forced her to see at close range what a life could so easily become if you weren't careful. What else did she think Wren would do?

•

Thessaly wasn't certain if Wren would want to talk the next day, but then Wren called and said, "Can I pick you up in a little while?"

"Sure," said Thessaly. There was a pause. "We good?"

"I think so," Wren said. "But I want to run something by you. Do me one favor: don't say anything till I get a chance to explain."

"Oh boy," Thessaly said. "Why do I feel like I'd better not look in the trunk of your car?"

They drove to the north side of the city, leaving behind the shopping centers and neighborhoods and restaurants for industrial buildings and prairie. Wren pulled into the parking lot of a big rectangular building. She got out of the car, and Thessaly, after a moment, followed.

"I looked at this the other day," Wren said, "but I don't have keys or anything. There's not much to see yet, anyway—it's just a warehouse, but it's climate-controlled and it has twice the space we're leasing now. And office space. And space for a tasting room, desks for staff."

"How can we afford it?" Thessaly said. "We're less than a year old and this is a big leap from your spare bedroom."

"Exactly," Wren said. "We need to grow. Bigger orders, build in a better margin for ourselves. Otherwise we're always going to be basically trapped on the hamster wheel: pay off one container to buy the next."

"But I can't ask my family for more. They already lent us a *lot*."

"Of course not. I'm looking into small business loans," Wren said.

"Come on, banks are barely giving those anymore," Thessaly said.

"Then we do it ourselves and raise our sales. We have to grow, and I don't really care how we do it. Let's quit testing the waters."

"I care how we do it," Thessaly said. "I'm a great salesperson, but we would need staff and we don't have the salaries for that."

Wren shook her head as if to shake away a mosquito. "If we hire experienced ones, they won't even want a salary—they know they can earn more on commission. If we don't do this now, Thessaly, I'm telling you, we could look up in five years and nothing will be different! We'll still be in our same old apartments, working out of my spare bedroom."

"So what if we are? Remember how Lionel got so insane about profits after we moved? If we keep expenses low, we have flexibility."

Wren's eyes sharpened. "Flexibility to do what?" she asked.

Thessaly suddenly felt trapped. "To do whatever," she said. "Move or hire or take time off . . ." She stopped. "Oh. You're worried I'll get all flighty and go make wine instead."

Wren didn't say anything. Thessaly looked up at the warehouse, which was square and ugly. She wondered if Wren was trying to push her out by making their work life as unappealing as possible. She didn't share Wren's vision, but she also didn't have a better one to offer. Sometimes it seemed to Thessaly that she had used up her moment of business inspiration the day she'd proposed they go out on their own, and she'd been on that leash ever since.

But then again: Wren had never steered her wrong yet. If it weren't for her, Thessaly might be the alcoholic wife of some post-Nick doctor. She might still be scurrying around Manhattan in the same patterns, never looking up. So when Wren said, "Let's just start imagining," she agreed.

The next week, they started interviewing salespeople. Their first real lead was Kara, a bartender who wanted to get out of restaurant hours. Kara was a few years younger than they were, a rare, or maybe the sole, Black wine professional in Madison. She had round tortoiseshell glasses, close-cut hair, and a bartender's emotional intelligence and inviting manner; buyers might forget it was a business transaction at all once she'd enthralled them with gossip from her days catering for famous bands when they came through town. "Mick Jagger's this *tiny* thing like as thick as my wrist," she'd said. "And Keith Richards is basically a walnut."

The only problem was her lack of experience. She needed a base salary and Thessaly persuaded Wren that Kara was worth it.

They were less unified when it came to their next choice. Alice was already working for a distributorship and importer far larger than theirs, run by Hank Ritton, a man Wren had crossed paths with back in her restaurant days.

"Why come to us?" Thessaly said. "She's got to be doing well with Hank."

"She said Hank's company's gotten too big and isn't challenging anymore," Wren said.

Alice was a rare bird for Madison. She had a blunt platinum pageboy with bangs and deliberate dark roots, and her face was lively and delicate, with eyes as bright as a fox's and a neat alert point of a nose. Her clothing was muted, her necklace strung with a heavy, smooth egg-shaped pendant, and her fragrance smelled faintly of cut figs. The whole look was a shock in this city, where people generally dressed as if they needed to be ready to go hiking on a moment's notice.

Something about Alice left Thessaly feeling unsettled. She didn't think she liked her—but she didn't have to like her. Alice herself might not be the trouble. The trouble was Wren. She got slightly fluttery as she escorted Alice into the office.

"I like what you guys are doing," Alice said, before they'd even asked her a question. "Such incredible taste. I can help you expand. A lot. I've got relationships all over this town."

"We want growth," Wren agreed.

"I'll tell you a secret," Alice said. "People are too nice around here. Makes competition easier."

"Won't you be frustrated," Thessaly asked, trying to take control of the conversation, "if you leave one place because it's too big and then the start-up turns into the same place you left?"

Wren looked irritated.

"Listen," Alice said, "I'll do what you want me to. I'm just saying I'm a top seller here, and I was in Chicago too."

"Where'd you work in Chicago?" Wren asked, her eyes roving the résumé on her laptop.

"Lowell Imports," Alice said. "The greatest people. Elizabeth made a mint in business and Gerry, that's the husband, loves fine wine. They started importing but figured out quickly they wanted someone else to run it." She flashed an intimate, buoyant smile. "When they decided to get out of the business, I was ready for a change myself."

"Madison must be a shock," Wren said, "after a city the size of Chicago." Two spots of color had risen in her cheeks, and she was focused somewhat hungrily on Alice as she waited for an answer. The interview had shifted, Thessaly realized with a small jolt. Wren was wooing Alice. Not the other way around.

"No, it was welcome," Alice said. "I always say Madison has the amenities of a much larger town but the ease of a smaller one."

"*I* miss the big city sometimes," Wren said.

"Oh my gosh, me too," Alice said, turning on a dime. She did it with such sincerity you could easily not notice she had only just stated the opposite. "But the other thing I say is that nobody can have everything all at the same time. Speaking of which, I do have one ask. Personally, I'd prefer to be on commission. I know a lot of time people like to start slow, but I'm not a slow-start type."

"Well, that's easy," Wren said after Alice had left. "We make an offer, right? She's going to add a lot of, I don't know, verve."

Thessaly looked down at herself, at her jeans and knit top and her silver bracelets. She still had some verve, didn't she? For the first time she wondered if she'd lost something in the past few years. Wren had gained plenty, that was true—but Thessaly had never stopped to think Wren might have somehow overtaken her. Maybe Wren was looking at Thessaly through a much less flattering lens than she'd thought.

But she didn't feel she could say any of this. Her feeling frumpy was not a reason not to hire Alice, who had all the skills they needed and who, even Thessaly could acknowledge, did have a certain presence. Alice could start pushing bigger, more commercial wines, letting Kara get comfortable with the book and allowing Thessaly to get back to the smaller producers she loved. When you put it that way, there was no argument.

Alice not only met the sales target they'd given her but exceeded it enough to earn a bonus. She was a brilliant salesperson. As they went through OND—Passerine's second but its first with their new employees—it became evident that there was no restaurant, bar, or store in town that didn't know her. No foodie, dancer, poet, or florist. Her sales didn't even slow as much as expected in the doldrums of winter and early spring; Alice was brilliant at refining each sales pitch to address the shifts in mood and weather. By the following summer, when she had been with Passerine for nearly a year, she was nearly outselling Thessaly on rosé, which required Thessaly to up her game just to keep the upper hand.

At the farmers' market Thessaly frequently saw Alice from a block away, laughing with a vendor and exclaiming over the heirloom plums or a jar of maple syrup. Somehow Alice always had a free ticket to wine dinners and fundraisers. Everyone loved her, Wren loved her, and with Alice and Kara firmly in place, it felt as if Thessaly ought to be able to relax a little.

Except for the warehouse. Wren didn't bring up the new space that often, just often enough to make it clear it was still her big goal. But every time she mentioned that the warehouse space was now fully built out, or that another space inside it had been leased, Thessaly secretly hoped someone else would rent the whole building, as if this would end the discussion. She had thought this company would be a way to make a living and learn, and she'd thought that doing both with her best friend would make it all the better. But she hadn't found the time—she told herself it was about time—to take classes, or even to ferment a random jug of grape juice in her basement. And her best friend seemed to have a new best friend, which was too embarrassing and grade-school to admit aloud.

There were moments when Wren pulled Thessaly into the office and laid out numbers—the working capital they had, what was coming and what was going out—with such grim determination that the warehouse and the speed of growth Wren was so insistent on felt like a guillotine above their heads. Where was the intimate little company they'd created, the nights of her and Wren dining out and gossiping about their old coworkers, the mornings quietly drinking coffee and working side by side until it was time to go out on sales calls?

Thessaly suspected she needed a boyfriend.

Alice found endless ways to echo Wren's skepticism of Thessaly's remarkable, but lower-selling, producers. Half the time Alice seemed to forget to sell them herself. But she never came right out and argued against carrying those wines. Instead, she expressed doubts with an air of surprise, as if she hadn't expected to have this opinion, either. "I *love* that bone-dry Txakoli," she said once, at a company meeting. "Love it. I don't even care that I have to work so hard to unearth just the right buyer for it. That's what makes it special."

"I don't find it too difficult," Kara said tentatively. "I can usually find a few good pairings on the menu and that does it." Wren barely seemed to hear.

Not to mention, Alice was conveniently always dropping by Wren's apartment. Every time Thessaly went by to pick up or drop off something, there was Alice, twirling in the second chair in Wren's office, tasting industrially produced samples Alice had brought by "just to try out," the two of them shrugging as if to say, "Why not?" So far, none of these terrible wines had quite persuaded Wren, thank god. But the days were numbered.

And yet Alice kept making money, a fact Thessaly had to remember no matter how many things had begun to grate on her nerves: her performative laughter, her label-dropping. Over time her whole schtick had started to seem more than a touch ridiculous—Thessaly had once seen her strolling downtown on a cool spring night wearing an actual cloak.

"I don't get the problem," Wren said, when Thessaly allowed

her misgivings to surface—just barely. "You just described a good salesperson. She can sell whatever we ask her to. She's a character. Plus, she's everywhere, and people see her and think of us. Like Legs."

They were sitting on Wren's front porch. "That's what people *think* is good sales," Thessaly said. "And it's why people hate salespeople. When I made my best numbers at Lionel Garrett, I didn't do it by bullshitting people and dressing like I was in *Lord of the Rings*. I did it by listening to what they needed and finding the stuff that helped them increase sales."

Wren's feet were up on the railing of her porch; it was barely sandal weather but already her toenails were painted a crisp pale blue and her heels were velvety. Thessaly had farmer's feet, and she hadn't remembered to get a pedicure. She'd bet Alice had remembered.

"Alice has good relationships all over town," Wren said.

"True," Thessaly conceded. "She does know everyone. But still."

"Are you sure this isn't about Alice not pushing all your weird little wines?"

"Kara sure does well with them."

"Her overall numbers are lower, though," Wren said. "Listen, it hurts when the market doesn't love what you love. But I think it's a good wake-up call. Can't you make this easier on everyone by choosing some less esoteric wines? I look at what sells in the grocery stores around here and I know it's mostly horrible, but if we get in there, we'll just clean up. We can even sell them decent wine without them knowing it."

"We have a balanced book," Thessaly said. "It has big easy ones and unique varietals that strengthen our reputation."

Wren shot her a look and Thessaly looked back at her. So there they were. Wren was Lionel and Thessaly was Jonathan. How had that happened?

"You want to get dinner?" Thessaly said. "Or takeout. Watch something dumb on TV." She missed doing nothing much with Wren. She missed how incensed Wren got over *Project Runway*. She missed them drinking big mugs of ginger tea after dinner and the way Wren always used the same mug. She even missed teaching her to bake puff pastry and croissant dough, which she shouldn't, because Wren was so persnickety about temperatures and weights that she drove Thessaly nuts. But she turned out perfect croissants.

"I'm meeting Alice downtown," Wren said. "Not for work, just to hang out. You want to come?"

"Sure," Thessaly lied. "I'll meet you there."

· CHAPTER 17 ·

In New York you could introduce yourself a thousand times and still know no one, but here in Madison, Wren was a known quantity. If she went out alone, she would end up knowing half the people in the bar. But it was more fun being swooped up by Alice and taken on an adventure. Tonight they met at a new restaurant just off the capitol square, the sort of place where the servers wore plaid flannel shirts and you could order eight different types of Scotch egg. "I could use something green," Wren said, peering at the menu.

"I know, right? They're coasting on a single beet-and-goat-cheese salad like it's 1995." Alice waved over their waiter with a dazzling smile. "You're Matt, right? Matt, we're dying for some vegetables to balance things out. Do you think the chef could whip something up?"

"Just a salad would be great," Wren said, but Alice waved her aside as she and Matt collaborated on what soon became an off-menu tasting menu of pea shoots and radishes and arugula.

"I'm sorry," she said as soon as he scurried off to the kitchen. "But I was trying to help the kitchen too. I couldn't let them serve a half-assed dinner to the owner of one of the most talked-about wine importers in the Midwest. They'd figure it out later and feel like idiots."

Against her better judgment, Wren laughed. But maybe the flattery was genuine.

As the months passed, Wren had found herself, for the first time in years, not *not* needing Thessaly, but needing her less. She hadn't known she resented Thessaly's importance to her until she was freed—just slightly—from caring about her opinions quite so much. Of course she still *cared*. When they managed to sit down to drink a glass of wine and not evaluate it, Thessaly still was the funniest person she knew, and she'd been the one to insist on Wren's worth before Wren was certain of it herself. But Thessaly could find friends anywhere she liked; she picked them up like pollen as she walked down the street. And Wren needed to grow up and expand her own circle too. Thessaly was her business partner and her best friend, but she couldn't ask Thessaly to be all things to her. Sometimes you needed an Alice instead, someone who'd never known her as a scared kid. Someone who liked to hit a new restaurant or two and demand a bit of a fuss.

One afternoon, she decided to take Alice to see the warehouse. Why did Thessaly not see the opportunity here? Was Wren crazy and Thessaly in the right?

At the warehouse they met the realtor, who lurked a few feet behind them while they walked through the remaining empty offices and the half-empty warehouse space. Every time Wren came here she expected to find its appeal duller than she remembered, but it never was. She loved the echoes and the smell of cold stone.

Alice strolled around on the concrete floors, studied the steel beams of the ceiling, nodding as Wren pointed out the potential tasting and meeting rooms, the admin space. When she finished, Alice shrugged as if there were nothing more to say.

"What do you think?" Wren asked.

"It all makes sense to me," she said. "I just don't know why you haven't rented it yet."

Suddenly Wren was afraid of being disloyal to Thessaly, who was, after all, the co-owner of the company and Alice's boss. She couldn't undermine her own partner in front of an employee. "I guess I'm still considering," she said. But even this retreat felt disappointing. She'd forgotten how good it felt to have a partner who enjoyed dreaming the same dream she did.

Alice was inspecting a bank of outlets in the wall. She didn't look at Wren when she said, "You can't pay for this place by filling it up with wines like Lachryma."

"No," Wren admitted. "You can't."

In early June, Alice threw a party. She lived in a beautiful mid-century modern house on the near west side that she had bought with her savings from Chicago. Wren didn't like the dynamic of her employee living better than she did, but she had to admit that Alice had amazing taste. The night of the party, Wren wore a green summer dress from a pricey boutique Alice had suggested.

She met Wren at the door with a grandiose hug. Behind her the living room was already filled with people. Her house was spare and lovely, painted in shades of ecru and sage and moss, furniture glowing in warm teak and mahogany and clean, faintly Asian lines. "Kara and Thessaly are here somewhere, looking gorgeous as always," Alice said, "as is someone I keep meaning to introduce you to. Also looking gorgeous, if such things interest you."

"Well, if I must," Wren said, because it was summer, because she was as well dressed as anyone here, and because tonight, such things did interest her.

"Wonderful, wonderful," Alice said. "Grab a drink and I'll track you down."

She found Thessaly by a platter of grilled shrimp. She looked Wren up and down and said, "You look amazing, Sparrow. New dress?"

"Yeah, thanks," Wren said. Suddenly she was self-conscious about how much she'd spent. "How long have you been here? Met anyone?"

"Sort of. I've noticed that I can spend twenty minutes talking with Alice's friends and not be asked to say a single thing about myself, except that I import wine," said Thessaly.

"That's like the only part of myself I want to talk about," said Wren.

The house was filled with people and music and pot smoke and the groups spilled out into the manicured backyard and the front porch. Once again Alice had unearthed people Wren had never discovered here in hippie Madison, people in seersucker, people in chic silk dresses drinking Sazeracs. They all had that very expensive look Wren had learned to like back in New York: the low-key one that cost thousands, the caramel highlights in the swingy blowout, the barely perceptible, secretly elaborate makeup, sprays of tiny diamonds.

A gust of unexpected confidence blew through her. Thessaly soon left, but Wren stayed, moving from group to group, somehow beguiling the shit out of people and waiting for the inevitable moment when they asked what she did and she had the pleasure of telling them. They were lawyers and software people, but she was something else, something romantic and well traveled, and all of them knew it.

She drank four glasses of wine and circled back to the man Alice had presented her with earlier, a tall, too-good-looking guy named Bill or Will or Jasper, whose hand Alice had literally placed inside Wren's, saying, "I'm sick of you two not knowing each other."

Around midnight Wren departed, taking with her Alice's gift. She never brought home guys right after meeting them—she believed in a few awkward dates first—but tonight she didn't care. She liked his smooth tanned skin and high cheekbones, his lupine eyes and big hands. She felt hot—not just turned on but *heated*. She felt confident doing what other women did and she decided she could do too.

She led Will/Bill/Jasper into her apartment and poured them each a glass of Cava that neither of them needed. It was just something to do until they could maneuver themselves beside her bed, taking off clothes and kissing, and as the last garment came off she took a step forward and gave Bill/Will/Jasper a gentle tap on the chest, which he rightly interpreted to mean he should lie back on the bed, and then she climbed on top of him, smiling at him in the dark. She congratulated herself for not drinking so much she couldn't feel anything, just enough to know she could do whatever she wanted to. Running her tongue over his neck, his collarbone, his smooth expensive-smelling chest, she thought about how she'd always heard how much men liked it when you took charge, but never before had the confidence to test the rumor. They were supposed to like it when you had things you wanted, things you asked for, and sure enough, he did.

•

In New York, Thessaly had been a late sleeper. Here, freed from an office culture that required her to drink heavily, she had redis-covered an ancient habit: she awoke at five-thirty and went to the farmers' market—providing her an excellent reason to duck out of Alice's white-collar executive salon and head home early. When she'd left, Wren was throwing back her head and laughing with some male-model type. Was this who Wren was into now, a guy like that, with dead eyes and highlighted hair? In New York, they would have rolled their eyes at a man like this. Discomfited, Thessaly had left without saying goodbye.

She'd been skeptical of the farmers' market when she first got here. She came from the land of hand-harvested kelp and creamy avocadoes, backyard lemons and overloaded persim-mon trees. But this particular Midwest morning was fresh magic after the long winter. She bought soft-ripened cheese and bags of snap peas and rhubarb, then walked slowly through the crowd of shoppers, trying to put her finger on what was making her nostalgic. It wasn't until she stopped at a stand piled with spinach and herbs and began to shoot the breeze about soil and rainfall that she realized it was the farmers: Her people! Her weathered, brusquely friendly people, handing her slices of cucumber to sample.

Back at home, she wound up making a vat of green and lemony soup. It was far too much for one person, even after she con-sumed three bowls: she'd made enough for a group of hungry field hands. On Monday she had to give some away. She dropped a portion off at Kara's house. Kara would enjoy it, for one thing. For another, Thessaly had no desire to share her beautiful soup with Alice, who would exclaim over it before taking two sips and then setting down her spoon. Thessaly had noticed Alice did not like food all that much. She performed enjoyment in it, but she never ate.

"Oh my *god*," Kara said, holding up the clear container to admire the golden broth and the green peas and barley pearls. "I'm going to have this tonight with a poached egg on top. Actually, I might have to have it before I come into the office."

Thessaly was so pleased, she hugged her before she left. She baked for anxiety, but she cooked for the pleasure of the seasons, for the way it filled her apartment kitchen with savory, sharp fragrances, for the right person's genuine pleasure in the gift. She didn't have to wait for the soup she'd made to show up on a menu or arrive at a warehouse. She didn't have to hound a shipping company about its location. She could just make it. Create it. She missed dealing in things she could touch and taste. She spent her whole life thinking about wine and yet it often seemed theoretical to her, just boxes she moved around place to place, line items on a spreadsheet.

A few weeks later, she was doing her lap around the market when a woman in kitchen clogs and lightweight pants and a colorless shirt glanced Thessaly's way.

"You're Wren's friend," the woman said. "You guys came into Heirloom a few times." She had beautiful eyes, brown and gold, with dark rims around the irises and unexpectedly feminine black lashes.

"Of course," Thessaly said. This was Zoe, who oversaw the sourcing of local cheese, produce, meat, and anything else the restaurant needed.

"I see you all the time," Zoe said. "Do you cook? Or just drink?" She had a side gig, cooking for a farm during harvest season, and she was looking for help in the kitchen.

"I used to bake," Thessaly said. "And I grew up making vats of whatever for the crew on my family's vineyard." She didn't know why she was saying this. She had plenty of work.

"It's just like a thank-you meal for the people who work there. But being out there is beautiful. You want to bring Wren?"

"No," Thessaly said. "I mean, she can't, she's pretty swamped." But she did not want to explain why she wanted to go cook on a farm for almost no money. She didn't want to hear that Wren thought Zoe was kind of homespun. She just wanted space for herself.

Thessaly drove out a week later in the warm summer air, through the fields and past dairy cows, to the one place where she didn't have to worry about shipping and inventory and miles and planning. She simmered new potatoes and roasted tiny Sungold tomatoes; sliced cucumbers and scattered them with olive oil and salt and mint. It was heaven. Inspired, she went home and made a new sourdough starter and even kept it alive.

Sometimes she wondered if Wren would run into Zoe and hear about this. She'd wonder why Thessaly hadn't told her about it. She'd think Thessaly was nuts for working on one of her few days off. At the very least, Wren would tell her to ask for a lot more money. Then Thessaly would have to find a way to hide the truth, which was that she would have done it for free.

The employees on these vegetable farms were largely Mexican, just like in Sonoma. So Thessaly called her mother for recipes. Thessaly knew her own food was still up and down—her beans needed salt, her rice needed a third rinsing—but she was proud of her salsas: mint-green, or brick-red, rich in herbs and chiles that created a finish both refreshing and sneakily searing.

The land around Thessaly on the days she drove out to cook on the farm was certainly different from California: so much flatter, its slopes easy and gentle and carpeted with greenery. But the smoky fragrance of the food, the green smells of the cut plants and occasional whiff of manure, the voices all around her in a mix of Spanish and English—it all induced in her a shining spear of longing until her eyes began to swim. She felt as if something hot and bright was separating her lungs, forcing her to make room for itself.

•

Wren was probably going to have to kill Thessaly. Once again, on a Sunday, she had disappeared, and this time she was ditching a wine dinner they'd bought a ticket for. Had it been a free ticket, Wren might have skipped out too when Thessaly had texted last minute: Couldn't Kara attend? But Kara was busy and this was not the first time Thessaly had blown off a weekend commitment.

Wren stepped out of her leggings and into her green dress, smoothing down her frustration. She and Thessaly attended one or two of these dinners a year, just to keep abreast of what other importers and distributors were doing in a small, competitive market. The whole purpose of a wine dinner was marketing: the restaurant got to show off a seven-course tasting menu and woo local tastemakers. The winemaker, whose wines were paired with each dish, introduced their prized vintages to chefs and drinkers to drive up future sales. Alice didn't want to attend; this was her past employer, and she said that going would have felt disloyal to Passerine. Plus she didn't think much of the producer, which had tamped down Wren's interest too. Oh well. Someone had to go, and Wren wasn't going to let the ticket go to waste.

The restaurant where the dinner was held was clean and bright and simple, with reclaimed wood and rough linen to evoke Scandinavian pioneers. Hank, Alice's old boss, was standing near the entrance when Wren arrived, greeting people and stroking his wiry auburn beard. He was a Madison transplant, who'd moved here from Fort Worth for college and never left. He got a lot of mileage out of being Texan, playing up the accent when it suited him and presenting the good-natured, heartless honesty of a man who'd castrated a steer or two in his day.

They did their Madison version of the European kiss, one quick pucker, no cheek contact. "By the way," she said, "I'm many months late saying this, but I hope it wasn't bad form to hire Alice. I'd have asked you first, but you know how it is. You can't talk to the current employer when someone isn't sure they're leaving."

Hank waved to someone behind Wren and started to turn away. Before he did, he added, "We knew she was leaving. All clear on our end." His face was smooth and bland.

Wren knew better than to say, "You did?" She wanted to seem in the know, but this was the Midwest; you weren't supposed to pepper people with questions. But she'd been certain Alice had said otherwise. She set her face to smooth and bland too.

Hank gave her shoulder a clap and they both moved on. At the table, she was seated between a pleasant-looking, light-haired guy in his forties and a woman with silver hair who immediately turned away to talk to her companion.

Tonight's winemaker was from the Finger Lakes in New York, which hadn't yet earned the same reputation as California and the Pacific Northwest. Wren nodded along, hearing nothing, as the winemaker talked and the servers poured in advance of the next course. Maybe it wasn't so bad that Thessaly had bailed. Maybe Wren was being overly sensitive. Because now that she had settled in, she was glad to be here. They were supposed to lean on each other, after all—that's the benefit of a partnership. And just because Wren found it impossible to delegate didn't mean no one else should. Thessaly was probably just being wise about where she spent her time and energy.

A golden-seared scallop arrived, served in a tiny pool of corn risotto and chewy lardons. It was a few weeks early for corn. Maybe they'd frozen it last summer, but still, she marked off a few points for lack of seasonality.

The man next to her leaned over. "How come they make this risotto taste like a field of corn concentrated in one bite and my risotto tastes like . . . my risotto?"

He was better-looking than Wren had noticed at first—with wry blue eyes and a nose that looked—not in a bad way, somehow—as if it had been broken once or twice. "What's your risotto like?" she asked.

"It's like all the rice grains huddle together for protection," he said. "Mostly from me."

"Ah," she said, casting a subtle glance over his hand for a wedding ring. He didn't have one, but he might be one of those married people who didn't wear one. "I'd say not to sell yourself short, but I get the feeling you aren't."

"I'm not," he said happily. "I'm genuinely unskilled."

"Well, for one thing, they probably use three times the butter nonprofessionals would, and I bet they puree a ton of corn kernels and press the cream out and then stir it in," Wren said. "There's a reason nobody does this sort of thing at home. It's exhausting."

"I'd love to get my cooks to do something like that, but we'd never sell it," he said.

His name was Martin, it turned out, and the cooks he was referring to were in a Wisconsin chain of steakhouses called Oberon, for which he was the beverage director. Wren managed to hide her surprise. She'd never been to an Oberon Steakhouse. It was one of those places where the whole point was consistency and familiarity. You got your ribeye and your mashed potatoes and your wedge salad and your premature cardiac event and it was the exact replica whether you were in Madison, Appleton, Racine, or Brookfield. What was he doing here?

"The founder's name was O'Brien," Martin said, "but no one expects great food from the Irish. No offense if you're Irish; I am. So they went with Oberon."

He paused, probably debating whether to mention where the name came from. But there were far too many English lit drop-outs in the wine world for Wren not to recognize her Shakespeare. "Nothing evokes a bloody steak like the king of the fairies," she observed.

"Luckily it's one of those names that just sounds good even if you forgot your high school production of *A Midsummer Night's Dream*. Which I did; I had to look it up when I got this job. How about you?"

"Oh, I looked it up years ago," she said, which made him laugh again. "I'm an importer."

"Ahh, like Hank," he said, and she considered this, flattered. A year earlier, Wren might have thought Oberon was too soulless and corporate, too big, for a small company like hers to pursue. And maybe it was. But everything was corporate now, including the chic restaurant in which they sat—a new breed of eatery put together not with spit and borrowed kitchenware but investors, thousands of dollars, and rigid corporate oversight. She couldn't overlook chains at this point, nor did she want to. Who was she to be a snob?

"Well, kind of like Hank," she said. They talked for the rest of the dinner, Wren saying nothing much about the wine until they got to one she liked: the Cabernet Franc, served with duck. It was unequivocally appealing, lively and well made, tinged with black fruit. She stopped talking and just tasted for a moment, letting the wine shape-shift.

"Even though I don't carry this wine, I'm professionally obligated to admit that it would be great with steak."

Martin nodded. "I have this one on our list. People tend to go for a California Cab first."

"I have some Italian reds you might think about," she said casually. "A few incredibly good-value Sangiovese. You should try them sometime." After dessert, she had her business card ready. They shook hands, she passed him her card as if he'd requested it, smiling easily into his bright blue eyes and promising to give him a call in a few days. Then she got the fuck out of there before she could screw it up.

The next day, Thessaly brought her a slice of apology pie. Wren would have liked to refuse it, but it was blueberry pie, which Thessaly knew she adored. When someone knew you this well and backed it up with pastry, it didn't feel worth holding a grudge.

Besides, they had to decide who was going to approach Oberon. Wren had made the connection, but she wasn't a salesperson. Kara was so new that it made more sense to go with Alice or Thessaly, who had experience working with larger accounts. And while Thessaly could sell big wines to big corporate restaurants if she had to, Alice might enjoy the challenge more. And lately, she was just hungrier.

"I want Passerine to have that account," Thessaly said. She paused delicately. "I do wonder how her general look will go over at a steak chain."

She had a point. The other day Alice had stopped in to pick up samples wearing tall flat suede boots and a peculiarly shaped linen dress with points in odd places, like a flattened star.

"I'll remind Alice he's kind of a straight-dealing guy," Wren said.

Later, Wren realized she'd been hoping for more of a fight on this. It worried her how easily Thessaly gave up control, or yielded on a decision, but maybe they'd always been different that way. Wren couldn't let anything go.

Alice took down Martin's info and promised to follow up. For a week or two, they heard nothing significant. Every time they asked, Alice mentioned a new email exchange, another possible meeting, but nothing firm. And so when Wren got a call from the Oberon corporate number one afternoon, she wondered why Martin was calling her instead of Alice.

"Just touching base," he said, after a few niceties. Then he paused. "Look, this is a little delicate. I didn't realize when we met who was on your staff. I'm not one to tell you how to run your business, obviously, but I respect you, and I didn't want to just disappear without telling you why we might not be able to work together."

Wren stared at her reflection in her laptop screen, her mind racing. "My staff? I'm sorry, Martin, I don't have the slightest idea what you're talking about. If there's something I can fix, I absolutely will."

"I've met your sales rep before," he said. "When I worked for a restaurant group in Chicago. All I can say is that Oberon isn't one of those hole-in-the-wall places that bend the rules. We do it by the book. No free menus with your wines already printed on them, no reps offering to buy a few hundred bucks of nothing from the restaurant if we'll just place a bigger order." He lowered his voice. "I'd lose my job."

"Did Alice offer you something like that?" said Wren. A bribe, she meant. That's what he was describing.

"Not this time," he conceded. "But maybe because I'm not letting the conversation get that far. I like you, but I'm just not . . . comfortable."

Ten minutes after hanging up, Wren texted Alice to come to the office for a meeting as soon as possible. She didn't text Thessaly. She told herself it was because Alice would be more forthcoming with Wren. After all, they were friends. But part of her knew that she just wasn't ready to hear what Thessaly would have to say: She had never liked Alice to begin with. And maybe she'd been right.

Alice arrived in her usual cyclonic fashion, layers of fabric and flyaway platinum hair, but the second Wren asked her about Martin, her mouth and eyes went still. "Look," she said. "I should have told you we didn't get along. I know from past experience he's kind of stuffy. But I honestly thought I could win him over. Especially after everything I've learned from you. And Thessaly."

"Did you offer him anything under the table?"

Alice shrugged. "I'm sure he told you that I didn't do a thing outside the lines. He said that, right? When I realized who it was, I knew he was super straight. In Chicago that kind of thing was no big deal. Frankly, this is why I wanted to work for you. Both of you." She leaned forward, her hands clasped over her knees.

Wren shifted in her chair and nodded, buying time. Maybe it was a misunderstanding. Maybe Alice had changed. Alice had made them so much money. She'd gotten them into as many restaurants as Thessaly. More. Wren didn't care that the money Alice made them often came from less prestigious and more commercial wines. Alice was security. Alice was a freezer with nothing but ice cream and salmon in it, a kitchen without a bean to be found.

"Look," Wren began, still searching for clarity. Then she glanced up at Alice and stopped. Why, at that precise moment, did Alice look so different? Suddenly this woman she had found so captivating, so confident and savvy, was nothing but a flat watchful gaze and bleached hair and a ridiculous outfit. Alice's black-plum eyes looked bottomless, pupils eerily undetectable.

Wren had seen this kind of person before, the kind who was entirely sincere and entirely untrustworthy. She'd grown up with one.

"Alice," she said quietly, "what am I going to find if I start following up with your accounts?" The depth of her anger, the near-violence of it, made her take a breath. She didn't like being angry; if she got angry, she would become distracted and inefficient and sloppy—at least she assumed she would. She'd never let it happen.

"For god's sake," Alice said. "In Chicago, I did what I had to do to sweeten the deal. Can we stop acting like I'm dumping nuclear waste into the water supply instead of doing exactly what you want me to?"

Wren got up and went into the kitchen, where she poured a glass of water and gulped it to calm herself. Her hands were shaking. When she'd taken a few deep breaths, she went back to the other room, where Alice was sitting, relaxed now, gazing out the window.

"You should go," Wren said.

"Okay," Alice said, shouldering her purse. "We can talk about this tomorrow."

"No," Wren said. "I'm terminating your employment."

Alice's face was a perfect mask of shock. "Come on," she said. "How will you get along without me?"

"Same as we always did," Wren said. She stood by the front door and watched Alice make her way slowly toward the exit, giving Wren time to recant. When Wren did nothing, Alice laughed to herself and shook her head.

Wren watched Alice stalk to her car and open the trunk. She took out several boxes of Passerine samples and dropped them with an unceremonious clunk in the middle of the street. When the last one began to tip over onto its side, Alice just stood there, arms crossed, and watched the box fall, two bottles spilling out onto the asphalt and rolling toward the curb. Then she looked at Wren, shrugged, and got into her car.

Wren didn't bother waiting until Alice's car was gone to walk out to the street. She was already finished with her. She righted the box and picked up the bottles that had rolled away and cracked. She opened the boxes and started looking through the labels. First, she'd note exactly what Alice had been carrying around. Then she'd compare it to what Alice *said* she had been carrying around, and start figuring out what she had cost them.

· CHAPTER 18 ·

Thessaly should have been consumed by the news that Wren had fired Alice without even speaking to her. She should have been delighted, honestly, that her personal cross to bear was gone, that her best friend would be her best friend again. But her sister called that same morning at eight-thirty central time, which meant six-thirty West Coast time. "Don't freak out," Ari said.

Thessaly's heart began to pound.

"I'm at the hospital with Mom and Dad, everything's fine, nobody's dying." There was rustling. "Mom," Ari said, "it's Thessaly. I know. I *know*. I'll tell her."

Thessaly couldn't breathe. An aneurysm. A heart attack. A farming accident.

"Sorry," Ari said. "He just fucked up his knee. But he's in surgery. He'll live."

Thessaly sat down and took a deep breath.

"Should I come home?" Thessaly asked. She took a seat on her front steps. There were cars parked on both sides of her tree-lined street, houses with hippie yard art. Suddenly it all felt very temporary to her.

229

"Maybe," Ari said. "Can you imagine Dad trying to direct the rest of the growing season from a wheelchair? I can help some, but maybe you can swing by?"

"I'll check with Wren," Thessaly said. "But you know her. She's got it all under control. Always."

"I can't tell if you're being sarcastic."

"I'm not."

Ari's voice was muffled for a moment before she came back. "Try, okay? Mom won't ask, but I'm needier than Mom."

The next day Wren sat cross-legged on the bed while Thessaly packed. "I can go with you," she said. "I'd be happy to." But she looked so distracted that Thessaly knew the offer had demonstrated superhuman will. Alice was out. Thessaly was out. It was down to her and Kara.

"I know," Thessaly said. She stopped folding a pair of jeans to make sure Wren knew she meant it. "But you need to be here."

"Okay," Wren said. "What about Italy? We're already cutting it close with their harvest and our conference in Chicago."

"Right," said Thessaly. "Shit."

They'd been invited to an industry conference that August to give a presentation on "women in wine" and sit on a panel with other importers. It was a big deal: a debut of sorts, and a clear indicator that someone outside of Madison thought they were doing something in the wine world.

"They're both a month away," Thessaly said. "Dad won't need me that long."

"Let it take the time it takes. We'll figure out everything else."

"Thanks," Thessaly said. "I'm sorry."

"You have nothing to apologize for," said Wren. "But *I* am sorry about Alice. You were—"

"It's okay." Thessaly didn't say the truth, which was that at the moment she truly did not care about Alice or anything related to her business. "We can talk about her later." Or never. She zipped up her suitcase and looked around to see what she was missing.

"Whenever you want," Wren said. She stood up. "He's going to recover and be fine," she said. Because of course this was Thessaly's great fear, the reason she was so distressed about a painful but not crippling injury. It was the shock of vulnerability. "And whatever you need, we can figure out together. Now come hug me. Don't skimp; it has to last you a while."

This was as direct and loving as Thessaly had ever seen Wren be, and it broke through all of Thessaly's nervous energy. She stopped darting around and let Wren put her arms around her, her own hands flat against her friend's warm, strong spine. She stood there for a moment, just breathing deeply, until she was ready to leave.

When Thessaly arrived home, Sonoma seemed grander. The trees taller, the skies bigger, the views more commanding. Eduardo, her father's right hand, looked suddenly older, as if he'd leapt ahead a decade. "Did your hair turn white just this week?" she asked after hugging hello. "You know this land as well as he does."

"Sure, but we also need the big mind back out there."

"You're the big mind," Thessaly said. "But I can be another pair of legs, at least."

They spent their days moving from field to field while she tried to get her bearings and take in all of Eduardo's directives. At the house, her mother produced cauldrons of summer minestrone and ratatouille, consumed with the idea she could heal David with vegetables, plus secondary vats of shredded chicken or pork braised in milk to give everyone enough protein to avoid collapse.

231

David roosted on the front porch, his leg propped up on an otto-man, surrounded by papers and constantly on his laptop, feeding in information about the crops and their progress. He had tried going out in the tractor with Eduardo, but the jolting was too painful and the possibility of reinjury too likely.

"Be me," he'd ordered her. "Me with a knee." And so Thessaly tried, by texting back and forth with Eduardo and driving up and down the hills to examine the vines and report back to them both with photos and info. Only half of what they said made sense to her.

Coming back to the front porch at the end of the day, she couldn't help but notice her father was strangely cowed, the look in his eyes almost frightened. He'd spent so much of his life with-out a major injury that it must have been astonishing to realize he was not invincible. It certainly was to her.

Eduardo's white hair, her father's voice suddenly soft and questioning—she had the feeling that she had been away for lon-ger than she'd expected, that time had zoomed forward in her absence. What were they going to do when her father died or Edu-ardo retired? Their land was the child their family would tend perpetually, and now, suddenly, the thing she might find herself stuck with. She didn't want to farm. She had spent years telling herself she was gathering knowledge, but suddenly she realized she could easily go another ten years, twenty years, without ever taking the leap. If she got stuck running the farm, how would she ever find the time to do anything else?

The one thing that eased her worries was the idea that if she did have to come back here, she could make wine with her fami-ly's fruit. Maybe by now, after all this time and her so clearly doing her filial duty, her father might think she'd learned enough.

Maybe she wouldn't have to go take a low-level job with a wine-maker but could build it here? That is, if her father would ever stop bossing her around.

She drank her iced tea with her father, and when he said things like "when you come back" she just nodded, not just because he seemed old and scared, but because maybe he was right.

•

It was high summer in Madison, the month of tomatoes and pink wine and endless ears of corn. Now would have been the time to make that corn risotto Wren and Martin had eaten at the wine dinner, and she almost picked up her phone to tell him so. But not quite.

Everything felt too quiet. Her nights loomed, wide-open and underpopulated, and she'd begun cooking to fill them. Her days were busy but hermetic, just her alone in a room in a frenzy to keep up. She hadn't realized how unmoored she would feel without Thessaly around. It occurred to her that she wasn't even sure of the last time they'd hung out together outside of work, and while at the time she'd felt relieved to be busy with Alice, to have a little social power, she now regretted it. She hadn't even thought to send something to Thessaly's family, and yet her family had welcomed Wren to their home so many times. Wren adored the Sonoma house; it was stocked with blankets and copper pans and pasta and goat-milk soap, all safety and abundance, like a spa that wouldn't kick you out.

She ordered a gift basket a solid week after David's injury, hoping no one would notice how late it was. She hoped Thessaly had not noticed a lot of things this spring. But she had caught her friend gazing at her sternly more than once, as if realizing for the first time that Wren was shallow, or venal, or simply not that worthy. For the first time in years, Wren felt Thessaly's presence not as comfort or partnership but as an observer, a judge, someone who looked at her and no longer saw Wren's best self, but the awkward pathetic girl who wasn't welcome at the sales dinners, the self Wren had spent years trying to bury.

Next Wren lasered in on Kara, acknowledging how much she had taken her for granted. Kara was competent and reliable. She didn't wave her numbers around, but she maintained her relationships well and kept selling, quarter after quarter.

Good god, what if she quit too? What if she got tired of being in this pod with only her grim boss Wren, no one fun or artsy to hang out with? A few days after Alice had left for parts unknown and Thessaly for Sonoma, Kara had turned up in a bright graphic print dress and dangling earrings—an effective job interview look. Wren eyed her suspiciously and then took Kara to lunch, where she plied her subtly about goals, feeling guilty that she'd let Thessaly worry about Kara while she lavished attention on Alice because Alice had ingratiated herself and apparently Wren fell for it.

Wren was no better than Gavin, expecting her staff to amuse her and flatter her, at work and outside too, and overlooking the ones who did not.

She wanted to tell this to Thessaly, the only one who'd understand why this Gavin realization felt like such a wake-up call. But on the phone the next day, Thessaly was distracted, clipped. Wren found herself asking inane questions just to keep her on the line. What was the weather like? How was Ari's tasting room going? Did Wren's gift basket arrive?

"Very nice," Thessaly said. "Dad said you must think he's an invalid to give him that blanket, which is his way of being touched."

"I did include a note to drape it over his broken matchstick legs," Wren said.

Thessaly laughed, but already she seemed far away again.

"Do you need to stay longer?" Wren asked. Perhaps if she offered the thing she feared, Thessaly would sense her generosity and refuse. Thessaly had understood more elaborate unstated bargains than that.

"I'm not sure," Thessaly said. "I keep forgetting what day it is. I had sort of a breakthrough." She told Wren a lengthy, incomprehensible story about nitrogen, which concluded with Thessaly sounding mystified that she'd solved the issue herself. "Wild, huh?"

"No," Wren said. "It makes a lot of sense."

•

Thessaly woke up every day in California equally certain that she must stay and that she must go home. But after a week, the household had settled down, and the conviction that she was needed faded. So, to Wren's evident relief and surprise, Thessaly flew back to Madison in plenty of time for her Italy trip and the conference, and Wren got to devote two weeks to practicing their presentation. They'd decided to tell the story of their company chronologically, pulling out the highlights of what they'd learned, what was notable about this moment and their business.

"Are we talking to people who find it novel that women can run an importing company?" Thessaly asked one afternoon. "Or to women who don't think they can do it too?"

Wren was standing in front of her, practicing their talking points. "Both, I think," she said.

By now Thessaly had checked in with all of Alice's accounts. There were some venues where a store owner or sommelier put in an order and then paused—a split second of uncertainty that suggested to Thessaly they'd been getting something extra from Alice and were waiting to see if she'd offer the same. Of course, she didn't. Time would tell whether this would end the relationship.

"We have to give Kara a bonus," Thessaly told Wren. "A good one too; no chintzy gift cards." Wren hesitated, just for a moment, but Thessaly crossed her arms and looked hard at her until she said, "Yeah, okay." Usually Thessaly would have been pleased at this small victory over how to spend their money, but so much was still unresolved between them that Thessaly couldn't even feel a sense of accomplishment.

Wren had gone after Martin with a full-court press and landed them a six-month tryout throughout the state. She delivered this impressive news without the slightest hint of self-congratulation.

For once they were grateful there was always so much work to be done. That made it easy to bury their heads in it and ignore the fact that their relationship was starting to feel like a struggling marriage. But what did you do when your friendship faltered? You didn't go to friend counseling. And Thessaly was tired of being the one who tried. She was tired of being the one who'd been ignored in favor of that charlatan Alice, of all goddamn people. She'd thought she was over it, but the more she had to have her face rubbed in it, at every account where she had to suss out Alice's dealings and save yet another relationship, the more pissed off she became. Sometimes when she went back to the office and heard Wren at her computer, she picked up the samples and left without saying anything.

The vision they'd once shared for Passerine was starting to diverge. Some of Thessaly's beloved but admittedly esoteric wines now seemed to personally offend Wren. They were too niche, too snobby, too impractical. "They sit in my warehouse, they take up space in my containers," Wren said. Thessaly tried to let this insult go, but how many times were they going to have the same argument? She didn't know how to resolve it.

Thessaly had been looking forward to Italy, and was telling herself not to be so suspicious of Wren's objectives for the trip. Clearly she hoped that Thessaly would minimize their involvement with small producers and pick up a batch of big, cheap ones. Which Thessaly would not do. She refused to sever her connections to producers who were doing something gorgeous and risky, or to artists like Valentina, one of their Le Marche producers, who'd designed her family's racy, gorgeous labels. Wren was right if you looked only at the numbers, but what about their reputation for taste? What about Thessaly's desire to show up and do this work at all?

"Say what you want about Lionel, but he knew how to grow a business. He knew he couldn't store wine in his garage forever," Wren said one afternoon. They'd left her house after what Thessaly prayed was their last practice session of their talk— when would Wren realize it was just a fucking talk, an event to fill the annual space in the schedule, and not a Nobel Peace Prize? Suddenly Wren's relentless drive to make the most of every opportunity felt a little provincial to her. Could she not fake the slightest hint of sangfroid? Had Thessaly taught her nothing?

This may have been why Thessaly responded the way she did when Wren found a way to bring up her other favorite subject. Again.

"Oh my god, how many times do we discuss the stupid warehouse?" Thessaly said. "It's not the bright lights of Manhattan. It's the north side of Madison."

"I'm just making a point," Wren said.

"Well, so am I. Go get a job with Hank if you want to work for a big company and be all suburban."

"Hank's pretty damn successful," Wren said.

"So are we! It's a lot easier to get rich selling Mega Purple. Someone *makes* our wines, practically by hand. Not us, but someone."

"See, that's another thing," Wren said. "These digs about how we don't make anything. I'm sick of feeling like you look down on this business and what we do. If you want to make wine, go do it already. Why'd you persuade me to do this if it was so soul-crushing?"

"Because I had to get the fuck out of there," Thessaly exclaimed. "It could have been anything, I chose this, you agreed, okay?"

Wren stopped walking.

"What?" Thessaly said.

"I just want to get this straight. This whole thing that's taken so much of our time and our resources and risked everything we built up, this thing you kept saying for years you wanted to do even when I gave you the chance to opt out, this could have been anything at all. It could have been, I don't know—"

"Beekeeping," Thessaly said. She'd had it. She'd had it with how Wren had to have everything done her way, for the reasons she wanted them done, with the people she wanted to do it with. "That was my first choice, but then the price of bees just skyrocketed so I went with you."

238

Wren looked stunned. Even Thessaly had to admit that it came out with a lot more scorn than she'd intended.

"Is this about the business, or is it about me?" she said finally, and Thessaly shrugged. She didn't know anymore. But she hadn't realized how Wren's face would look if she said even a little of what she'd been feeling.

So she lied. "It's just the business," she said. "Alice." She made a gesture that conveyed little except fatigue.

Wren said nothing for a beat. Thessaly felt, and could tell Wren did too, that they were brushing up against something they didn't want to touch. She felt it when they both decided not to pursue it too, because that was how well they knew each other.

"Go to Italy," Wren said, as if this had been in question. "Change of scenery. Go enjoy salty goat wine, or whatever. Just come home ready for that conference."

· CHAPTER 19 ·

The problem arose in Le Marche.

First Thessaly arrived in Florence and charged through two and three visits a day, wishing she hadn't scheduled a Wren-paced trip. By the time she saw Valentina in Le Marche, she was so burned out she almost didn't hear Valentina say they'd be bottling a few days later.

"The truck travels around from place to place, parks right there." She gestured toward the driveway. "They bottle it all up, pack it all in cases, and we're done."

To Valentina it was just a cheap, reliable way to bottle wine on-site. That was all it should have been to Thessaly too, because this had nothing to do with importing. She had never considered in depth what these portable bottling businesses did: they made it possible for small growers without much infrastructure to package wine. The people her father grew for would never use them; they owned or rented their own facilities. But the little guys, the start-up producers scraping together a half ton of fruit and a bunch of used barrels . . . some of those winemakers relied on these machines.

People like her, she couldn't help but think. If she ever made wine. Which she didn't.

And yet she wanted to see it in action anyway. Possibly even needed to see it. The problem was that it was coming the same day Thessaly was supposed to leave Florence for Chicago. The bigger problem was that she wanted to stay and observe a process that had nothing to do with their business, instead of going to the conference, which had everything to do with their business, and that she and Wren were already at the edge of a cliff.

Maybe she could do both. She found another flight that left late the same day as the bottling and got her into Chicago the morning of their panel, instead of the day before. Afraid to call, she shot Wren a text making the case that this would be easier for jet lag—she'd jump straight in, no time for her exhaustion to register.

Her phone rang immediately. "That's ridiculous," Wren said. "You can see those trucks here too, you know."

"But then I have to take more time off work and go do it," Thessaly said, in a burst of inspiration. It was technically true, but she couldn't tell Wren that she cared more about this than anything they would say at a convention center. "You know there's never time. This is all arranged and right here."

"The timing could be a lot better." Wren paused, waiting for her to speak. When Thessaly said nothing, she added, "But I guess we can make it work."

"Thank you," Thessaly said, relieved. "Thanks, Sparrow."

"I'll see you in Chicago," Wren said, and then she hung up.

•

That evening Wren practiced the talk again. She asked Kara to deliver Thessaly's part, in case she wasn't back in time. Kara read the pages, frowning, and then said, "Why don't you practice giving the whole thing?"

"But you'd nail it," Wren said.

Kara shrugged. "So will you." She crossed her legs beneath her and pushed her glasses to the top of her head.

Wren still hoped Thessaly would make it, but Kara was right—she could do the presentation alone, if she had to. Every time Thessaly had faltered, or let her down, she'd been forced to rise to the occasion—and it had worked out. Look at the wine dinner at which she'd met Martin: Where would Passerine be if he hadn't opened her eyes to Alice? She was endlessly grateful to him, once she stopped being mortified.

She'd gone to his office to give him a hybrid thank-you and apology in person, intending to tell him Thessaly would be his contact in the future, but then, looking at his steady blue eyes, she decided to handle this account herself. If he wondered why, he didn't let on.

"I wouldn't want anyone to keep something like that from me," he said. "I'm a rule-follower. It's one of the most boring things about me."

Maybe that was why Wren, who felt a lustful, blooming sensation in her chest at the recognition of a fellow rule-follower, had since found herself putting on lipstick to email him.

"Try it again," Kara said. "Just you."

Wren cleared her throat and began again.

•

On the day of the bottling, Thessaly drove to the winery with a box of fancy chocolates for Valentina. She'd expected to settle in at a table in an arbor until the truck arrived, but the place was bustling with activity: people attaching hoses to the massive stainless-steel and earthenware vats, stacking flexible woven baskets in the driveway for hauling empty bottles.

"We provide the bottles, labels, corks, screw tops," Valentina said, showing her around. "Everything but the machine."

The machine in question was a curious mix of modern industrial and faintly medieval. A long, open-sided truck came trundling up the gravel and began unfolding like one of those toys that turns from a robot to an airplane. They raised the sides to create a shaded platform and revealed a production line as long as the flatbed. Baskets of empty wine bottles went to one end of the truck and pallets awaiting the filled bottles were on the other; people placed empty bottles onto the conveyor belt and at the other end people plucked off the full ones and placed them into cases.

Thessaly watched the bottles jostle along the conveyor belt. She watched the liquid rise to the precise same spot in each bottle and the corks or metal screw caps plunge down and seal them up. She watched people move in a soothing rhythm, back and forth, watched the pallets fill and be carted away.

She was first dimly, and then acutely, aware of time moving forward, the hour of her departure edging closer and closer. She was supposed to be here for only a taste of this, not the whole thing. She had to go. This was the flight she could not miss. She'd promised.

Valentina hung back and let the bottlers do their work, but Thessaly found herself looking over at her more and more, how Valentina watched over everything, hands on her hips, her long dark hair in a ponytail. Valentina had once been a mere in-law to the winemakers, but now she was a vital part of turning this mass of glass and metal and juice into bottles, cases, and pallets of wine. Into product and livelihood. What did Thessaly do? She transported things other people made.

Only now did Thessaly realize how unglued she had felt ever since she'd come back from Sonoma. Or, to be honest, since well before then. She allowed herself to imagine staying here, finding some way to help. She allowed herself to acknowledge—just to herself—how little she wanted to leave this for Chicago. For Madison. She stood there in the hot sun and allowed herself to imagine a phone call in which she would blow up her own life. This wasn't just missing an event; it would be admitting to Wren that the tensions between them were much bigger than they had allowed themselves to say.

But she couldn't get herself to leave. Not even knowing what it meant.

Agitated, she left the shade where she'd been filming the process on her phone and approached Valentina. "What can I do?" she asked, gesturing toward the truck.

"Ready to jump in?" Valentina said, smiling. "I figured you couldn't resist. You can take these to him." She indicated several baskets full of empty bottles waiting to be filled on the conveyor belt and a man standing at the loading end of the truck.

"Grazie," Thessaly said, and picked up the first basket.

Wren could give the presentation. She was a clear and confident speaker now. Wren claimed a conversation was always more compelling than a monologue, but Thessaly wasn't so sure.

She knew there was no reason for her to remain here, except that she just . . . wanted to be here. To be here and do this. To be in a place growing the way she knew how to grow and learning to make something of it.

When was the last time she'd felt this pure kind of desire?

Nick. That was the last time. It had been so long, and she barely thought about him these days beyond an occasional fragment, but now Thessaly let herself flood with memories. For a long time she'd focused on nothing but the aftermath of their split, and how ashamed and embarrassed she was about it, but now she saw it differently. The split wasn't what mattered about that relationship. She'd missed the whole point. She should've been thinking about how it felt to experience that kind of pull toward someone or something. Had she respected the immensity of that desire back when it was happening, she might never have ruined it.

She didn't look at her watch; she didn't look at her phone. She barely let herself see the movement of the sun. She hauled baskets, got into and out of the way, snapped photos of the bottles produced by magic, until, finally, the truck flipped up its side panels and the people hopped up into the flatbed, and the whole thing rumbled off, down the side of the mountain. Thessaly waited till it was gone, said goodbye to Valentina, and headed slowly to her car.

Her flight was long gone. She'd checked out of her Airbnb. For the moment, she was totally unmoored. The only thing to do was find a hotel in Florence and rebook her flight.

Now it was starting to sink in. She wished she hadn't eaten; her body felt unsettled and uneasy, ready to reject everything.

She found a parking spot in the village and called Wren.

"You're supposed to be on the plane!" Wren said when she picked up. "Is it delayed?"

"Well, I'm delayed," Thessaly said. "I won't be back in time. I'm sorry." Her voice sounded hollow and false.

"*How* were you delayed?" Wren said.

"I just stayed too long," Thessaly said. "I knew what I was doing, but I wanted to watch. And it really is kind of amaz—"

"Stop," Wren said. "I don't care."

"I know," Thessaly said, but her heart began to pound. Now that it was happening, she was terrified. "I'm sorry. I know it's my fault, but I'll be on the next flight out of Florence and I can meet you in Chicago. You can tell me how it went."

"I'll do the talk alone," Wren said. "But I'm heading back to Madison the next morning. You can rent a car or grab a bus or whatever."

"Okay," Thessaly said. "I'll text when I know my flight. If I get there before you go, I'll come find you."

"You're not listening," Wren said. "You could walk in the room while I'm still *giving* the talk, and I would tell you to find another way home."

Thessaly nodded like a simpleton, as if Wren could see her, but nothing came out when she tried to speak. She'd done it, she thought miserably. Something caught in the back of her throat like a hook and tugged. How in the world had she convinced herself that Wren would ever forgive her? She must be a better saleswoman than she'd realized.

· CHAPTER 20 ·

Wren played the part all through her talk, the Q and A, and the subsequent gladhanding—professional, relaxed, solid. She ran into several of her old colleagues and greeted everyone with autopilot smoothness: a cheek press with Greg, who finally seemed grown-up and was apparently doing quite well as director, though there had been near-total turnover since they'd left. She gave Legs a tight hug. In his tattered leather he looked more dissolute than ever, yet somehow never any older. "Great talk," he said. "I told a bunch of people I knew you when. Where's your other half?"

"She's in Italy," Wren said. Legs gazed at her, waiting for more, but Wren smiled and changed the subject by asking how Lionel was.

Legs frowned. "Not great," he said. "No one knows what the issue is, maybe just age. Maybe cancer. You know Lionel: He won't admit he's mortal till he's dead. I'd keep an eye on the trades."

She could not have guessed how this news would feel: Wren had thought she'd burned away any trace of compassion for or emotional connection to Lionel, but tears sprang to her eyes at the idea of this man being diminished to nothing. They had all worked desperately to please him, to satisfy his sheer want, of everything—how could that be leaving the world? Even if she had kind of hated him sometimes too. Legs gave her one last hug and then everyone moved on to the next event.

In an instant, the adrenaline that had kept her going receded. She returned to her hotel room and slept for two hours.

Two days after the conference, Wren was back in her office and watching the door, knowing Thessaly must be home and on her way over. They were going to have to make some choices. But Wren didn't feel as scared as she once did. She wasn't agitated anymore. She felt cold and clear. She put on a crisp work dress and eyeliner and fine gold hoops.

Around nine-thirty she heard Thessaly's voice out on the front porch, pausing to talk to Kara. Then she listened to them say goodbye as Kara left and the front door slammed.

Thessaly poked her head into Wren's office. "How was it?"

At the sight of her face, Wren's heart lurched, ruining her sense of calm.

"It was great. Some sales questions, but with Kara there it was fine." She was daring Thessaly to try, just try, to take the bait and say all was well.

"Thank you for doing it," Thessaly said, looking shamefaced. "I'm sorry I left you to do it alone."

"I was fine alone," Wren said.

"I know," Thessaly said. "But we were supposed to do it together and I bailed."

Wren nodded.

"You look good," Thessaly said. "Meeting today?"

"It's already done."

Thessaly sat down in the other office chair. "What was the meeting?"

She looked young, Wren thought. Younger than usual. Wren felt much older.

"I signed the lease on the warehouse and the office space we looked at. Last office left in the building and I got a great deal."

Thessaly had the nerve to look astonished. "You did what?" she said. "You just went ahead and did that?"

Wren was about to list all the arguments she'd said before, but all she said was, "Yes. I did."

Thessaly took a deep breath. "I know you think I deserved this. But I changed one event without your input. One talk. You just blew up our business model. That's bullshit and you know it."

"We can order more, sell more. It's safer this way."

Thessaly gave her a look full of coldness. "Stop acting like it's about safety. You're just getting back at me."

"You showed me what you want!" Wren exclaimed. "You've been showing me for *months*. And if you think this isn't all about safety for me, then I don't know who the hell you've been hanging out with. It's easy for you—you've never felt at risk of anything real in your life. This was literally a whim for you. This is my whole *life*."

Thessaly was pale, two spots of color staining her cheeks. Wren took a breath and lowered her voice. She looked at Thessaly's shining dark eyes and her shaggy hair, her perpetual half smile, which, for once in her life, was now absent.

"I don't know what you want me to say," Thessaly said finally. "I really did want to do this with you. It wasn't a lie."

"But you don't want to do it anymore," Wren said.

"I can't," Thessaly said. "I've wanted to stay in the company because of our friendship, but now I think we're ruining that too."

"Stop," Wren said abruptly. Everything she'd felt before this moment—her clarity of purpose, her courage to confront, come what may—all of it had left her. "Don't talk like we're enemies."

"Okay," Thessaly said. Then they sat there, saying nothing, for as long as they could stand to.

PART 4

the one thing that teaches you everything else

· CHAPTER 21 ·

How long could a person hold on to her anger? For months, Wren learned that fall after Thessaly left, as she hired a salesperson to replace Thessaly, ensured Kara was content, and trained her new admin person to start in October. By the holidays, she was operating a new version of her business. Sometimes she stewed, allowing herself to believe Thessaly was at fault, but other times she admitted to herself that she'd caused it to happen too. It never made her feel much better.

That winter it became imperative that Wren paint her former home office. She needed a guest room. Or a home gym. She'd figure it out later. Almost experimentally, she took down a picture frame to see if the paint was discolored behind it. Then she took the rest down too. Pretty soon she had removed the curtain rod and shoved all of the furniture to the center of the office and did the same to the living room too.

This was how she knew she was out of sorts: before she'd even registered the need to buy brushes or drop cloths or even paint, she'd already torn the place apart.

After she got home from the paint store, she called and asked Hank for a meeting. She wasn't sure what she wanted from him, except to figure out if she had options, any options at all. Maybe she just needed a good job, not all this responsibility: the career version of a post-divorce bachelor pad, not a long-term purchase, just something with a pool.

"I can keep doing what I'm doing," she said to Hank in his office. "I mean, it's working. Or liquidate, go anywhere I want. I suppose I'm coming to you as a colleague more than competition."

Hank regarded Wren cannily. "I'm always the competition," he said. "Say, for instance, when you poached Alice from me. I'd already fired her, but I let you find out on your own why you might regret it."

Wren felt a junior-high kind of shame. Hank gave her a moment to experience this fully. "If you quit," he said, "do it smart. Not because you panicked."

"I'm not *panicking*," Wren said, suddenly annoyed. "I think we're all entitled to a little light flailing now and then."

Hank laughed. "Come on, now. You're really going to break your lease, sell off your inventory, notify your producers, fire your staff?"

Hearing it, she knew she would never allow such a thing to happen.

"Didn't think so," Hank said, and poured her a glass of wine.

After that she went home, to a house that was sparkling clean, so there was nothing to keep her busy. She was starting to get hungry. It was a little late for business, but she called Martin anyway. She'd been chalking up each little bit of information about him in a mental notebook, which she considered now: He'd grown up in Philadelphia, the son of a steamfitter and a high school math teacher. On his days off he sometimes walked from one end of the city's isthmus to the other to explore the neighborhoods he couldn't examine as closely while driving. He had no children, but an ex-wife who'd moved to Portland and left him with an ancient Saint Bernard mix he pretended not to love, except that last week Wren had seen the chef at Oberon hand Martin a doggie bag that turned out to be the steak scraps he took home for the dog each Friday as a treat.

"I probably interrupted your dinner," she said, once he'd picked up. In the background she heard voices talking and dinnerware clinking.

"Nah, I'm at the restaurant," he said. "Just heading out. I know I owe you an email—"

"Actually, I'm not calling about work," she said. Her fingers clasped the edge of the kitchen table. "Remember how bad you are at making risotto? I'm pretty good at it."

There was a pause. "I always figured you had to be," he said.

The key with risotto was the right kind of rice and plenty of stirring to release the starch and make it creamy. "A lot of people fake it with heavy cream," she told Martin, "but an Italian will say the only acceptable thing is some butter at the end."

They were in her kitchen, standing in front of the stove. Wren had set out all the ingredients on the counter before them. Martin had shown up still dressed for work, his shirtsleeves rolled up, carrying a bottle of white Burgundy, and they'd poured two glasses and then paused, gazing at the ingredients. An onion, chicken broth, butter. A lemon. A dish of rice.

"This is a nice place," he said, looking around. "Extremely clean."

She was thinking he was one of those men who got better-looking the longer you knew him. She was also thinking that he never seemed uneasy, never seemed to second-guess himself, and she wanted it to rub off on her. "I've been on a bit of a tear," she said.

"I'm flattered," he said. "Unless you did it for someone else." He was looking rather searchingly at her. The light picked up the platinum in his lashes and the hair on his forearms, the heavy silver watch on one wrist.

She did want to make risotto sometime, maybe even tonight. But not right now.

She took a step closer to him, close enough to feel the invisible wave of warmth from his skin, the faint scent of lime from his neck. Martin looked surprised, but only for a moment. So she took another step. He reached up and touched her, watching her face as he laid one fingertip with shivering lightness behind the hollow of her jaw, and she had to stop herself from making a sound in her throat, embarrassed that it took so little. She hadn't felt like this maybe ever; she didn't know what to do with it.

She kissed him to buy time, just to figure it out, and instantly forgot what she'd been figuring out. He tasted like the first sip of wine. How long did they have to stand here kissing in this bright kitchen, how long did she have to have her hands on his shirt instead of his skin? She should have kissed him as soon as he entered the house. She wanted to take him straight into her bedroom and quit wasting time. She hadn't realized what this would be like.

His hands were at her waist now, just under her sweater. "I'm sorry," she lied, yanking her sweater up and over her head the instant he touched her bare skin. She dropped the sweater on her sparkling clean floor. "I'm not usually like this."

He looked slightly stunned, but a second later both of his hands were back on her bare skin again, cupped around her waist, and he glanced down as if he weren't entirely in charge of them. "Is this—"

"Definitely," she told him. "Completely." She stopped unbuttoning his shirt. "Is it for you?"

He looked at her as if he would have gone through a wall if one were between them. "Definitely," he said, "Jesus, completely," and picked her up to wrap her legs around his waist. He took a few steps as if to whisk her off somewhere, but then he had to take his mouth off hers and look up to get his bearings. "I don't know where I'm taking you," he said. She started to laugh. "This isn't even my house."

· CHAPTER 22 ·

Thessaly had been back in Sonoma for most of the season before she realized she might have overcorrected. Her first morning back, her father woke her at five, handed her a cup of coffee, and said to be out front in five minutes. She was still on central time, so her body felt as if he had woken her at three a.m., but there was no point in arguing. He took her up to a tiny parcel, neatly roped off. Its soil was rich and dark and lined with rows of plants that would one day be heavy with fruit but for now just looked like witches' hands, empty sticks.

"None of the employees will touch this land without specific directions from you," he said. "There you go." Then he headed back down the hill.

The hill was steep enough that much of the work had to be done by hand, since a vehicle might tip backward. It made you wonder why anyone would plant here at all. But Thessaly, gazing up at the neat rows of waiting vines, knew this impossible square of land was a gift. The vines loved this harsh landscape the same way they loved being barely watered by rain and routinely shorn of most of their fruit—grape vines loved the right kinds of stressors. That was what made them great.

•

A few months later, Thessaly went out to dinner with her family. By now it was August and she'd been in Sonoma for eight months, several of which she'd spent babying her plot of land. Next to Ari with her sleek pageboy and crisp white pants, Eleanor's dancer's bun and brushed silver earrings, Thessaly and her father looked like farmhands being treated to a nice dinner by their bosses. She tried to hide her scraped, torn hands from the waiter.

Thessaly had spent months trying to persuade their father to expand into winemaking. Now that she was in a position to make the transition for real, it felt more intimidating than ever. Nevertheless, she thought maybe she could take the next steps if she did it with her family.

"We have the land, we have the grapes," Thessaly said now. "I'm pretty sure we can get one of those bottling trucks up the side of the mountain."

"You have to be more than pretty sure," Eleanor said. Her mother seemed to be waiting for something else from her, but what? Was there some secret code to unlock her father?

"Well, obviously I'd confirm before I rented one. Dad, what do you think?"

"I'm tired of being asked questions I've already answered," her father said, sawing at his pork chop. "I gave you a piece of land. I gave you the chance to earn something. So earn it."

In the morning, Thessaly went downstairs at dawn. Her mother was already up. "Morning," she said, pouring her a cup. "How's the half acre?"

"Fine," Thessaly said. She couldn't keep the petulance out of her voice. So childish, she thought, listening to herself.

"And Wren?" Eleanor asked. "When's she coming to visit?"

Thessaly paused. "She's super busy." She hadn't wanted to tell her family that she and Wren weren't even speaking. She suspected they loved Wren more than her anyway. "Don't worry, we'll finish paying you back, Mom."

"Of course you will," Eleanor said. "That was never in question. But without Passerine, you're . . . drifting a little."

Thessaly heaved a great sigh. "I'll figure something out."

Eleanor set down her coffee cup with a sharp click. "For years you've said you were going to make wine, yet you keep doing anything else but that. Now your only plan is to come back to us so we can do it for you?"

"With me, not for me! I just need time."

"Oh for god's sake. Your dad would've given you seed money a decade ago," Eleanor said. "Or called twenty different people to get you a job with a winemaker if I'd let him. But this is your career, not ours."

Thessaly stared at her mother, who gazed coolly back. She had always considered her mother analytical and tough in her own way—but she'd never realized how tough. She'd had no idea that her warm, soup-making mother had been observing her cowardice and uncertainty for so long, and the realization filled her with shame.

"I wasn't waiting for you to learn how to ask for permission the right way," Eleanor said, more gently. "I wanted you to figure out how to do it for yourself. Are you going to, or not?"

The obvious answer was yes, of course, she was working toward it like always. But Thessaly suddenly felt adamant that she was not going to just say what sounded good. If she told her mother she was going to go off and make wine somehow, some way, it would be the truth.

She called Ari that night instead of Wren. She wasn't close to her sister but saw her as an authority on most things. "I was just about to call you," Ari said. "Want to take a road trip?"

"After harvest," said Thessaly. "I have some stuff to figure out first."

"Obviously. There's a place in Paso that might be fun. Some customers said there's a new producer who used to be an assistant winemaker in Mendocino—Lila, something Czech."

"Just a winery?"

"More of a wine neighborhood. To be honest, my customers didn't love it, but I think it's straight up your alley."

"Did Mom put you up to this? I just found out she's been the one keeping Dad from helping me make wine all this time."

"I figured," Ari said.

"You knew?"

"Believe it or not, we don't spend every waking minute discussing you. But I assumed."

"And now you're taking me on this trip because you feel sorry for me," Thessaly said.

"Oh, quit being a baby," Ari said. "Because you lost your best friend and you need it, obviously. I've never felt sorry for you a day in my life."

The day of their trip to Paso Robles, she climbed into Ari's car feeling giddy with freedom. The harvest was done and suddenly she had so much time to fill. "This is incredible," she told her sister, and promptly fell asleep.

She woke up four hours later. "Sorry." She sat up and peered around. "Are we in the right place?"

"Maybe," said Ari, glancing between the road and her phone. They were in what might generously be called an industrial park. Trucks and flatbeds littered the parched landscape.

Finally they saw a big sign, white letters on a rusted plate, reading "Tin City." Tin City was apparently a mix of metal warehouses, construction, and nothingness.

"Well, now I kind of get why my customers didn't like this," Ari said. "The people who come to my place want to be somewhere shiny and upscale and European. This place looks like a box factory."

"I think it looks interesting."

"Of course you do. You still listen to Bikini Kill."

They parked in the shadow of a corrugated metal building with a patio set with picnic tables and umbrellas, scattered with people drinking beer in the sun. Past the brewery they found another building of half the size but the same no-frills construction, the fluted metal painted leafy green instead of silver. They opened the door.

Both paused in the doorway, their eyes adjusting to the dark interior and the dizzying change of scenery. The inside of the place took its cues from a nineteenth-century bordello. The walls were pansy-center navy, the curtains green velvet. There were ornate mirrors and sprays of silver birch, pale velvet fainting couches and love seats. A large oval tabletop perched on a wrought-iron base that looked as if someone had dipped a pile of twigs and branches into metal.

It was one of the oddest tasting rooms Thessaly had ever visited, a cross between Neverland and Deadwood. It looked nothing like the work of a European, New York, or Californian winemaker or even some hedge-fund millionaire. There were no long wood tables, no fake Provençal vibe with yellow pottery and fleur-de-lis wallpaper. She inspected a row of bottles on an antique sideboard, labeled with images of the small of a person's back, a curve of fruit and fabric. She did not have the slightest idea who'd come up with this. But she would have known instantly it was a woman.

The winemaker's name was Lila Czerny. She was in her late thirties, small except for a round second-trimester belly and a fuzzy halo of caramel-colored hair.

This woman was making her own small-batch wine. This woman had her own eclectic tasting room. This woman was doing everything Thessaly had ever wanted to do. And she was not a grave German, a weathered American farmer, or an elegant Frenchwoman of a certain age. She was not much older than Thessaly.

As they sat down to taste, Thessaly began to feel slightly crazed with possibility. Why were these wines so strange? They all felt as if they should be familiar—a Chenin Blanc, a Sauvignon Blanc Lila described as "breakfast wine," and Rhône blends—but none was exactly what you expected. They had an edge, a flash of electricity.

Nothing in this place looked like any of the things Thessaly had spent her entire life admiring: the winemakers were young and scruffy without being picturesque; the tasting room almost embarrassingly feminine. She wondered what she would have made of this place five or ten years ago, when she'd cared about impressing Lionel and Jonathan. She tried to picture Wren's reaction to the striped fainting couch, the repurposed furniture.

"They're kind of strange," Thessaly said. "But they're gorgeous."

"I told you," Ari said, glancing at her reflection in a massive old mirror framed with gilded serpents. "I knew this was your kind of place."

· CHAPTER 23 ·

Thessaly had warned her that the San Luis Obispo airport was minuscule, but Wren hadn't believed her. The entire airport was one diminutive building in the middle of a grand expanse, the mountains visible at a great distance. After she left the terminal, Wren stood beside her rental car and looked around for a moment, getting her bearings. Then she got in and set the GPS for the address Thessaly had given her.

"You sure you don't want to come?" she'd asked Martin that morning. They both knew it wasn't a real question.

Martin had been standing at the kitchen counter, buttering her sourdough toast. He never made toast for himself, but it somehow tasted better when he made it for her.

"Well, I want to," he said. He set down the butter knife and pulled her to him. "But you don't need me there. Think of all the inside jokes you'd have to explain."

"You'd catch up," she said, but of course he was right.

She hadn't laid eyes on Thessaly, not in real life, for nearly three years. She didn't even look her up online. Her anger had faded, but in its place was left a mix of sadness, a general queasiness, and guilt. Whenever she heard second- or thirdhand what her old friend was up to, Wren adopted a frozen smile like a wife hearing about her ex's new baby. Even Thessaly's name in her inbox could send a jolt of discomfort through her. Thankfully, those emails arrived less frequently, since Thessaly was paid out and the business had been fully transitioned to Wren.

It had been a shock when Thessaly emailed and invited her out to Paso. The email was brief, just asking Wren if she wanted to come see what she was up to. It came in April, a depressing month in Madison, one of false spring and snow flurries. Wren knew she had to go; to say no would mean cutting off even the possibility of friendship. In the weeks that followed, she'd spent more hours thinking about this meeting than anything else, even work.

Tin City wasn't kidding about the tin. It looked like Thessaly was working for a forklift manufacturer. As she drove farther, past breweries and restaurants and other winemakers' places, Wren started to understand the appeal. The buildings felt bracing and clunky and yet she liked the way their metal and concrete were set off by the golden light and the surrounding hills. This group of industrial buildings was so much more approachable and less manicured than the Sonoma landscape of Thessaly's childhood. It was something new, something that hadn't been polished and perfected yet.

She parked her car and looked in the mirror. Her brows were knit and her eyes looked panicky.

A tap on her window startled her. There was Thessaly, standing outside her car door, grinning. Her hair was longer than Wren had seen it, wavy and lighter than before, but her face was that same face, her broken-bridged nose, her full mouth and bright dark eyes. Her hands were on her hips; she wore jeans and a jacket and a white T-shirt and brown lug-soled boots. "I was inside freaking out when I saw you out here tweaking in your car," she said when Wren rolled down the window. "Let's just hug and do this thing."

"*Are* we hugging?" Wren said, hoping it came out sounding lighthearted. She could tell from Thessaly's reaction that she'd missed her mark. Her face beat with blood like a heart. She shook her head and started over. "It's good to see you," she said, and opened up her arms.

Thessaly smelled the same way she always had, some mix of lemon and sage and soap that Wren had never noticed consciously before. She might never have noticed it, if they'd continued to live their lives in tandem.

They spent the next few hours walking around, Thessaly introducing her to everyone they met. There were a dozen or so brewers and winemakers in Tin City. Thessaly's boss—the only female winemaker—came barreling out of the building to meet Wren.

"Wren, welcome!" Lila said. "Drink everything!" Even as she shook her hand enthusiastically, she was also talking at Thessaly about filtering a field blend and the flatness of the grenache blend and several other things Wren didn't even catch.

Wren wondered if Thessaly had found it hard to go back to working for someone. She didn't think she'd ever do it herself. But if Thessaly minded, she hid it expertly. The only time she was anything less than upbeat was when Wren observed how hard the job must be. "It's so fucking hard," Thessaly said, quite seriously. "Like endless. But it's all I want to do."

She led Wren past amphorae full of aging Chenin Blanc and barrels of Grenache and Mourvèdre and Zinfandel and they began working their way from one warehouse to another, like a block party. They stopped for tastes of wine and beer and cider, oddball things like bottle-aged Sémillon and Syrah that didn't taste like Syrah from anywhere else in the state. The wines were young and bright with berry and dark wood and spice, the big wines Thessaly had always loved more than Wren did. They had a Pinot Grigio that invalidated every eye roll about Pinot Grigio Wren had ever given; it was so bright she could hardly stop sipping at it.

Then Thessaly hauled her along to an empty lot down a curving road. There were construction vehicles, currently not in service, and the beginnings of a timber frame.

Thessaly headed to the middle of the lot and stopped. "So here it is," she said. "It's mine. Well, it's going to be mine."

Wren made a show of turning and looking and exclaiming, but in her head she was filled with contradictory feelings she didn't want to admit. She felt jealous, inadequate. Thessaly was taking this leap solo, whereas Wren had needed to hold hands with a friend. She also felt melancholy: Thessaly would never be her partner again—she knew that—but seeing it so clearly filled her with an unexpected grief. That part was over.

But more than anything she felt pride. She'd long ago wondered if Thessaly would ever start making her own wine, and she was almost there.

As Thessaly paced out the space for the tasting room and barrel room and office, she was talking in a headlong rush, about labels, about acidity, about all the treasures you could find in salvage yards. Then, abruptly, she paused in front of Wren, hands on hips and feet planted apart. Her expression was suddenly doubtful. "What do you think?" she asked. "I want your opinion."

"You do?"

"Of course." She cocked her head. "Hey. Do you think I'm going this deep into debt and starting this thing up without your opinion? Jesus, tell me what you think."

Wren finally allowed herself a smile, a real one, feeling relieved and grateful and slightly overwhelmed. Because Thessaly still wanted her opinions after all, because she had taken on an even more daunting project than Passerine, and because she had evidently decided it was time for them to be friends again, one way or another, and she was right.

Thessaly's house was fifteen minutes from Tin City, a stucco two-bedroom in a mid-century neighborhood, surrounded by lavender and sagebrush and rosemary bushes. She haphazardly parked her truck ("It was immediately clear this work demands a truck") in the driveway and swung Wren's suitcase out of the bed in the back. Then they went inside and Thessaly started cooking while Wren changed into leggings and a sweatshirt.

Dinner was simple and delicious. Thessaly rubbed a hanger steak with olive oil and salt and pepper and chopped rosemary and grilled it while Wren sliced fennel and lemon and crunchy, bitter fronds of frisée. "We can go out to eat tomorrow," Thessaly said, as they set the food down on the table, "but I thought you might need to crash tonight. Grab those glasses, would you?" She waved in the direction of some wineglasses hanging upside down beneath a cabinet and disappeared into the basement for several minutes. She returned holding a Burgundy-style wine bottle, unlabeled except for a handwritten white sticker, which she turned away from Wren after she opened the bottle and poured.

The wine was a deep dark red, and Wren picked up her glass and took in the allspice and pepper and the wood and the berries.

When she drank it, she expected something fat and cooked and hot, but it wasn't, not at all. It had a bracing acidity instead, almost too much.

"What do you think?" Thessaly asked. "This isn't the very first wine I made—the first one I did with a little of the Syrah I grew on my dad's land. It was kind of a chemistry project more than a good wine. This one is technically my second wine, but it's the first I made here in Paso, and the first time I had to source the fruit and so on. Then I borrowed Lila's press and bought a few barrels and basically just did it."

"I love it," Wren said.

Thessaly laughed. "No, you don't. You think California reds are hot and inelegant."

"You just thought I thought that. I only think hot, inelegant reds are hot and inelegant. But this is lovely. It's so well structured. Maybe slightly high in acid, but aging'll integrate it."

Thessaly smiled, though she seemed to be thinking something she wasn't saying. "You may be right," she said eventually. "Let's eat."

They sliced their hanger steaks and tore pieces of sourdough bread to run through the juices and the herb-scented olive oil. The wine was disappearing fast, and Wren knew she might regret it after all the tasting they'd done before—they'd spat, but still—but she didn't care. It was not going to harm her beyond a headache in the morning. And this was so silky and bright and changeable that she kept returning to it to see how it had shifted.

"When's opening day?"

"October, I think," Thessaly said. She poured more for both of them and lifted the bottle. It was down to less than half. "Barring any delays. I've been aging wine for a year so we have a release to open with. I'll start with rosés and Chenin Blancs while the reds get where they need to be. Lila's introduced me to a lot of growers, and I'll see what they have extra of, so I can get a good price. Plus, it's a fun challenge, figuring out what to do with it. Blend it, or let it be a field blend, so we make a wine out of exactly what was growing in one specific spot . . . I'm not sure. There're so many things you can do."

"Well, let me know if you need a distributor in the Midwest," Wren said.

"I will. But I might be too small for you. Legs keeps saying I should be in touch, but he's just being nice. Maybe in twenty years, when I'm big enough for Greg." She rolled her eyes.

"Legs'll probably get you in those contract riders for touring musicians. Your wine, unfiltered Camels, and no red M&M's." Thessaly laughed. Wren added, "But you'd be big enough for me. I mean, yes, you'll be the smallest. I've let a lot of the tiny guys go since you left; I just knew I'd never feel secure taking tons of risks. But you're different. You are not a risk."

"Thank you. I'm going to have you write that down so I can get it tattooed on my arm."

Wren paused. "This isn't going to fail. But even if it did, which it won't, you'd find a Plan B."

"No, you always had a Plan B. I have no Plan B. If I think that way, I really will fail."

"Well, I needed to have one more than you did. You'll inherit land someday and you could sell it if you want, you could borrow from your dad, and so on. I'm not saying any of that is a lovely scenario. But it's there. I used to resent it about you. Then I kind of loved that about you, because it made me feel more secure by association. Now it just is." She was slightly shocked to hear herself saying everything she'd ever thought. How rare it was to have someone to whom you could say everything.

Thessaly watched her for a long beat. "I don't think I would have done very much without you," she said eventually. "I don't think I'd even be here—I'd have been too chickenshit to jump in. I know you're right that I have some financial safety net, but I'm doing this on my own. All of us are—we're all assistant brewers and assistant winemakers, and we have to lean on one another to navigate the permits and stuff—but my family's not involved. It's just on me. Which is petrifying. I can't let myself think about it."

"You're completely capable of doing this," Wren said.

"I honestly don't know if I am," Thessaly admitted, "but some idiot let me try, so here we are."

Wren poured more wine, reluctant to end the bottle, and left the last glass's worth in the bottom. "You want to take a walk?"

They put on sweatshirts, because the temperature dropped to the forties at night, and brought their glasses with them. Thessaly lived in a winding neighborhood nestled at the base of some foothills, no sidewalks, and they walked along the edge of the road for a long time without talking.

Thessaly started to speak, and Wren braced herself for something profound. "So I googled Alice the other day," Thessaly announced.

"Mother of god, you didn't. Is she selling cars or something? Multi-level marketing?"

"Guess," Thessaly said.

"She's heading a midsize beverage trade association outside Atlanta. She has a string of failed restaurants and pissed-off investors. No—no, wait. She runs a wine-based travel agency, like organizing bus tours and getting kickbacks on tastings."

Thessaly started to laugh. "You googled her too, admit it."

"I didn't."

"Well, you're almost exactly right anyway. She runs a wine-as-wellness business. Like, she takes people around for massages and Chardonnay and presumably at least one rejuvenating vagina steam per day. Which might be nice, except the wine she's using is garbage."

"Huh. And here I thought I was exaggerating."

Back at Thessaly's house, they retrieved the bottle with its last few ounces to share and brought it out back. They sat in chairs at a patio table, looking up at where the lights still shone above the hilltops. Wren wished there was more wine, even though she knew what she really wanted was just more of this. The wine was good and young and new and well made, yes—but so was the moment. The pleasure in this wine was inseparable from sitting here, and as trite as being together and sharing wine sounded, it was also simply true.

This was what had drawn them both in, Wren thought: The way the best wines—the obscure, specific ones—were so many things at once. She and Thessaly never stopped thinking forward to the next harvest and the next vintage, and yet they never forgot that wine was timeless too, still made much as it had been thousands of years ago. (Earlier that day, Thessaly had shown her how to remove the plugs from the barrels and listen for the activity of fermentation, like a midwife or a witch.) As they drank, she knew they both were thinking that this wine, like all the wine they loved, had transformed the intangibles of place and time and effort into a real thing, a thing that did not exist before. When the bottles were gone, it would never exist again. Others would arrive, but never this one, never again.

Of course, she thought, peering into her glass, wine people could access these poetic strains of meditation because a lot of them walked around with a faint to middling buzz at least forty percent of the time.

Thessaly nudged the bottle to Wren's side of the table. "All right," she said, "do the last pour, would you?"

Wren picked up the bottle and poured, and as she did, she caught a glimpse of the label. She didn't expect to see anything printed beyond a varietal and date, but on the white label there was a haphazard doodle of a songbird, inked in one corner in Sharpie.

Wren really did not want her eyes to fill. It would ruin the moment if she got all trembly. But she was only human.

"You've really grown as an artist," she said, to cover it up. "That chicken is spot-on."

"That's really been my focus. Just years of sketching poultry."

Wren took another taste, to see how much lovelier it tasted now. "How much more do you have of that?" she asked. "Enough to sell?"

Thessaly laughed, her lovely white teeth shining in the dimness. "Nope," she said.

"Oh, too bad," Wren said. "Maybe just enough to have some more this weekend, then."

"Not even that," Thessaly said. "That was the last bottle I had. I scraped the money together for the fruit, begged and borrowed the equipment, and bartered some sweaty miserable work in exchange for use of the bottling truck. And it came out so gorgeous I couldn't believe it. I still can't. I saved it for you, and that—" She gave an eloquent shrug of one shoulder. "That was it."

Wren's throat felt full and hot; her eyes swam. She wished she had something for Thessaly too, something as important, something as generous. But Thessaly's expression was wholly content. She was not missing a thing they didn't have at this table, in this place, looking up at these hills.

"You've done an incredible job," Wren told her.

"Thank you," Thessaly said. "So have you."

It had grown late. Tomorrow they would sleep in and baby their red wine headaches and spend the day driving around tasting Zins, Rhône, and Bordeaux varietals and blends, and they'd meet endless winemakers in Thessaly's new community until at the end of the day they would be desperately sick of reds and want nothing but seltzer and gin and tonic. But for now, they just sat without talking and drank the last of the wine in their glasses, glancing back and forth until they each had one sip left. Thessaly shrugged and tapped her glass to Wren's. They drank, and then it was gone.

• ACKNOWLEDGMENTS •

I am incredibly grateful to Zibby Owens, Anne Messitte, Kathleen Harris, Jeanne Emanuel, Madeline Woda, Bridie Loverro, Graça Tito, Chelsea Grogan, and the rest of the Zibby Books team for their skill, generosity, and willingness to try new things. I owe tremendous gratitude to Leigh Newman for acquiring the novel and believing in it enough to tease out every necessary story beat that I could no longer see and calmly enduring my nitpicks and freakouts. My thanks to Heidi Pitlor for her insightful and transformative feedback, and to Dave Cole for a supremely detailed copyedit that tackled the endless wine names, regions, and varietals. Thank you so much to the Zibby Books authors for making our WhatsApp thread a place in which to admit when we want to throw our manuscripts into the nearest body of water. And so much gratitude to Jane Delury and Julie Chavez for being my emotional support writers. Little vests with your names on them are being manufactured even as I type.

Pestering people about their jobs in the wine industry was so much fun that I had to force myself to quit calling them and start writing. *How to Import Wine* by Deborah M. Gray was extremely informative about the nuts and bolts of the job. Ann Avant, Carla Betz, Clarke Boehling, Brian Carroll, Damien Casten, Neal Dessouky, Alleah Friedrichs, Meredith Griffin, Caroline Guthrie, Jasmine Hirsch, Bill Hooper, Tom Loup, Sam McDaniel, Molly Moran, Erin Pooley, Jim Prosser, Stacy Sandler, Andrew Shapiro, Sarena Stern, and Terri White were sparkling conversationalists, gracious about my endless questions, and much more generous with their time than I had any right to expect. Any inaccuracies are all mine.

Corrie Malas is my dream interviewee and collaborator, insightful and wise and incredibly observant about all the things I wanted to know. I owe her years of drinks and as many reads of her future books as she might desire.

Sara Roahen was my tour guide, host, and advance researcher for a Central Coast wine tour that made all the difference in where this story wound up.

Thank you thank you thank you to Alison Weatherby, Susanna Daniel, and Sarah Yaw for reading with literary insight, humor, and encouragement.

So many thanks and bottles of wine to my agent Sarah Burnes for her generosity with her time, editorial feedback, and steadfast professional guidance.

My love and my gratitude to Steve O'Brien and Holly O'Brien for being my people and making me laugh at least once a day.

And all my love to my community in Madison and beyond: friends, family, writers, readers, eaters, cooks, wine sellers, and wine drinkers.

· ABOUT THE AUTHOR ·

Michelle Wildgen is the author of the novels *You're Not You*, adapted into a feature film starring Hilary Swank and Emmy Rossum, *But Not for Long*, and *Bread and Butter*, and editor of the food writing anthology *Food & Booze*. Wildgen's reviews, essays, and stories have appeared in publications including the *New York Times Book Review* and Modern Love column, *O, the Oprah Magazine*, RealSimple.com, *Salon*, *Best Food Writing*, *Best New American Voices*, *Triquarterly*, *Story-quarterly*, and elsewhere. Formerly executive editor with the award-winning literary journal *Tin House*, Wildgen is now a free-lance editor and cofounder with novelist Susanna Daniel of the Madison Writers' Studio.

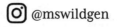 @mswildgen

www.michellewildgen.com

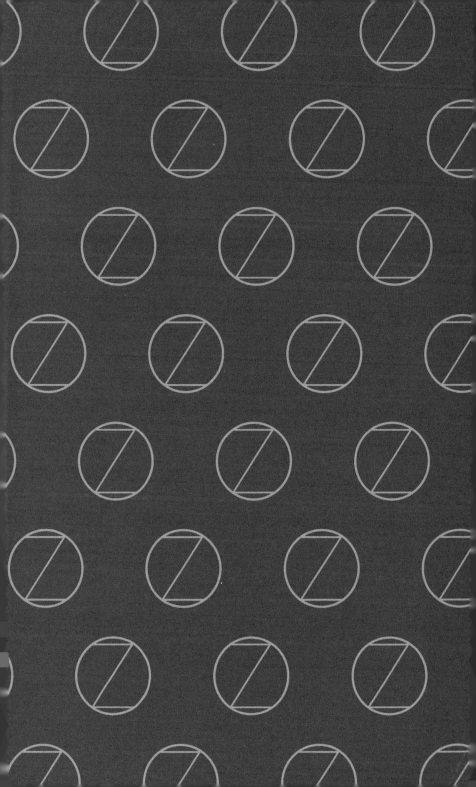